Praise for

the complex art of being Maisie Clark

"[Maisie's] inner voice captures the confused, unfiltered thoughts of a teenager—full of self-doubt, sarcasm, and bursts of confidence—in this thoughtful, character-driven story of growth. A well-realized coming-of-age story that celebrates art and the journey to accepting yourself."

—*Kirkus Reviews*

"Sabrina Kleckner delivers a heartwarming, giddiness-inducing journey in search of what it means to define your identity, proving that coming of age is not only a complex art but also a masterpiece of coloring outside the lines!"

—Matthew Hubbard, author of *The Last Boyfriends Rules for Revenge* and *The Rebel's Guide to Pride*

"*The Complex Art of Being Maisie Clark* is a warm, heartfelt, and creative exploration of art, family, and the ways people change. Maisie's art-school journey takes her from surface-level attempts at reinvention to a deeper understanding of both herself and the people closest to her. With complex, three-dimensional characters, a vividly rendered world, and a story that's both humorous and profound, this book, like Maisie herself, is easy to love."

—Elizabeth Holden, author of *Mighty Millie Novak*

"Maisie Clark may be searching for her artistic style, but she's mastered wit, charm, and heart. There's a warmth to Kleckner's sophomore novel that invites readers to root for the bold and vibrant Maisie as she navigates her first semester of college and finds her voice. With a lovely sunshine-meets-grump pairing, an endearing sibling dynamic, and characters who feel like friends, *The Complex Art of Being Maisie Clark* is compassionate and real."

—Kalie Holford, author of *The Last Love Song*

"Vibrant, hilarious, and sweet, *The Complex Art of Being Maisie Clark* deftly captures the excitement and awkwardness of the transition between high school and university. Through Maisie's sharp and utterly engaging voice, Sabrina Kleckner paints an honest, empathetic portrait of a girl struggling and determined to define her own style as an artist and as a person. A web of unique and tenderly drawn relationships form the heart of this story about art-making, connection, and self-discovery."

—Leyla Brittan, author of *Ros Demir Is Not the One*

"Heartwarming and charming—readers will be taken in by Maisie's list to change her life and enjoy the ride as she learns that life, college, and even creativity cannot be defined or reinvented by a list. It's a testament to starting over, not by force but by choice, and the emotional roller coaster that comes with that decision. Throughout her highs and lows, readers will cheer as Maisie finds just exactly who she is and, more importantly, who she wants to be."

—Gretchen Schreiber, *Ellie Haycock Is Totally Normal*

the complex art of being Maisie Clark

SABRINA KLECKNER

flux®

Mendota Heights, Minnesota

First Edition
First Printing, 2025

Book design by Karli Hughes
Cover design by Karli Hughes
Cover illustration by Ana Bidault

Flux, an imprint of North Star Editions, Inc.

This is a work of fiction. Names, characters, places, and incidents are either the product of the author's imagination or are used fictitiously, and any resemblance to actual persons living or dead, business establishments, events, or locales is entirely coincidental.

Library of Congress Cataloging-in-Publication Data
Names: Kleckner, Sabrina, author.
Title: The complex art of being Maisie Clark / Sabrina Kleckner.
Description: First edition. | Mendota Heights, Minnesota: Flux, 2025. | Audience term: Teenagers | Audience: Grades 10–12.
Identifiers: LCCN 2024054601 (print) | LCCN 2024054602 (ebook) | ISBN 9781631639203 (paperback) | ISBN 9781631639210 (ebook)
Subjects: CYAC: Self-actualization--Fiction. | Art schools--Fiction. | Schools--Fiction. | Family life--Fiction. | London (England)--Fiction. | England--Fiction. | LCGFT: Novels.
Classification: LCC PZ7.1.K638 Co 2025 (print) | LCC PZ7.1.K638 (ebook) | DDC [Fic]--dc23
LC record available at https://lccn.loc.gov/2024054601
LC ebook record available at https://lccn.loc.gov/2024054602

Flux
North Star Editions, Inc.
2297 Waters Drive
Mendota Heights, MN 55120
www.fluxnow.com

Printed in Canada

Mitchell Kleckner—

I keep writing books about siblings, so in part, they're probably all for you.

Chapter One

I enjoy existing. Generally. But I did not spend nine months developing eyes in a womb for them to one day witness *this.*

It started at the door leading up to my brother's flat. When I stepped inside, my view was obstructed by neon green streamers. They hung from ceiling to floor, and I got a mouthful of plastic as I tried to claw my way through. Directly on the other side, not two inches from my face, stood the source of my horror: a massive cardboard cutout. Now I yelp, backing away—and into the streamers, which my feet catch on. A second later, I hit the wood floor, hard, and pain shoots up my elbow. I try to stand, but I'm thoroughly tangled, and—

The rod attaching the streamers to the ceiling falls, barely missing my head as it smacks the ground. The world goes green and then dark as more streamers fall across my face. I scream again, less out of fear and more out of annoyance, because *I am not in the mood to die today.*

"Maisie?"

I wiggle, trying to rip free, until hands grab my shoulders. "Gently! Maisie, please."

I pull the last strands of plastic off my head and sit up, coming face-to-face with Benji, my brother's boyfriend. He's brushing streamers off my arms—slowly, taking care not to rip them.

"Are you all right?" he asks as I catch my breath.

"I was gone for two hours." I scowl, rubbing my elbow. "Not even two hours!" Now that I'm no longer falling all over the place, I realize the decorations adhere to a . . . theme. The cardboard cutout is a massive Shrek. Large *Shrek* posters are taped to the walls, covering the usual white paint. There's a cake on the kitchen table. I can't see what's written on it from here, but the frosting is the same inedible-looking shade of ogre green as everything else. I sigh. "It's too early for this."

"It's four p.m."

I struggle to my feet, kicking a few spare streamers toward the door. My gaze lands again on the cake. From this angle, I can make out the mud brown letters crafted from icing:

MARRY ME?

"Oh my God?" I spin back around.

Benji, who is normally the epitome of casual, hesitates. "Cal and I have been dating for ten years. Surely this isn't surprising?"

I gesture wildly at the cutout, which towers over me. "Where did you *get* this? No one just sells six-foot-tall Shreks. Did you put in a custom order? Or—don't tell me you *made* it?" Benji designs clothes for a living, but he's a skilled artist in many mediums. When we first met, he spent most of his time spray-painting buildings across London. From his sudden and suspicious quiet, I have strong concerns he branched out recently in his creative pursuits. "Oh my God, you did, didn't you? You totally built this from scratch!"

"I don't know why you're in a twist. Handmade decor is romantic."

"Not when it's *Shrek*!" I stare at him. Everyone in my family is an artist. For my brother, Calum, it's a hobby. For my parents, it's a job. For me, it's everything I've been and everything I hope to become. The point being, I know art, and Benji's work generally makes me want to throw my pencils out the window. Okay, not really. But also sometimes really, because (don't tell him, I'll never live it down) he's the best artist I know. So this mess of streamers, that horrific Shrek, the questionable cake . . .

"I get it. You decided to propose, and now you're freaking out. You're having a breakdown in the form of *Shrek*."

Benji scoffs. "First off, I don't 'freak out.' I am historically known for my composure. Besides, what is there to freak out about? Your brother is—and I say this lovingly—as skittish as a poorly adjusted cat. Has designing a proposal that won't send him running for the hills been a challenge? Yes. Are *Shrek* and the world financial markets the only two topics he voices strong opinions about? Also yes. Are either of those interests ideal backdrops for heartfelt vulnerability?" Benji pauses. "I'll admit the cake looks a bit . . . child's birthday–esque. And the streamers are clearly a hazard. I'll scrap those because murder isn't my intention. And—well. The cutout was a choice. I've made a lot of choices." He rubs at his temple. "Oh, it's not good, is it? This is not good at all."

"It's fine. I mean, it's nightmarish, but we can fix it." I grab a trash bag from the kitchen. We both snatch up handfuls of green streamers and start stuffing them out of sight. The cake and cutout prove more difficult to toss in haste, until I have the brilliant idea to run my finger through the brown MARRY ME? icing. The streak left behind looks . . . not appealing, but if my erratic brother were to walk into the flat in the next ten seconds, there's no way he'd guess this had been the setup for a proposal.

Benji stares at the smudged cake. "If I were superstitious, I'd call that an omen."

"Good thing you're not, then."

"Quite." He scratches at his neck. "Unless, of course, the omens are real and they're laughing."

I roll my eyes. Benji was right when he said Calum doesn't like a lot of things. *Shrek* gets a pass, possibly because "Get out of my swamp!" is a sentiment my brother intrinsically relates to. But music is "distracting." Vacations are "unproductive." His idea of a good time is spending the day at London's finance museum, which is embarrassing to admit, and I'm not even him. The point being, Calum doesn't bother with most pursuits or people, but he does bother with Benji. And if that isn't a sign of undying commitment, then I don't know what is.

I tie off the trash bag. "If Calum was going to run for the hills, he would have already. Just be cool, yeah? You're generally good at that—ignoring these last three minutes."

Benji scoffs again. Then his gaze catches on something behind me and he frowns, nodding his chin toward my suitcases by the door. "Not to divert attention from this embarrassing moment that I'm enjoying immensely, but didn't you already leave? There was an awkward hug. You tripped over the threshold on your way out."

"My—scarf. I forgot it."

"What scarf? It's August."

"My summer scarf!"

Benji raises an eyebrow. "Maisie Clark, don't tell me we've finally found something you're afraid of?"

"I'm not *afraid*."

I'm not. Check-in for my university dorm opened an hour ago, and the only reason I'm dragging my feet is because Calum said he'd help me lug my stuff over. I crashed at his and Benji's flat this summer because, despite a ten-year age gap, my brother and I are actually pretty close. His work schedule is intense, though, so I haven't seen much of him during these two months. I'm not surprised he's late.

Which, it's fine. It's good I have some time, because I got sweaty on my impromptu walk through Kensington Gardens and now makeup is dripping down my face. I blot the foundation with a paper towel and reapply in the living room mirror, but it refuses to stick. Somehow I'm oily and dry all at once. The thick liquid slides off my cheeks but condenses like congealed cheese between my eyebrows. I see Benji watching me through the mirror. Judgmentally. I point the tube of foundation at him. "There's nothing wrong with wearing makeup."

"Of course not." Benji pauses. "You just look like you hate it."

I do hate it. My face itches, and I can't rub my eyes without smudging black all around them, but I need to grow up, and people don't grow when they're comfortable. It only hit me after I completed my art school applications: I'm a very good fraud. The portraits I submitted for my portfolio are technically advanced. They tell a cohesive story. They are also a lie, because although they were painted by my hand, they're not *mine.*

How do I explain this? My family runs a shop in upstate New York. Glenna's Portraits is a wonderful place; it's my favorite place. I've helped out with the paintings since I was a child, often doing the sketches and base coats before Dad finished them off. But because we worked together, I needed to match his style for consistency. When I was twelve, it was fine that my art looked like his. It was *supposed* to look like his. But I'm eighteen now, and as I stood in our workshop choosing bits and pieces for my college portfolio, I wavered over whether to include a whimsical commission of Mr. Montgomery and his poodle for a solid three minutes before realizing *it wasn't one of mine.*

That's the problem. I'm so good at matching Dad's style that I even confuse myself sometimes. At this rate, my tombstone will read: *Here Lies Maisie Clark, Best Known for Exquisite Line Work and Copying Other Artists.* That's not what I want my legacy to be, so I've made a decision. I'm going to give up portraits. Forever. Instead of studying figure drawing and oil painting at university, I'm only going to take classes in mediums I've got no experience with. And if I can't find my voice this year—far away from Glenna's, at the prestigious London College of Art—then I'll quit art entirely. I'll transfer to a nonspecialized school and study something broader while I still have time to pivot. Art will become a just-for-fun thing for me, the way it is for my brother. And maybe I'll always feel like a failure, but at least when people say to Mom *Oh, your daughter is a [insert career here]?* she'll be able to answer *Yes!* as opposed to *I don't know?* when asked who painted the landscape over our fireplace.

One year.

No one knows about my ultimatum—not even my best friend, Alicia. I've said it out loud to make it real, but only with my door locked at night. It's for my sanity, keeping this decision secret. If people knew, they'd have something to say about it, and the whole reason I'm in this mess is because I need to learn who I am on my own.

Anyway—the makeup. In order to find my style, I have to push outside my comfort zone. So, I have a list. My TRY NEW THINGS list. I've already completed steps 1–4:

TRY NEW THINGS

1. STOP HELPING OUT AT GLENNA'S.
2. GO TO AN ART SCHOOL FAR FROM HOME. MAYBE IN ANOTHER COUNTRY.
3. NO PORTRAITS OR OIL PAINTINGS. ONLY SIGN UP FOR CLASSES IN MEDIUMS YOU HAVE NO EXPERIENCE WITH.
4. EXPERIMENT WITH YOUR APPEARANCE AND CLOTHING.
5. MAKE NEW FRIENDS (BECAUSE ALICIA IS GOING TO).
6. ALWAYS SAY YES. EVEN WHEN YOU DON'T WANT TO.

It's a solid plan. I know it is, but Benji's been watching me all summer with his eyebrows raised. Now he waves a hand in my direction. "I'm not your mum. Dress how you like. But if you're doing all that because you think you're supposed to, instead of because you want to, then the only thing you'll get from this crisis are photos you'll cringe at in five years' time."

I shake my head. Benji's online store sells out in minutes every time he drops new clothes. The fusion of Japanese and English architecture he embroiders onto fabric is not just impressively intricate: It's *him*. There's a precision to his style that comes from being exactly sure of who he is, and it makes his designs recognizable from a mile off.

"It's not a crisis." I pull out a red lipstick. "I'm just trying new things. Figuring out what I like. You wouldn't understand."

"Please. Teenage Benji thought facial piercings were a requirement for being bisexual. Don't stick metal through your eyebrow unless you're prepared for an infection and a scar."

"*That's* what those marks are? I always thought you were stung by a bee. You know—twice. Vertically."

He shoots me a rude gesture and then tosses the garbage bag over one shoulder, Santa-style, before starting toward the door. "Let's go."

"Where?"

"The rubbish bin. And then your dormitory."

I shake my head. "You don't have to come." It's over an hour past check-in, and I haven't heard from Calum. Aside from being untimely, my brother texts like an old man—and that's only when he remembers it's a feature on his phone. I won't be surprised if he completely ghosts me. But that's fine. I'm supposed to be branching out on my own.

Benji slips on his shoes. "Did you know? An ex once described me as a seed stuck in her teeth. Annoying and impossible to dislodge."

"Gross? I hope you shoved her into a well."

"Oh, no," he says cheerily. "She dragged me round for two weeks in Year 9 and then ripped my heart out. The point being, fourteen-year-olds are unbearably poetic and you'll be hard-pressed to get rid of me." He opens the door. "I'll carry you if I must."

Chapter Two

Benji doesn't carry me to university.

We take a taxi.

First, to the admissions building to get some official documents and keys, and then to my dorm. It's only a few minutes' walk from the main campus and maybe a half hour by tube from Calum and Benji's flat. It'll be a reasonable commute once I'm not laden down with luggage.

The dorm is pretty in a haunted manor type of way. Think old red brick and vines crawling up the side. It's wider than it is tall—only five floors, but my room is up there at the top. When we walk through the front door, my eyebrows pop up. The rickety stairs look barely wide enough to step on with two feet, and they lead straight up into musty darkness. "I already almost died today."

"That's the spirit." Benji starts hauling up my first suitcase. I grab the second. With each ascending step, I'm very aware that if he falls backward, I'll be squashed like a bug underfoot.

In the end, no squashing occurs. My suitcases make it around all the landings—barely. When we reach the top, Benji is panting, his hair disheveled. I'm melting, and the puffy sleeves of my yellow dress are sticky with sweat. The fifth-floor air is heavy and claustrophobic—heat rises, and this is London. Air conditioning in my room won't be a thing.

"See?" Benji says, still wheezing slightly. "Uni is a magical place."

"Those stairs are a hazard. Someone's going to break their neck."

"No, no. The corridors are too narrow. You'd get stuck between the walls before you hit the ground."

"Reassuring."

When I try the door handle, I find it unlocked. My roommates must already be here.

Or, not roommates in the way American universities work, where everyone sleeps in the same space. Inside the first door are more doors. Seven total, but two open to bathrooms and one to a kitchen. The other four lead to individual rooms, because I'm sharing a flat with three people as opposed to a bunk bed situation. Having my own room was a luxury I didn't expect when I received the information on student housing a few months ago, but a part of me was also disappointed. When I pictured college, I imagined cramped living quarters and no personal space and bonding with my roommates over the misery. This situation is colder. More isolated. In order to talk to people, I'll have to knock on their closed doors or corner them in the kitchen. Not as ideal for #5 on my list: *Make new friends (because Alicia is going to).*

We run into a mom in the hallway. She's dressed in a crisp white suit that pops against her brown skin, tall heels that make my ankles hurt just by standing in their presence, and an airbrushed makeup look that my unpracticed hand could never achieve. She introduces herself simply as, "Natalie's, you are?"

"Um. Maisie?"

She stares at me up and down with an unreadable expression. Then she turns to Benji. "You're not also a student?"

"Ha. Just her brother. Or—not by blood. Or marriage.

But I wouldn't call us friends. Enemies? She does bully me. This is more information than you asked for." Benji flushes slightly. He's never implied we were family before, and his stumbling may have come from Natalie's mom raising an eyebrow at the admission. We don't look like siblings: I'm white and Benji is Asian. He's ten years older than me, and right now we're like day and night with my bright summer dress and his aggressive summer blacks. He's right, though. We're not friends. The age gap is too large; we're in different phases of life. *Enemies* is a joke. I'm constantly rolling my eyes at him, but if anyone else were to look at him funny, I'd chuck them out the window. *Brother...*

Yes. Of course that's what he is. I constantly have the urge to shake his shoulders in exasperation, but he's often the first person I want to call when life goes wrong.

"Right." Natalie's mom points a manicured nail at me. "My daughter is a serious artist. No noise after ten p.m. She will report you if you disrupt her studies or sleep." Then, without another glance, she brushes past us and out the front door.

"You hear that?" Benji says once she's gone. "Only day drinking for you."

I roll my eyes. "Don't you have an embarrassing proposal to get back to?" It would probably sound more like a dismissal if my hand weren't clamped around his elbow. Benji needs to go—it's the only way I can get on with the whole stepping-out-of-my-comfort-zone-in-order-to-find-my-artistic-style thing. But once he leaves, I'll be *alone.*

He doesn't shake me off. Not physically, anyway. "The day drinking was a joke. But while we're on the topic: Drugs are bad, condoms are good—"

"Oh my *God.*" I push him toward the door.

He clings to the threshold. "Never cut your own hair past midnight. Don't let a stranger tattoo you in a club! In a drunken moment, you may think to yourself, 'The physical properties of matter are no match for me. I can heat this curry in its original container without worrying over melting points.' But, hypothetically, once you have burned your arm, vomited everywhere, and force-evacuated the building at three in the morning—"

"Benji."

"Yes, yes, you're too eighteen to listen to me." He taps my shoulder. "But call when you make poor decisions. Or when you don't."

I hug him. He's annoying and the worst, but I'm only telling myself that because I have to let go. I don't want to—I swear I don't move my arms—but one moment I'm grasping someone solid, and the next I'm clutching at nothing, standing in the corridor alone.

It's fine.

I'm alone, and it's fine.

It's where I wanted to be.

I spend the next several hours unpacking, organizing everything in my wardrobe, and buying groceries and dorm room necessities. The sun has long set when I finally work up the nerve to befriend my flatmates. The thought of knocking on strangers' doors with a smile pasted on my face like a desperate saleswoman is uncomfortable, but is it even a growing moment if you don't feel like you're going to die?

The room next to mine belongs to a boy. His skin is bone-white, almost vampiric, and he's wearing a shirt and trousers that look like they belong in a previous century. "Henrold" is what I hear when he says his name.

"Sorry—Henry?"

He shrugs.

"Harold?"

"If you like." He's holding a lizard. When I ask if it's real, he repeats, "If you like," before slowly closing the door.

Right.

I try the next room. It's another boy. This one is blond and blue-eyed. He isn't holding a lizard, which is encouraging. Less encouraging is that he's naked.

I blink.

Yes, I'm seeing correctly. I thought maybe I wasn't, because why on earth would someone open their door to a stranger without at least putting on underwear, but it's not a trick of the light. He's *naked* naked. No fabric. Just freckles.

"All right?" he says casually, as though this is a normal interaction on a normal Friday evening between two people who are wearing clothes. His hair is wet, like he just showered, which at least makes more sense than "Henrold," but *grab a towel, bro?*

This time, I'm the one to shut a door in a face. My hopes are significantly lower as I trudge up to room number three. I knock, and the door swings open of its own accord, as if it wasn't fully closed. At first, I don't see anyone inside. The bed is bare. The wardrobe is open but empty. And the desk—

It's occupied by a girl. I don't mean she's sitting in the adjacent chair: She's *on* the desk. Like, crouched on top. There's no need to ask her name: She looks exactly like her mom even though she's clearly trying not to. Instead of long dark hair, hers is shoulder length and bluish green.

Instead of a power suit, she's in black spandex shorts and a baggy Florence + the Machine T-shirt. There's an orientation folder by her knee confirming what I already know—*Natalie Agrawal,* the left corner reads.

"There's a man." She doesn't turn to look at me. "He's been lurking outside our dorm for half an hour. I'm considering dumping a drink on his head."

I step forward, but in order to get a clear view, I'd have to climb onto the desk next to her. Seeing as I was just flashed by one roommate, I figure I shouldn't turn this into a chain reaction by attempting gymnastic maneuvers in a dress. "It's not someone moving in?"

Natalie shakes her head. "He doesn't have luggage—only a briefcase. What do we think? Water? Or Ribena?" She has both drinks on her desk.

Lurking outside the dorm, a briefcase...

"Does he have dark hair?" I ask suddenly. "Intense eyebrows? Posture somewhere between 'I'm awkward' and 'I'm emotionally constipated'?"

Natalie finally looks at me. "You also saw him from your room?"

I roll my eyes—not at her. "That's my brother."

Natalie's hand inches toward the Ribena. "Well, you'd best collect him before someone else does."

I back out slowly from the room and run down into the dark outdoors.

Calum is indeed staring up at the dorm. He's in his work clothes like always and holding a briefcase with both hands. I stalk up to him and smack his elbow. "Were you going to stand out here until someone reported you for trespassing?"

He blinks. Slowly, as though taking a moment to

register my presence. His usually sharp eyes seem dull, which might have something to do with the intense circles beneath them. I don't know if they fired a bunch of people at his corporation or what, but in the past when I've visited him, Calum's always been able to clear his evenings for me. This summer he's been so swamped (I won't make a *Shrek* joke) that we've had exactly two dinners together.

"Hello?" I snap my fingers in front of his face. It's been a solid seven seconds since my initial question. "I didn't need you to drop me off at university, but you did say you'd come. You couldn't have texted that you were going to be a million hours late?"

"My boss took my phone."

"*What?*"

He shrugs half-heartedly. "We have to maintain confidentiality until a deal goes through next week. She took my laptop, too."

"That's definitely illegal. Besides, you work in finance, not as a spy. At least, I'm eighty percent sure you're not a spy." I pause. "Benji's birthday was questionable. You got us out of that escape room in five minutes—which, by the way, ruined all the fun. The point *being*, if national security isn't at risk, then your boss can't take your things. And she can't keep you in the office until—" I check my phone. It's nearly ten p.m., which is earlier than I expected. Lately he's been working past midnight.

Calum ignores me. "Did you unpack?"

"Don't change the subject."

"Are your roommates fine?"

I hold up my phone so he can see the clock. "Can't you just quit?" I'm talking about his job.

"Can't *you* just quit?" He's talking about me. On another

day, he might have said it with the hint of a smile, but tonight he sounds irritated. Possibly because this is not the first time I've brought up his work schedule recently. Or the hundredth.

I cross my arms. Honestly? I don't care if he's pissed. Calum looks ready to keel over, and it makes something urgent choke up my throat. This is why I need to find my artistic style. I don't want to become him: working a miserable job with miserable hours while convincing myself I'm not miserable. As much as he claims to enjoy finance, my brother did not choose his career because he wanted it, and if *Calum* is bending under the pressure of making a practical decision over a passionate one, then how could *I* handle it?

"You used to have a life. More of a life." I lean against the rough brick of my new dorm, feeling the bright sting of it. "You had hobbies. Well, a hobby. When was the last time you updated your web comic? And you had friends. *A* friend, if we're not counting Benji. Does Rose even know you exist anymore? When was the last time you hung out with her? When was the last time you went anywhere that wasn't home or work?"

"Maisie—"

"I don't know how Benji puts up with you. Well, I guess it's easy since you're literally never around—"

"*Maisie.*"

Okay, that was low. True, but low. "Sorry," I mutter. "You just . . . do need things. Like sleep. And regular meals."

"I took high school biology, thank you."

Did he? When he was sixteen, Calum ran away from home. I didn't see him—or hear from him or even know where he was—until he was twenty-two. It was a whole thing: Mom found out he's gay, got scared of how it'd go down in our town, said he couldn't ever be public about it, and everything spiraled from there. Oh! And I was only six when he left, so no one told me any of this was happening, which meant I spent years wondering what I did to make my brother stop talking to me. Fun times! I'm not still bitter! Anyway, things aren't perfect now, but Calum's somewhat back on speaking terms with our parents, and there's less tension all around. Of course, that doesn't change the fact that he had to fend for himself before he was ready, and I know that's why he won't quit this job that doesn't let him be a person: It would take a lot more than hundred-hour work weeks and an unreasonable boss to convince him to give up high pay at a stable company. I *know* all this, but I also know he could have a more balanced life if he weren't so terrified of change.

Calum looks like he's about to say something snippy, but then he yawns against the back of his hand.

"I'm unpacked," I say. "My roommates are human people. Everything's under control, so you should go home before your boyfriend breaks up with you and I'm forced to choose sides in the aftermath. Don't put yourself in that situation—we both know Benji's more fun."

Calum yawns again, this time into his elbow. "Yes, well."

I scoff. "You're just going to let me have that?"

"Of course Benji's more fun than me. Why would I date someone *less* fun than me?"

That's a fair point. Instead of admitting it, I shoo him down the steps. "You've yawned like six times in the last minute, which really can't be healthy. I'll see you later. Maybe this weekend?"

"Maybe in a few weekends." Calum yawns again. "Eventually I should have a Sunday off."

"A whole day? Goodness. Whatever will you do?"

He glowers. "I don't have to spend it with you."

A part of me hopes he doesn't. A part of me hopes he sleeps.

"Go," I say, and he really must be exhausted because he doesn't hesitate again before stepping away from the dorm.

I wait until he's out of sight before heading back inside. We're different, Calum and I. At sixteen, my biggest problem was the one-star review a client left on Glenna's site after I messed up a portrait. When my brother was sixteen, he was scraping together money for a one-way ticket to our aunt Lisa's house in Scotland without knowing if she'd take him in. Of course we're different, but at our cores we have the same DNA, and Calum gets so tangled in his head. He agonizes over every decision, to the point where he often doesn't make them at all, and then settles for the default path even if it's the less ideal one. I don't want my life to unfold by default. I don't want to be suffocated under the weight of my indecisions.

I love Calum, but I don't want to be anything like him.

Chapter Three

The weekend is a rush of figuring out my new neighborhood and attending orientation. There isn't much time for bonding with my flatmates or working on my self-growth, but I only freak out over that briefly. Life will settle down once routines are established.

Right?!

My first class on Monday is photography. I hate photography. There's no getting your hands dirty. No spending days up to your neck in blending and shading. You just aim a camera, snap a picture, and . . . art!

Don't come for me.

Besides, I *want* to be excited. What better way of pushing out of my comfort zone than by partaking in activities I don't enjoy? This is all part of my plan, and since the whole make-new-friends thing has been a bust so far, this class is my first real chance to branch outside of myself.

The studio is in a red brick building that looks similar to my dorm. It's a small space, which would have been fine if our first lesson wasn't "photograph boring objects in this room for two hours" (I'm paraphrasing).

I try to be excited, but I've spent my life working to capture the feeling of an upturned lip, the slightest frown line, a glazed-over eye. Objects are never the subjects of my paintings because they don't have emotions of their own. Yes, yes, an ominous chair or humorous tablecloth adds to the atmosphere of a scene, but wood and fabric don't have the complexity that people do. I usually find myself rushing through my backgrounds in order to get to the good stuff.

Today, there is no good stuff.

Not to mention, there are *a million* minutes left. Or somewhere around there. I'm not into math.

"What's your name?"

I jump slightly and turn to find Dr. Lazar behind me. She looks like a stereotypical artist—blunt bangs, a loud dress, and chunky green earrings that match her nails and shoes. She got right to business when we arrived: handing out cameras, giving a quick tour of the darkroom down the hall, going over rules and expectations. She seems no-nonsense, which I like. I *liked,* until her hard stare turned on me.

"I'm Maisie?" My palms are sticky. I wipe them on my electric pink overalls (I'm trying something new, okay?), which is a mistake: They leave dark patches.

"Maisie, the most important aspect of photography is looking at your subject. Are you properly studying what's in front of you?"

Today we're exploring Polaroid cameras. The film develops automatically, which is why Dr. Lazar chose it for our first lesson. She wanted to "see what I'm working with."

She points to my photos. "How many have you taken?"

"I don't know?" The camera pumps out ten pictures before you have to insert a new film roll. I've reloaded a few times. More than a few. Seven? Eight?

Dr. Lazar gestures around the room. "We've been here less than fifteen minutes. No one else has gone through a single roll of film, yet here you are with a stack of photos as high as your elbow." She flips through my work. "These are sloppy, and that's putting it nicely. Did you consider the angles? The lighting?" She holds up a blurry shot of the floor. "What story were you trying to tell?"

Story? There's nothing in this room but dust and chairs. "I—"

Dr. Lazar plucks the camera from my hand. "For the rest of this lesson, you will study your classmates and the space around you. Learning to watch is far more important than learning to take."

"But—"

"If you are not mature enough for my methods of teaching, there is still time to swap your schedule."

Wow. I *want* to swap my schedule. I want to fall in a hole, because, yeah, I wasn't as careful with my work as I should have been, but I've never done photography before! If Dr. Lazar expected us to spend ten minutes setting up each shot, shouldn't she have said?

Then again, maybe she's right—I'm *not* mature. That's the only reason I don't walk out of here without a second thought. She wants me to leave, so of course I'm going to stay.

Ha.

So there.

My stubbornness doesn't feel good. It feels pointless, because I'm pretty sure the only person actually bothered by my continued presence in this room is me. My face is hot for the rest of the workshop. I don't make eye contact with anyone. I don't talk. I just stand in a corner and keep carefully calm. Once we're dismissed, I power-walk to my room where I'm alone enough to cry.

"Maisie!"

It's nine p.m., and I'm sitting on the front steps of the dorm, my phone balanced on my knees. Alicia's in Iowa;

it's been a nightmare to stay in touch with the time difference.

I wave, and she grins—all bright teeth and dimples. She got into her dream university to study poetry, and from the pictures she's texted, it seems like she's been having the best time. So when she asks about me, I paste on a smile and say, "Everything's great!"

"Yeah?"

"Yeah!" I turn the conversation back on her. "What happened at your orientation? Why were you in the *woods*?"

She groans. "It was supposed to be a *bonding experience.* You know, camp for a week while doing team-building exercises. Which—the idea sounded nice on paper, but after three days without bathrooms, it really went downhill. Although maybe that was the point—you can't exactly ask someone for a squat shovel and pretend you're still strangers after."

"Squat shovel?"

"You know, to dig a hole to—" She stands abruptly on her bed and bends as if to sit on a toilet.

"Alicia! I didn't need a visual example!"

"That was *not* a visual example. Trust me."

I snort. "Did you make friends, at least?" The question comes out of my mouth both rushed and scrunched-up, because Alicia's been my best friend since that day in pre-K when we staged a joint revolt to take back all the colored pencils from Jenny Rainy. In elementary school, I was the artist; she was the writer. As we grew older, I would break down to her because of my family; she would break down to me because of her unrequited crushes. We fit like puzzle pieces: better together. But when will we be together again? These aren't summer programs where I'll come back from London and she'll come back from Iowa and we'll fall into our usual routines. High school is over; there are no more routines.

Alicia doesn't seem to be wallowing like I am, though, because she continues on with her usual passionate tone, describing her campus and cafeteria and the hot girl in room 308 who totally winked at her maybe. I let her talk because it's good to hear her voice and see her happy, but—squat shovel aside—it sounds like she's in exactly the right place for her, and the more she elaborates, the more I think about how the main reason I chose *my* university is because it's far from home.

When we say goodbye, I stay sitting for a while on the steps, trying not to feel like my whole life is a mistake.

"Shit."

I hear the curse before I feel the foot—directly in the center of my back. The pain hasn't quite registered when there's another thump on my shoulder, and then someone topples past me and down the steps.

My first thought is *How annoying* and my second is *Ouch?* and my third is *I wanted to wallow out here alone, but now you are sitting there holding your ankle.*

Ruiner of My Evening Plans looks familiar. He's got pale freckly skin and floppy brown hair and a sharp jawline. His ears are heavily pierced, and he's wearing too many layers for summer. I suddenly realize where I've seen him: Aside from apparently living in my dorm, he is also in my photography class.

"Hello?" I rub my shoulder. "Did you not notice me on the steps?"

"Obviously. That's why I'm now on the ground." He glowers. "Doorways aren't chairs, did you know? People walk through them."

"Thanks for the heads up." I gesture at his ankle. He's still gripping it tightly. "Are you okay?"

"It's fine."

"The fact that you haven't stood up yet makes me think it's not fine."

"I'm taking in the view."

"Yeah, because cement really blossoms this time of year." My orientation packet included a list of numbers to call in the case of an emergency. Ruiner of My Evening Plans is speaking too casually for me to think he's seriously injured, but it is a little concerning he still hasn't moved. I point at him the way I might at an untrustworthy child. "Stay. I'll be right back."

Of course, this is when he decides to stand. He's able to take a few steps, but his jaw clenches hard when his right leg bears his weight.

I point again, this time at the pavement. "Don't be reckless. Sit if it hurts."

"It's walking, not cliff diving."

"I'm serious."

"So am I." He turns his back to me and starts down the street.

I throw up my hands. If he wants to limp off into the dark, so be it. We're not friends; I don't even know his name! It's not my business if he wants to be irrational.

I convince myself of this for a solid three seconds, but it's not in my nature to leave someone alone who clearly shouldn't be—ruiner of my evening plans or not.

"Where are you going?" I call after him.

"Away." That's a bit of an exaggeration, considering he's moving at one mile an hour. I catch up to him in two strides.

"Shouldn't you be heading in instead of out? It's Monday night. There are classes tomorrow."

"Thanks for the concern, random person I don't know."

"I'm Maisie."

"Didn't ask."

As we round a corner onto the main road, I realize he's heading for the tube station. This isn't a Tesco run—he's traveling a ways across the city. Or, he wants to. We haven't even gone two blocks, and he's already slowed significantly, putting less and less weight on his foot. When we reach the steps descending to the platform, he stares down at the florescent-filled depths and falters.

"Can we go back now?" I ask.

"You can go where you want."

I block his path. He shoots me a tremendous glower.

"Yes, I'm very frustrating." I stand my ground, crossing my arms for emphasis. "I'm also stronger than I look. If you try to dodge past me, I *will* push you back upstairs."

"What do you *want*?"

"To know where you're going."

"It's not your problem."

"It is somewhat my problem." Not that I want to admit it, but I *am* the reason he tripped.

He leans forward. For a moment, I think he's going to push past me despite the warning, but he just grabs onto the stair railing to take his weight fully off his foot. "I'm leading an art class. If I don't show, they'll fire me, and—" He hesitates. "I need the job, okay?"

Some of my annoyance fades. London is expensive. My parents are helping me out with food and necessities, but not everyone's that lucky. I pull out my phone. "What's the address?"

"Huh?"

I shove Citymapper at him. "Where are you working? Type it in."

He does, and I check the route. It's twenty minutes by tube and another ten by foot. I nod back in the direction of the dorm. "Go and get your ankle sorted. I'll take over your class."

He stares. Long enough for it to become uncomfortable. "You can't just do my job."

"I'm a quick learner."

"That's not what I meant."

"I know what you meant. I like art. It's no big deal."

He's still staring—too intensely, the way someone does when they're trying to catch a lie.

My first instinct is to go for more sarcasm, but I no longer think he's trying to be difficult. I don't hear pride under his snippiness. I hear fear. I think he's desperate, and I think he's in pain, and I think that's a nasty combination that often leads to clouded judgment.

"Listen." I point at him and then at me. "You're injured, and I'm not. You're supposed to run an art class, and I'm an art student. Clearly the universe is telling you to go home."

His expression is unreadable; I keep going. "You can either continue on like this and make your ankle worse, or you can let me go instead. Disaster-case scenario and I get you fired, I'll find you a new job. You can hold me to it; you know where I live."

He's still hesitating. Absurd, since there's only one right option here. But if he's unsure, even after all this, then there's probably a reason—whether I can see it or not.

The silence stretches for so long that I stop thinking he's going to respond. His eyes are down, first on the stairs, then on his injured foot. Finally, he mutters, "Have you tried?"

Now I'm the one saying "Huh?"

"You don't sound British. You sound like me. So I'm assuming you're also on a student visa. Have you tried getting work? It's hard when you're not a citizen. There are limitations."

I cough. "I actually am a citizen. My mom's Scottish, so I have two passports."

His eyes turn murderous.

I hold up my hands in surrender. "Okay! You hate me and you're not going home. Fine, but you're also making destructive life choices, which, unfortunately for the both of us, means I can't just leave you alone. So there appear to be two options: We can either stand here arguing for the rest of the night, or we can go to your job together."

His eyes narrow, like the suggestion threw him off but he doesn't want to show it. I'm also a little thrown off—I didn't expect that offer to come out of my mouth, but now that it has, it's clearly the most logical solution.

"It's one night," I press. "You obviously care about this job, and from the way you're leaning on that railing, you're not going to make it on your own. I'm here already. It's no big deal. Let me come."

He shuts his eyes and breathes in. Out. "Fine," he mutters, but it was unnecessary.

I already knew I won.

Chapter Four

At this point, you might be thinking, *Maisie, stop meddling in other peoples' business. This isn't your problem, and not everyone wants your help.* You're probably right, but hey. I came to London to have new experiences, and shepherding an injured stranger to his night job across the city is definitely a first for me.

Getting to Eli's (yes, Eli—he begrudgingly allowed me his name once we were in transit) workplace is a team effort. The tube is fine. So is leaving the station (thanks, escalators!). The ten-minute walk is less fine, because almost immediately, his ankle decides to go fully on strike and he has to hop forward with his fingers deep in my shoulder. I suggest we take a cab, but he mutters something about it being a waste of money when we're already almost there, so we continue on despite my better judgment. It doesn't help that he's fairly tall and I'm fairly not. His balance is off because of his foot, and my balance is off because of his height, and the fact that we don't go tumbling into oncoming traffic is honestly commendable on both our parts.

In the end, we do make it. And although we hardly spoke on the trek, you can't be that close to someone's armpit for a prolonged period of time without bonding at least a little.

"Eli?" An older woman stands at the entrance of the pub on my right, squinting into the darkness.

Eli straightens without letting go of my shoulder and gives a lackluster wave. "That's me. Hello."

I frown at the interaction. "Is this your first day?"

"Yes," he mutters. "Which is why I couldn't just not show up."

The woman steps toward us, going from confused to concerned in the span of a second. "What's happened?" she asks, giving Eli a once-over. She's short and skinny and looks older than my parents, but she moves quickly, and her eyes are sharp as ice. "Are you injured?"

Eli shakes his head, which is bold considering I'm currently being pressed into the pavement by his fingers. "I rolled my ankle, but it's no problem—I'm fine to lead the class."

"This does not look fine," the woman says, gesturing at our configuration. Her eyes lock with mine. "You are—?"

"Maisie. I told him to go home."

Eli glowers at me, but the woman shakes her head. "Mrs. Beverley." She turns back to him. "You should have rung."

"It happened on the way over. There wasn't time—"

"Dear, I hired you for an art class, not to defuse a bomb. Sit down. You're about to tip over."

The pub has outdoor tables. I assume the class is taking place inside because the chairs in this area are all empty, and there's a sign on the door stating RESERVED FOR PRIVATE PARTY.

Now that his job doesn't appear to be on the line, Eli becomes more amenable. He lets me lead him to a chair without protest. Once he's down, his head drops, too, and it's only now that I realize how hard he's breathing.

Mrs. Beverley reaches toward his leg. She's still a few inches away when he flinches. Hard.

I frown. I'm not a doctor, but that can't be good. She didn't even touch him.

"How do you know each other? From the university?" Mrs. Beverley doesn't go near Eli's ankle again. She simply claps a hand on his shoulder and looks up at me.

I nod.

"You're also an art student?"

I nod again.

"Can you crochet?"

"I—*crochet?*"

"Yes," she says impatiently. "We're making tea cozies tonight. You are, anyway. I'm taking him to A&E."

My mouth opens and then closes. I don't know what a tea cozy is, let alone how to crochet one. I'm also trying (and failing) to picture Eli, with his scowl and many piercings and all-black outfit, leading a class on crochet. Not that men can't crochet—my dad, in fact, is quite adept at it—but *Eli*...

There's really nothing funny about this situation, but I can't help it—I smile. Eli's not looking at me, but he seems to sense it because he suddenly rolls his eyes.

"Well?" Mrs. Beverley snaps her fingers. "Crochet—can you? I'd cancel the class, but the students are already here."

"Um." I clear my throat. "Not exactly..."

She sighs.

"But!" I hold out a palm. "I can do other types of art. Portraits." One night of backsliding into familiar territory won't ruin my growth. Right? "I could come up with a few quick drawing exercises," I continue, "and all we'd need are some paper and pencils..."

Mrs. Beverley waves a hand. "So long as it's something you can lead comfortably. The class is two hours, but you can let them out early, considering the circumstances. There are extra supplies in the coat closet, and Bill, the bartender, is familiar with the students. He can help out if you need it. I'll pop in to explain the change in schedule. Stay here?" She darts into the pub before I can respond.

After that whirlwind, the subsequent silence feels charged. Or maybe that's just because Eli's breathing hasn't eased. If anything, it's gotten worse.

"How bad is your ankle? Really?"

"Oh, you know." His voice is monotone. "Not great."

"Why . . . ?" I'm not entirely sure what the rest of that question is. *Why did you keep walking if you were in this much pain? Why are you still trying to act like you're fine?*

He doesn't answer. The careful blankness to his expression reminds me a little too much of Calum, and if I've learned anything from my brother, it's that sometimes it's okay to press someone for a response, and other times it's really not.

Mrs. Beverley comes back a few moments later. "I've called for a cab." She hands me a slip of paper. "Here's my number. Ring if you need anything." She pauses. "Can you handle this?"

Can I? Half an hour ago, my plans for the night were to cry in my bed because my photography professor hates me. Now I'm agreeing to teach an art class? In the medium I promised to give up forever? My hands are vibrating with anticipation or motivation but definitely not fear, because it doesn't matter if I can do this—I have to. Fake it till you make it, right?

"All good," I say. "It'll be fine!" I rush toward the door but then spin back to look at Eli. "Hang on. Your phone."

"What?"

"Can I see it?"

He stares at me suspiciously but reaches into his pocket. Maybe he's too tired for another argument, or maybe the wide smile I've affected to inspire confidence is less easygoing and more terrifying.

"Unlock it," I say.

After he does, I snatch it, type in my number, text myself so I have his, and then wave my contact information at him. "Message if you need to. At the very least, let me know when you're back at the dorm. I'll sit outside until I see you, otherwise."

He shrugs half-heartedly, which is not the assured confirmation I was hoping for, but hey. It's something.

Okay.

Art class.

Can I lead an art class?

I can lead an art class.

I square my shoulders and walk into the pub.

Chapter Five

Maybe something should have clicked after "crochet" and "tea cozies," but a lot's happened and we're in a pub! At ten p.m.! I assumed this was one of those classes for twenty-somethings—you know, drink while you paint and paint while you drink. But it's a Monday night, which is a bizarre time slot for something like that.

Of course, now that I'm standing in front of the students, everything makes sense. There are about thirty of them, and they are not in the young adult demographic. They are in the old adult demographic. I'm talking seventy plus.

Eli. A little warning would have been nice!

Not that it really matters. Until a few years ago, most of our clients at Glenna's were older, anyway. I can work with this.

Mrs. Beverley, thank God, already passed out paper and pencils. She said she explained the schedule change, but I figure I'm still supposed to introduce myself.

"Cool." I clap my hands together. The noise is louder than I expected, and silence falls at the tables closest to me, heads turning to attention.

This is fine. I mean, I've had zero preparation, I've been doubting my art skills, and a part of my brain isn't here because it's outside with Eli, who's sitting too pale and sweaty on that chair by the curb, but it's *fine*.

"Hi? I'm Maisie? I'm from New York, but I'm studying at the London College of Art? Nice to meet you?"

No one responds. Maybe they really wanted to make those tea cozies, or maybe I'm overthinking this.

"Um," I continue. "For this class, we'll . . . portraits? Yes, we're drawing portraits of each other. So . . . choose a partner? And if you don't have a partner, raise your hand?"

A part of me doesn't expect them to listen. I'm at least fifty years younger than the youngest student, and there are *a lot* of them. If they wanted to stage a coup, it would be all over for me.

But then I hear them breaking into groups, and wow. Is this what power feels like? Give me any more and I might become insufferable.

After a few minutes of shuffling, three people have their hands raised. I pair up the two sitting closest to each other, but that still leaves one woman in the corner.

"You can work with me." I wasn't planning to partake in the exercises—it's one thing to teach this art form I'm supposed to have forsaken, and another to actually pick up a pencil—but it *would* be helpful to have an example to pass around.

The instructions are simple. We're starting with rough drafts, but the catch is they can't take their eyes off the face of the person they're drawing. They also can't lift their pencil off the paper. The product will be a mess, I assure them, but the idea is to get used to *looking*. As Dr. Lazar (who sucks but unfortunately did make a decent point) explained, in order to capture an image, you need to pay attention to your surroundings. And you can't do that if your eyes are down.

I give them five minutes. After the timer is set on my phone, I sit down across from my partner. She's on the older end of the students, which is saying a lot. When I ask her name, she doesn't respond. I'm not sure if she can.

That's fine. I don't mind silence as long as it's not

awkward or intimidating. Now that we've gotten to work, the vibe is relaxed. It's miles from photography, where everyone moved around rigidly, hardly daring to breathe. The noise level varies throughout the pub—my table is silent, but our neighbors are riotous.

When the timer goes off, I show my sketch to the room. This is a warm-up technique I learned from my dad, so naturally the lines on my page are reminiscent of his. I try not to think about that as I address my audience.

"It's a bit wonky," I say, pointing to the crooked angles of the eyes and how the neck is way too long, "but it's a good base to start with. Now you're going to use a darker pencil to trace over the outline and add detail. You can look at your paper this time, but don't forget to also look at the person you're drawing! We'll go for fifteen minutes."

When I return to my table, it's no longer just my partner there. Two older men have taken the chairs next to us. "Thought we'd join," the one with glasses says.

"Get that insider advice," the one with the cane chimes in.

Okay? I don't know how to respond, so I kind of wave and then lean over to peek at my partner's paper. "Don't just look at my eyes," I tell her. "Make sure to also consider the space between them."

"Yes, Margaret, make sure to also consider the space between them," the man with the glasses repeats, like we're in kindergarten.

I'm so taken aback I almost don't notice when Margaret flips up her middle finger at him, which then takes me aback about six thousand times more.

Am I about to bear witness to an old person fight? Should I have established anti-bullying policies? Or—

"Are you *friends*?" I ask.

"Margaret wouldn't say so, would you, love? But it's a small circle at this age." Glasses Man grins at her. Then he turns to the other man. "How're you liking your portrait, Ollie?" He tilts his paper forward.

I'm expecting something unserious, considering these are clearly elementary school students trapped in eighty-year-old bodies, but when I lean over to take a look, my eyebrows shoot up.

"You're an artist." It's not a question—he's clearly experienced. The lines are confident; he wasn't afraid to press the pencil hard into the paper. And even though this is just a sketch, I see the beginnings of distinct features that resemble the man with the cane—Ollie.

"Exquisite, Georgie. Museum material."

"Shall I offer it up to the V&A?"

"Hang it over your bed instead. You're severely lacking in company."

"Why are you taking an art class?" I ask, louder than necessary. Georgie clearly has more experience than me; he could be leading this lesson instead of participating in it.

"Mrs. Beverley," he responds without missing a beat. "She's got a massive crush on me, and I enjoy making her flustered."

Ollie elbows him. Possibly because I'm speechless. "There isn't much nightlife for our demographic," he explains. "Ironic, considering we're up later than most everyone else. This class is a good way to pass the time."

Huh. It never occurred to me older people might want to do things like this. I assumed they enjoyed staying home in front of the TV. Maybe some do, but probably others would enjoy these types of spaces if more were available.

My timer goes off. I stand and walk around the room, trying to mimic the way my art teachers would glance over people's shoulders. Some of these students are clearly beginners. Others are quite skilled. I tell them to switch partners, and we do the whole exercise again.

After four rounds, the mood starts to drop. It hasn't quite been two hours, but this feels like the time to call it. "Sorry about the schedule change," I say, and I do mean it, more than I did at the start, because I can tell this class is important to them. "Everything should be back to normal for next time, though!"

My tablemates say goodbye as they leave, as do other students I didn't talk to. They thank me for my time and tell me they enjoyed the lesson, even though I'm sure it was lackluster compared to what they usually get.

Still, I smile.

I smile a lot.

Leading that art class gave me a rush of adrenaline. I don't know why—maybe from the high of knowing *I did that, look at me go,* or from the relief of *I did that, and no one was accidentally set on fire,* or maybe simply because it felt good to slip back into a comfortable medium after a day of lessons I hated. Whatever the reason, I'm buzzing as I help Bill the Bartender clean up.

After, I head outside to call a taxi. The exhaustion hits once we're rolling back toward the dorm. I pull out my phone to check the time, and it's only then that I see the texts.

10:58 p.m.

The Ridiculous Boy (Eli):
Hi

The Ridiculous Boy (Eli):
Is it fine
The Ridiculous Boy (Eli):
The class

God. I was so firm about him reaching out, and he did—he listened, but then I didn't respond. His messages are from more than an hour ago.

12:10 a.m.

Me: Hi!!
Me: Sorry!!!
Me: I was getting everyone out the door and didn't see this!!
Me: Everything went well!!
Me: Heading home now
Me: You??

The Ridiculous Boy (Eli):
Will be here a while
The Ridiculous Boy (Eli):
My ankle's broken

I shouldn't roll my eyes. I do, because this dude! I didn't even know you could walk on a broken ankle. Maybe he's unlocked a really depressing superpower.

Me: Is Mrs. Beverley still there?

The Ridiculous Boy (Eli):
I keep telling her to leave and she keeps telling me to shove it
The Ridiculous Boy (Eli):
You know
The Ridiculous Boy (Eli):
In an aggressively polite way

That doesn't surprise me. I was only in Mrs. Beverley's presence for five minutes, but it felt like she was holding up the world.

The Ridiculous Boy (Eli):
Sorry for ruining your night

Me: I didn't mind helping out!!
I actually really enjoyed the art class

The Ridiculous Boy (Eli):
Don't do that

The Ridiculous Boy (Eli):
Tonight was shitty and not just for me

Me: It's fine!!!

Me: Besides it's my fault you tripped

The Ridiculous Boy (Eli):
It's not your fault I tripped

Me: I was sitting in the doorway!!!

The Ridiculous Boy (Eli):
I wasn't looking where I was going

The Ridiculous Boy (Eli):
And anyway you covered my job

Me: BECAUSE I BROKE YOUR ANKLE!!!!!!!!!!!!!!!!!!!!!!!!!!!!

The Ridiculous Boy (Eli):
You practically carried me across London

The Ridiculous Boy (Eli):
At least let me buy you coffee

My fingers pause on my phone. A boy wants to buy me coffee. A ridiculous boy who had me pulling out my hair multiple times in the space of a few hours, but hey. Like he said: Tonight was shitty, and not just for me.

Me: We can do coffee

Chapter Six

It's Wednesday, and since Dr. Lazar does not yet believe I am worthy of her cameras, I'm forced to stand in a corner of the photography classroom like a toddler in time-out while everyone else snaps away at the floorboards. Or the ceiling. The vases on the tables? It's hard to pay attention when my face is hot and itchy, and it's not like I can ask the other students what they're up to. As you might imagine, this punishment is doing wonders for my social game.

At least Eli isn't here to witness my shame. He must still be dealing with his ankle. We do have plans to meet up this Friday, though, for coffee. I definitely don't spend the rest of the lesson thinking about that.

I truly don't spend my afternoon class thinking about it; I'm more preoccupied with the fact that metalworking is somehow even more embarrassing than photography. For the full period, I try hard to make eye contact with the other students, and the other students try harder not to make eye contact with me. Maybe it's my outfit. I went far outside my comfort zone today with black lipstick, a spiky choker necklace, dark shorts over ripped tights, and a lacy crop top. *I* was intimidated by my reflection in the mirror this morning, so it's not unreasonable that others might fear me, too.

On Thursday, I go for a softer look—lavender jeans with a powder-pink top and a knitted white cardigan—but I still can't get anyone in my lessons to hold a conversation with me for more than five seconds. Maybe it's because the question that always follows *Name?* is *Why are you taking [insert class here]?* and people can see the weird hesitation in my eyes as I try to come up with a less confusing answer than *Because I hate it.*

So, I end up spending the rest of the day alone. In silence. It's not new, doing art in silence. But it is new, doing art alone. Back at the workshop, Dad and I could go eight hours without speaking. But he was always there, just to the side of me. Mom was always a few paces away, taking calls with clients. Alicia tended to join us as well, writing at the table I liked to sketch at.

She texts me as I'm walking back to the dorm.

4:02 p.m.

Alicia Miller: I got into the poetry society!!!!!

Alicia Miller: Which means I get to help edit our university's literary magazine!!!!

Alicia Miller: Unlikely any of my actual writing will get featured because they never choose work by freshmen, but this is the first step!!!!!

A bitter feeling pools in my gut. My first reaction to Alicia's news should be *YAY!!* but instead it's *Oh.* I *am* happy for her—Alicia's been talking about that poetry society since before she even got into college—but the thing is, if I can't match her success in the next few hours with something like *I've joined a secret club that meets in an underground storeroom once every three months at exactly 2:02 a.m.,* she'll realize she's winning at college. And if Alicia realizes she's winning at college, she'll realize I'm *losing* at college, which means she'll stop texting me as much because she's a good person and won't want to rub her victories in my face. And if she stops texting, we'll start to drift, and once we start to drift, we'll keep on drifting until the day we look back and discover we're no longer friends . . .

Me: YAY!!
Me: That's so great!!
Me: Congrats!!

Alicia Miller: THANKS!!!
Alicia Miller: How are YOU???
Alicia Miller: How's your first week of classes?

Me: Not bad!
Me: I also joined a society!
Me: The Society of Paranormal Believers

It's not a lie. Well, I haven't *joined* yet, but I'm going to the interest meeting tonight. The thing is, I was anticipating this: Alicia winning at college. If it wasn't the poetry society, then it would have been a first date, meeting her new best friend, or getting an A on a writing assignment. Alicia left Crescent Valley because our town is small and she is big. She was always bursting through the seams of it: the oldest in our grade, top of all her classes, confident in her abilities, outspoken in her opinions. I knew I'd have to work hard if I wanted to be on par with her this year, and so I figured I'd start by pursuing an activity she wouldn't expect.

Alicia Miller: You joined WHAT?!
Alicia Miller: Maisie Clark
Alicia Miller: You hate everything paranormal

She's right. I do. And it's her fault: Alicia loves all things horror and went through a phase in middle school where she dug into the paranormal lore surrounding the woods of Crescent Valley. I don't *really* believe our town is haunted, but after one too many stories in sixth grade about howling on windless nights and flashlights that flickered off and on, I went through my own phase of not wanting to walk alone outside after the sun went down.

Me: I figured it was time to get over my ghost thing haha
Me: What should I wear???
Me: For ghost-hunting
Me: Ghost-watching
Me: Ghost-something
Me: I'm not actually sure what the goal is
Me: Of this society
Me: Beyond "ghosts"

Alicia Miller: Send me options!!!

As I walk out the door several hours later, I text Alicia a photo of the outfit she helped me assemble: black leggings with a black top and a baggy gray jean jacket that Benji made me for my birthday last year. The back is hand-painted with an image of Edinburgh Castle amid the cherry blossoms, since spring is the time of year I most love to visit my aunt in the city. It's my favorite piece of clothing, but I haven't worn it in months because it clashes with my TRY NEW THINGS list. I'm about to meet up with a bunch of strangers to look for evil ghosts, though (or nice ghosts, I don't know), and the soft press of familiar denim reminds me I'm not alone in this city, even if I am alone tonight.

When I arrive outside the student center, there is a crowd of around twenty people wearing everything from flip-flops to sneakers to heels. The closer I get, the drier my throat becomes: Everyone is clumped in groups of twos or threes, like they all came here with at least one person they know.

"Hi!" I say brightly, shoving my way next to two girls I vaguely recognize. They're in my photography class, which in hindsight should have caused me to turn and run. So I suppose it's on me when they pause, look at each other, and then burst into laughter.

Well. That's not what you want. My cheeks burn. At least it's dark out. The smile stretching my lips doesn't waver, but after several frozen moments, it starts to hurt.

"Sorry," one of the girls says. She's blonder than me and taller than me and is pulling off red lipstick better than me. She steps aside so I can join the huddle. "Maisie, right? I'm Elsie, and that's Grace." She tilts her head toward the other girl, who has shoulder-length brown hair and sparkly purple eye shadow that matches her sparkly purple crop top. "I'm so curious about you, actually. I'd never show my face in a course I was terrible at—let alone keep with it after the professor humiliated me. So it was a surprise to see you again in photography yesterday." She looks me up and down in a slow way that makes me wonder if I'm wearing something wrong. "No judgment," she adds in a voice that very much implies judgment. "I'd simply love to understand the thought process."

The smile doesn't leave my face. I push more enthusiasm into my voice. "I like trying new things."

"Oh!" Grace says. "American. How cute." Her voice does not imply she thinks I am cute.

Before I can respond, the crowd starts moving in the direction of the tube. I stand frozen for a moment, but then Elsie curls her hand, beckoning me forward.

"Come," she says. "Tell us about your life. I'm *dying* to know more."

I don't want to tell Elsie and Grace about my life. My gut is screaming at me to leave this evening behind, but #6 on my TRY NEW THINGS list is *Always say yes. Even when you don't want to.* Besides, if I leave before snapping any photos for Alicia, she'll know I didn't have it in me to stick with this society, and that failure will look more pathetic than if I'd just not come at all.

My arms unclench from around my stomach. Maybe I'm making assumptions. Elsie and Grace are not giving off good vibes, but we might find common ground once we know more about each other. I raise my chin, trying to stretch myself taller.

"Yeah," I say as casually as I can. "Okay!"

The tube ride is not okay. I spend it squeezed between Elsie and Grace, who ask me questions ranging from vaguely rude to outright belittling (How did you get your hair to lie so . . . flat? Is there an art form you *are* proficient in?). Then they promptly abandon me the moment we reach London Bridge.

Which . . . fine. According to the society organizers, we're here for a tour of some tombs, and Elsie and Grace don't need to see me getting squeamish over that. As we walk toward the river, I try to ignore the fact that I'm alone at the back of the crowd by snapping photos of the moon over the Thames. When I lower the saturation, they look impressively eerie, so I send the most haunting ones to Alicia.

The tour isn't terrible at the start. A guide goes through the bloodier aspects of London Bridge's history, which I don't particularly enjoy hearing, but Alicia's relayed creepier information to me on darker nights. It starts to become less fine when we're suddenly told to head under the bridge and into an old plague pit—which, what?? And then it becomes *really* not fine when costumed actors with chainsaws jump onto the path in front of us. I know it's fake, because I'm not five years old, but I can't stop thinking about how everyone else on this tour is shrieking and clinging to the arm of a neighbor while I'm standing alone.

The group has only walked a few feet forward when I slip back out, my ears ringing from the loss of heavy screaming. My eyes sting. I want to call someone. Alicia.

Except I can't call Alicia. She can't know I'm on the verge of a breakdown. I can't call Mom or Dad: It's eleven p.m. and I'm in a plague pit with strangers and I've already been judged enough for one night. Benji wouldn't judge me, but he would tell Calum I'm randomly crying under a bridge in central London, and I don't want my brother to know I couldn't get through one week of university by myself when he went through years on his own.

So that leaves... no one. There's no one else I can reach out to.

Well.

I stare at my texts. The most recent is from Alicia.

Then I've got some from Benji, and then from Mom, and then from a group chat between me and Mom and Dad. Below that is my thread of exchanges with Eli. We're supposed to meet up tomorrow. Somehow, my fingers find themselves messaging him tonight.

11:25 p.m.
Me: You wouldn't want to get coffee now instead of at a reasonable hour tomorrow??

I don't expect a response. It's far too late on a Thursday, but my phone buzzes thirty seconds later.

The Ridiculous Boy (Eli):
Sure

Oh. I was so convinced he wouldn't reply that I wasn't prepared for the fact that he might. The feeling isn't one of dread, though. It's more . . . nerves. And after tonight, with the Society of Paranormal Believers, the difference is noticeable. Nerves are uncomfortable, but dread *hurts.*

Clearly it's not worth putting myself in situations that hurt. Like, I knew I would hate this ghost society, and I went anyway. I knew Elsie and Grace weren't very nice, and I let them be not very nice to me. For what? All I really gained from this evening was a barrage of insults. So maybe #6 on my TRY NEW THINGS list—*Always say yes. Even when you don't want to*—needs modification. Maybe it should be: *Say yes more than you say no.*

I glance again at my phone.

Me: Are you at the dorm?

The Ridiculous Boy (Eli):
The library
The Ridiculous Boy (Eli):
There's a café here

Me: Cool!
Me: I'll meet you there!

The Ridiculous Boy (Eli):
Cool

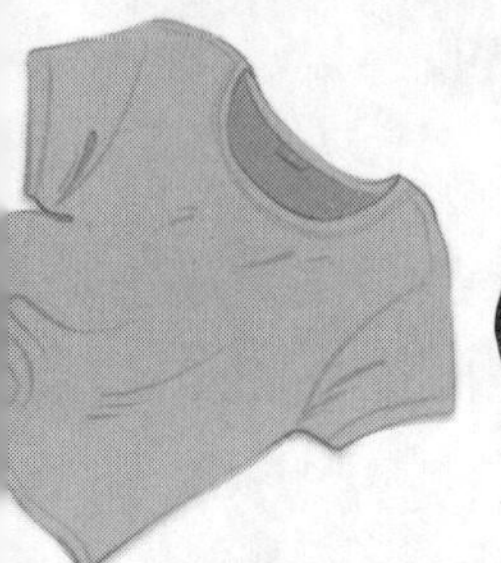

Chapter Seven

The café in our college library is basically an arrangement of metal chairs, wobbly tables, and paper cups. By the time I arrive, it's closed. The library itself is also verging on closed: Although some students are still buried in the studio spaces to our right and left, half the automatic lights are off, and the sole staff member on duty is asleep at her desk.

"Not to be a bad influence," I say when I spot Eli at one of the rickety tables with his head in a textbook, "but the only other people here are either sleeping or crying. Can we go somewhere else?"

He hesitates.

"I won't, like, get you drunk or anything." I cough. "I just mean I'd like to do something fun, and I'm not getting 'fun' from that sign in the corner with the big SHHHH."

I wait for him to shoot me down. He doesn't, but his response of "Where do you want to go?" is not horribly enthusiastic.

Several museums flash through my head. They'll be closed at this hour, though. London has night markets—I've always enjoyed wandering through them, devouring street food—but Eli's got crutches and a bulky cast on his leg. "Do you like board games?"

He raises an eyebrow. "A library isn't your idea of a fun time, but board games are?"

"Board games in a library are very different from board games in a pub."

"I thought you weren't going to get me drunk."

My cheeks heat. "That's not—I wasn't implying—you're *intentionally* misinterpreting—"

His lips twitch up for a fraction of a second, as though beneath the deadpan expression, he actually does know how to smile. Then he ducks his head and places the textbook in his bag. "All right."

It takes a moment for my hackles to lower.

I expected more of a fight.

I should probably admit something here: While I like the *idea* of a board game pub, I don't actually know how to play board games. At home when I was little, "family time" was pulling out the watercolors and painting in the forest outside. And then Calum left, and our house got colder. I can't remember doing many fun things with my parents between the ages of six and twelve. When I wanted to have a cozy day, I'd go to Alicia's, but board games weren't a thing at her place, either. To relax, we'd watch movies with her parents or work on various creative projects in her room. But while this pub feels uncomfortable, it's in a growing way, not in a dread way. And although Eli is really as much of a stranger as Elsie and Grace, my instincts are not sending out *Run away!* alerts around him like they were with them, so. At least there's that.

"What do you mean?" Eli asks once we're settled at a table. He points at the wall to my left. It's covered in bookshelves, but instead of novels, they're filled with loudly colorful boxes. "Monopoly? Candyland? You've at least played *chess*?"

"I can do chess," I amend. "I'm actually pretty good."

The thing about going to a tiny school in the middle

of nowhere is that the curriculum was kind of whatever. My eighth-grade math teacher incorporated chess into a lot of her lessons and even held a grade-wide competition at the end of every year. It became a whole spectacle. Like, I'd never seen kids get so hyped over math, but the winner didn't have to do homework for the last two weeks of school, so, valid. Anyway, (hair flip) hello. Crescent Valley Middle School's eighth-grade Chess Champion, at your service.

I grab the game from the shelf, and we get set up and ready to go.

"Have you used timers before?" I pull them from the bottom of the box.

Eli shakes his head. "We don't need those. This isn't an actual competition."

"It is if I actually beat you."

"Oh. You're one of those people."

"*Those* people?"

"You don't like to lose."

"Of course I don't like to lose. Who likes to lose?" I gesture for him to make the first move. "The sooner we start, the sooner I can destroy you."

He rolls his eyes. "You spent all that time on Monday calling me unreasonable, but you're oddly confident for someone who doesn't play board games."

"Declaring I'm going to murder you at chess is not the same as declaring you can walk on a broken ankle. I hope the doctor yelled at you."

"Multiple doctors. For multiple hours." There's no bite to his tone, but there is something firm, like *Please stop now.* I do stop. He's got his injured foot propped on a chair and has made no more attempts to be reckless with it, and

I don't need to shout at someone who's already received the message.

He picks up a pawn. The game begins.

And then it ends.

In four moves.

"What the hell?" I sit back, staring at the board. His attack was a precise slaughter across the field—he took out only the pieces he needed and did it so quickly, almost carelessly, that I couldn't see him calculating between moves. "Are you some sort of chess genius?"

He clears the board. "I used to compete."

"*Professionally?*"

He hesitates. Then he pulls out his phone. After typing something in, he shoves it across the table at me and becomes very interested in my captured king in his fist.

It's an article. From *ESPN*, detailing the appointment of a fourteen-year-old women's grandmaster. The kid in the photos is wearing a dress and has longer hair than the guy sitting across from me, but they've got identical scowls.

"You're a *grandmaster?*" I press the phone back into his hand. Carefully, because he showed me something more than just chess. "Seriously," I continue, "you let me go on about being a master while you're an *actual* master?" I hold an arm in front of my face like a fainting maiden. "Don't even look at me."

It's very small, but I see it. He smiles. "I'm not the best. Just—you know. Not bad."

"Right, because *ESPN* writes articles about 'not bad' chess players. Go *away*."

He begins to return the board to the box; I grab it back. "No, no. We're not done here. Can you win with your hands behind your back? Or if I'm loudly singing in your ear?" I pull off my elastic headband and toss it across the table. "Can you beat me *blindfolded?*"

He stares at the headband but doesn't pick it up. "To be clear." He pauses. "From that article. If it wasn't clear . . ." He trails off and does not, in fact, make himself clear.

"Yes," I say anyway. "Your name was different. And other things. Do you want to talk about it?"

"No." His glass of Sprite (which he ordered after muttering "I have been warned that mixing alcohol with painkillers will be less of a fun time and more of a death time") is empty, but he still attempts to take a sip. "It just wasn't clear. If it was clear. But if it was clear, then—"

"It was clear." He's trans. I didn't expect to be handed something delicate by someone I hardly know—I tried to be careful so I wouldn't fumble it, but obviously I did fumble it. "I'm sorry. I mean, I didn't want to say the wrong thing, but I should have said something—"

He shakes his head. "It's fine. I just wanted—"

"To be clear?" I tried not to say it. I really did, but come on. I had to.

He pulls my headband over his eyes—whether from embarrassment or to move on from the subject, I'm not sure.

I tap his foot under the table. The uninjured one—I'm not a monster. "It was clear," I confirm one last time for him. "And I was serious about the headband. Can you win with it on?"

He shrugs. "It's been a while since I've played."

The fact that he doesn't say *No, Maisie, I could not possibly beat you without looking at the chess pieces, how ridiculous of you to even suggest it* makes my eyes bug. How can anyone play without seeing the board? He'd have to be able to hold all the positions in his head and remember exactly where we've both moved...

"Why did you quit?" I ask, feeling a sudden need to understand. People don't get this good at something unless they love it.

He can't see me with the headband over his eyes, but I can see him. I see the way he flinches. After a pause, he mutters, "Sometimes that's just how it is."

He doesn't elaborate, but he doesn't need to. I love portraits. I gave them up anyway. That's just how it is.

Enough. Tonight is supposed to be fun. Tonight, I'm supposed to win!

I pick up a pawn.

He ends with my king.

What sorcery is this?!

Chapter Eight

It's been two weeks since the start of the semester, and my TRY NEW THINGS plan isn't progressing as smoothly as I'd hoped. I haven't seen Henrold since that first encounter (a part of me wonders if I imagined him); Naked Boy (Marcus) sleeps at his girlfriend's most nights; and Natalie never leaves her room unless it's two a.m. and she's burning something in the kitchen (usually popcorn; once, inexplicably, Sour Patch Kids). Eli is also difficult to crack. Although we're in photography together, Dr. Lazar keeps her classroom silent and I never see him outside of lessons. I think he works off campus most afternoons and evenings.

So #5 on my list—*Make new friends (because Alicia is going to)*—is still a bust. At least my classes have been more fruitful. Kind of. Aside from this school being far from home, the other reason I chose it is because of the curriculum. They don't let students choose a concentration until their second year, which gives everyone the opportunity to take classes across disciplines in order to get a better sense of where they want to focus. It means I was allowed into a bunch of courses I have zero talent for or experience in, and... well. The results are as mediocre as you'd expect.

Metalworking is terrifying. I have lots of ideas for pieces that could totally lend to my own style, but I don't have the technical skills to pull them off. The best I could do on Wednesday with our ninety-minute lesson was cut out a handful of circles. I was going for spirals, but when

I attempted to maneuver the metal more precisely around the electric saw, I nearly sliced through my thumb.

So.

Circles.

Ceramics isn't deadly, but it sure is frustrating. I spent a week carefully handcrafting a flowerpot that Dr. Amato deemed "interesting," only to drop it as soon as it came out of the kiln. In order to receive a proper grade on the assignment, I had to remake the whole thing, which involved three late nights in the studio with only my yells of annoyance for company.

Abstract painting is actually going okay. Maybe because acrylics on canvas is something I'm used to. Whatever the reason, Dr. Dumont stopped me after class yesterday to ask if she could hang my first project—a series of palm-sized prints titled "Blues"—outside the studio as an example. It was nice to be complimented like that, and it's even nicer that my paintings already have a distinct style. I could easily point them out in a messy room full of student art, which is a huge step up from my work back home. But the reason my work stands out is because, despite my best efforts, it's less abstract than it should be. I'm used to painting in a realistic style, and those techniques apparently don't just leave my brain when I'm exploring a new medium. So with my brush I still summon Dad, and the similarities are even more frustrating in abstract painting than they were back at Glenna's, because at least I *liked* portraits. I don't get the same joy out of scribbling freely over a canvas as I do from spending two hours zoomed intimately into the whites of an eye.

Not that it matters. I mean, the important thing right now is finding my own style. *Liking* that style can come later. My mom claims that if you try a food fifty times, you'll eventually come to appreciate it. I'm sure I'll develop a taste for my classes if I keep at them.

Well. Maybe not photography.

On Friday, Dr. Lazar hits us with a big announcement. "I don't do traditional exams. Instead, you will spend all term on one project. A draft will be due at the end of October, and you will receive initial feedback. Your final grade in this course will depend on what you do with that feedback."

She passes out the assignment sheet. "Photography revolves around the viewer and the viewed. I want you to take that theme and distill it into a more concentrated topic of your choosing. Together with a partner, you will craft a series of ten photographs and write a joint paper detailing the ways in which your work inhabits the idea of perception. Yes, you heard correctly: a joint paper. Photography is rarely a solo endeavor. You must learn to collaborate with others in order to create a cohesive vision." For some reason, her eyes seem to seek out mine. Then she directs her gaze back to the class at large. "As I said, your project will not be officially marked at the midterm, but I expect you to turn in a completed draft before November."

Ten photographs and a joint paper don't sound like a lot, but Dr. Lazar doesn't play around. If we want a good grade, we're going to have to take this seriously.

At least it's a partner project. And Eli is in this class. I beeline over to him—partially because he's not Grace or Elsie, but mostly because he actually likes photography. I'm still banned from touching the cameras, which is more annoying than embarrassing (I'm lying), but after spending some time trailing after Eli, I kind of understand why Dr. Lazar put me in purgatory. Last class, everyone (but me) spent an entire period photographing specks of debris on the studio floor. Boring, I know. But somehow, by catching just the right angles of light, Eli managed to turn dust and stray hairs into strands of gold. I never could have achieved something like that from the way I was rushing about during our first lesson. I probably couldn't have achieved that even if I took all the time in the world. So thank God he agrees to work with me on this project. Not just because I want a good grade, but because passion is contagious. If anyone can help me learn to appreciate photography, it'll be someone who loves it.

We start brainstorming in the library after class. The space is broken into study rooms and studios, some of which can be booked out in advance. We didn't do that, but luckily there are open areas in the main atrium, which contain a smattering of mismatched furniture. Eli and I drop our stuff at an empty table sandwiched between two couches. And then it's awkward. We haven't hung out one-on-one since our not-coffee night, which means I haven't hung out with *anyone* since our not-coffee night. I'm generally comfortable around people, but small talk is a muscle that gets stiff with disuse. My body feels big and clunky; I don't know where to put my hands or feet. It doesn't help that these couches are way too low for this table.

"So. Perspective?" I manage.

Eli nods. "Perspective."

"Right." I balance my notebook on my knees, and then reach up to set it on the too-high table. "Perspective."

"Perspective," Eli repeats.

This is going great.

I clear my throat. "You should probably—since, I mean. Cameras." Those weren't sentences. I'm not even sure they were words, but what I was going for is that any good group has a leader, and Eli is better than me at photography; he literally has a camera around his neck right now. If someone's going to take control of our project, it should be him.

Eli doesn't respond to any of that, of course, considering it occurred inside my head. Instead, he says, "Why are you taking this class?"

I blink. "What do you mean?"

"You obviously hate it. Every time you look at a camera, your nose scrunches." He taps the strap around his neck and then gestures at my face. "You're doing it right now."

"I'm not." I am. I blush. "Shut up."

"I'm serious," he says. "There are so many classes at this school. Why did you choose one you hate?"

"Is it a crime to try new things?"

"No—"

"Then there you go." I'm not trying to be sharp with him. I think I'm just pissed because he likes photography and I don't. Which, I *know,* is 1) literally why I wanted to work with him and 2) not an appropriate reason to snap at someone. "Sorry." I shake my head. "You're right. I don't like photography, but I'm trying to branch out from portraits, which is all I did back home."

"What's wrong with portraits?"

Oh, you know, just an inescapable family legacy I've got nothing of value to add to. I match his gaze. "What's wrong with chess?"

Eli pauses. Then he changes the subject like I knew he would. "Whatever. Just promise you'll take this project seriously."

I scoff. "Why did you partner with me if you think I won't?"

"I didn't partner with you. You partnered with me."

Wow. My eyebrows go to my hairline. "Sorry, I think I missed the part where I chained you up in the classroom until you said yes?"

"Would you really have let me say no?"

"What kind of question is *that*?"

We're both glowering now, and this is my fault. Eli and I got along the night of the board game pub, which made me forget how badly we *didn't* get along the night of the art pub. He's stubborn to the detriment of his own health and, well. I'm stubborn, too.

I cross my arms. "Yes, I'm taking photography even though I hate it. Maybe that sounds unserious to you, but all of my classes matter to me. I wouldn't be here if they didn't." I don't go into my ultimatum—I haven't told anyone about that, and I'm not going to hand it over to some guy I barely know just to prove a point. If Eli thinks I'm not a dedicated artist—well. I'd rather be seen as a joke than as a copy of my dad. At least jokes have their own punch lines.

Eli doesn't respond immediately. He often leaves a beat between exchanges. At first, I thought it was a nervous thing, but he doesn't give off distressed energy like Calum does when I throw an argument at his feet. When Eli's quiet, I think he's just thinking.

"My art class," he says finally. "The one I teach? I'm leading a photography lesson on Monday. You should come. Maybe it'll help us figure out an idea for our project."

The way he phrases it—*our project*—makes me take a breath. He cares enough about doing well on this assignment to work through it even while we're clashing. Art matters to him. Maybe as much as it matters to me.

"Okay." I nod. "Text me the details."

He nods back. "I'll text you."

"The details."

"The details. I'll text you."

I didn't know it was possible to have an awkward phone conversation without being on the phone, but here we are. We have both been nodding for way too long. Someone needs to hang up.

I shoot to my feet. "Cool. Sounds good. See you Monday. Bye!"

5:12 p.m.

Alicia Miller: Just got my first paper back in Uncovering Shakespeare…

Alicia Miller: It's an A!!!!!

Me: HELL YEAH

Alicia Miller: How are your classes going??

Me: They're okay!

Alicia Miller: What are ceramics and metalworking like? Are they as fun as portraits??

Me: They're fine!

Me: What did you write your paper on??

Alicia Miller: Are you sure you want to ask that question????

Alicia Miller: Because you can't cover my mouth and scream BORING when we're on opposite ends of an ocean

Me: Pretty sure I can survive one conversation about Shakespeare

Alicia Miller: Famous last words…

Chapter Nine

When Eli said he was leading a photography class, I pictured the art pub with its dim lighting and worn wooden tables. I did not anticipate chaperoning a field trip of elderly people to one of the most crowded tourist destinations in the UK. I should have known there was a reason Eli waited until this morning to send me the details. I don't waste any time in replying:

9:23 a.m.

Me: Tower Bridge???

Me: How are we supposed to keep track of twenty-nine senior citizens in the wild???

Randomly Good At Chess Boy (Eli): This is London, not the jungle

Randomly Good At Chess Boy (Eli): Besides Mrs. Beverley will be there

Me: She's not exactly young!!

Me: And your ankle is broken!!!

Me: If they escape, you do realize I'll be the one who has to chase after them???

Randomly Good At Chess Boy (Eli): They're grown adults, not chickens staging a coup

Me: Have you met Georgie and Ollie?????????????????????

Anyway, that's how I end up at Tower Bridge on a muggy Monday afternoon. We couldn't go late enough at night for the crowds to thin because the upper deck of the bridge closes at six, so when I come up from the tube, the sun shines down as strong as the September air burns hot, and it feels even stickier than it should because of all the people. I want to yell some more at Eli for choosing this location, but the thing about a loud and packed photo spot is there's unlimited material to capture. Tower Bridge, of course, and London Bridge behind it. The Shard in the distance, the busy boardwalks to the left and right of the Thames. His students will have plenty to play around with, and so will we for our project.

Eli and his elderly crew are crowded together by the base of the bridge. As hot and sweaty as I am, I can't help but smile when I see Mrs. Beverley. I get the sense she's lived in London forever, but with her neon pink visor and travel backpack, she looks like a tourist.

"Good to see you, love." She thrusts her bag at me before I have a chance to respond. "Pass these out, won't you?"

Inside are disposable cameras. I hand them out to the students. Although it's been less than a month since I've seen them, they greet me like a long-lost granddaughter.

"Have you been eating well?"

"What's that you've done with your hair?"

"It's blistering out—are you wearing sun cream?"

Eli sits on a bench a few yards away. I watch as he gives instructions to the students clumped around him. For some reason, I figured he'd be a graceless teacher—maybe because we keep having graceless conversations—but he explains everything with the same ease that he has while handling the cameras. When he's finished, the crowd ambles off toward the bridge and I amble over toward him.

"Hi." I thrust my hands into the pockets of my overall dress and then take them out when the fabric goes all squiggly.

"Hi." He looks up at me. "I think we should split up in case anyone needs help. Mrs. Beverley is taking a group up to the walkway. I'll stay down on this side of the bridge. Would you go to the other end? We can meet in the middle later to talk about our project."

I gesture at the receding backs of the students. "I thought they weren't chickens."

"I'm asking you to supervise, not corral."

"Ha. Haha. Hahaha." The laughter comes on slowly, a trickle into a gargle into a flood, because at first, I think he's joking. He's *seen* me in photography, hasn't he? He's aware of how that class is going for me, yet he's suggesting I take on an authoritative role?

The laughter comes until my stomach's screaming. "Sorry." There are tears in my eyes. I wipe them with my forearm. "You do remember I was banned from touching the cameras in class, right?"

"You can turn a gear, right?" He matches my intonation. "Some students might need help winding up to take their photos. No PhD necessary."

"Okay, but—"

"Didn't you want to branch out from portraits?"

That's the most annoying point he could have thrown at me. He knows it, too. His raised eyebrows are what make me turn in a huff and flounce away toward the bridge.

Whatever. If he doesn't mind me messing up his class, then I don't mind, either, so I walk across the river and wait for someone to need me. As Eli predicted, a few students ask for help winding their cameras and that's basically it.

"Thank you," one says to me. She's small and bony, with movie star sunglasses that take up half her face. "How long have you been a photographer?"

I don't laugh this time, only because I don't want to be rude to a stranger. "Oh, no—I'm just in a course at university."

She nods knowingly. "I'll tell my granddaughter to look out for your work. She's only fifteen, but she wants to be a photographer, too. What's your name?"

"Maisie. Maisie Clark. But, I'm not—" I can't finish the sentence, even though I should. The likelihood of me ever being good enough to have "work" in this field is a joke at best. But this woman is looking at me and not seeing my dad, and I don't want to shatter this new version of myself. Even if it is a misinterpretation.

The woman turns away, carrying my false image with her. Soon she's too far for me to call after, to take it back. The realization makes it harder to breathe, yet somehow also like I finally can.

After that old woman unmoors me, I wander, letting the loud crush of people lead me where it pleases. Eventually, it spits me out near Eli. He's toward the center of the bridge, looking out at the water. "Well?" he says when he spots me. "Did the world explode when you touched a camera?"

"No." The students are working with disposables, but he's brought his fancy camera that I saw in the library. It hangs on a thick strap around his neck and looks old but well cared for. I hold my hand out toward it. "Maybe I need to try a more powerful one for the universe to take notice. Can I?"

He hesitates.

"Sorry." I draw my arm back.

"No, I mean." He glances at it. "Just be careful."

"Are you sure?"

He nods.

Both his hands are full of crutches, so I have to take the camera off his neck. No natural disasters occur when I grab it, but Eli freezes when I step into his space, the way you might in the presence of a large bear or venomous snake. Absurd, since I'm definitely too small and bouncy to be terrifying. Once I've got the camera, I quickly step away. There's an awkward pause. Instead of lingering in it, I hold the lens up to eye level and point it at his face.

He scowls.

"What? You can take pictures of people, but they can't take pictures of you?"

"I don't take pictures of people," he says. "Architecture, usually. Or landscapes."

"Well, faces are more interesting than random bolts of metal." I bend low so I can catch his whole body. "Smile!"

He twists, suddenly, away and toward the water. It wasn't meant to be graceful; it was meant to be an escape. But it is graceful, his injured foot angled in the air and the good one spinning on its toes. I catch him in profile, before he can turn completely, and his one visible eye looks back at me through the lens. Not glowering. Just looking.

"Give it back now," he says.

"One more."

The scowl returns.

"Just one." It's the portrait artist in me. I've painted

everyone from babies to seniors older than anyone in this class. Sometimes my subjects are ecstatic to step into the workshop. Other times, they've been dragged by a parent or partner and look like they'd rather be anywhere else. Everyone wants to be seen at their best, though—even the people who don't want to be seen at all.

I lower the camera. All the way, so I can look at him unobstructed. "I want to take one you'll actually like. Can you show me how?"

He scoffs and turns again to the water.

I go with it. "Your whole body? Half?"

"Neither."

"Come on, I can hear Dr. Lazar already." I put on my best imitation of her voice. "*These are sloppy, and that's putting it nicely. What story are you trying to tell?*" I go back to my usual register. "If you want to get a good grade on this project, the first step would be showing me how to take a proper photo."

I've got him. I see the defeat in the slow shake of his head. Eli glances back at me, and I'm guessing I look as immovable as a wall, because after a final standoff he rolls his eyes and starts giving instructions:

1. Lie down. Yes, on the sidewalk. Yes, someone's probably pissed there at some point. You're the one who wanted to do this.
2. Closer to me. Too close. Stop. I said stop!
3. Bring the exposure down. Not that button. Not that button. Not that—just give it to me.
4. Can *you* tell the wind to blow in the other direction? Then why would *I* be able to tell the wind to blow in the other direction?
5. Tilt the lens slightly. Not that far! Okay, right there.

6. Did you take it? "Right there" meant you could take it!

I like the first photo better. I guess that makes sense: The first one is my version of him, while the second one is his. "Can we use these?" I ask, flipping back and forth between them in the viewfinder.

He stares blankly.

"For our project," I clarify. There are two photos of Eli—the one I captured and the one he orchestrated. His version is calmer: He essentially blended himself into the bridge by having me line up the angles of his body with the angles of the architecture, so neither stands out more than the other. My version is more chaotic: He's blurred slightly from the movement of his spin toward the water, and the look on his face is candid.

The contrast makes me think about perspective. Dr. Lazar talked about the viewer and the viewed, so maybe we could home in on that by exploring the differences between two versions of a photo? One directed by the artist, the other by the subject?

I explain the beginnings of my idea. It's good—maybe even great. It reminds me that I know art, actually, even if my classes are unfamiliar and I haven't grown to like them yet. When I'm done speaking, I expect Eli to agree that I'm a genius and we should start on this immediately. But he just frowns. "What are you saying?" he asks.

"I told you!"

"I mean, what point are you making? I like the idea of two versions of a photo, but that's only a concept. What are you trying to say with that concept about perspective?"

My mouth opens and then closes.

What point are you making?

He's right. I've come up with a way to say something,

but not with something to say. Have I ever said anything with my art? I like portraits because they tell stories, but they were never *my* stories. I've always painted them in the vision of others. Maybe that's why my work looks so much like Dad's: We both learned to make art for our customers instead of for ourselves.

What are you saying?

These past few weeks, I've been treating voice and style like they're interchangeable, but they're not, are they? Style is how you say something; voice is what you say. Like, when I think of Benji's art, it's beautiful, but it also has a purpose: He merges imagery from the two places he calls home. In doing so, you're able to see where they overlap and where they don't. Calum's web comic is stylistically distinct, but it also explores home—what makes one, who makes one, how to find one. As for my portraits . . . if I was never saying anything of my own in them, did they ever have any real substance?

Eli's camera feels like an anchor, suddenly, dragging my neck down toward the rocky waters of the Thames. I yank the strap from my shoulders and drape it back over his. Then I step away. "I need some air."

His eyebrows draw together. "We're outside."

"Yeah. I'll just—I'll be back."

I won't be back. Eli knows it: He tilts his head slightly as I step into the crowd, the gesture a question.

I don't answer. I let the tide swallow me whole.

Chapter Ten

Mrs. Beverley is old, and Eli is injured, and I abandoned them to round up twenty-nine senior citizens alone. I do feel guilty, but I couldn't stand being looked at for a second longer. If Eli had stared hard enough, he'd have seen my cakey makeup and cute overall dress were draped over nothing of substance.

I don't look at myself as I stumble back through London. Not in the shop windows, or in the reflection of my phone screen, which buzzes in my pocket—presumably with annoyed messages from Eli for disappearing on him mid-conversation. Not in the dark-paned glass of the tube. Not even in the floor-length mirror mounted on the back of my flat's front door. As I barrel inside, I'm only thinking about my bed and the covers on top and how I want to burrow underneath, so it's a miracle I don't face-plant over the person spread stomach-down on our hallway floor.

My toes are half an inch from Natalie's feet when my hand shoots out to catch my balance against the far wall. Thank God our corridors are narrow; I refuse to be the cause of more broken ankles. "Hello?" My panic sounds like anger. "What are you *doing*?"

"Wallowing," Natalie responds from under a sea of turquoise hair.

I want to yell that there are fifty thousand other places she could have lain down that would have been better choices than the public hallway of our entryway. Instead, I say, "*Why?*"

"My sister."

Some of the red leaves my vision. I didn't know Natalie had a sister, but I do know sibling drama. There have been times when Calum has exasperated me so thoroughly that I've also been tempted to lie down where people might step on me. "You had a fight?"

"Worse." Natalie rolls until her cheek is pressed into the prickly gray carpet. "She got into medical school. *Stanford.* The nerve."

I blink. Congratulations are obviously not in order, but what am I supposed to say? *Condolences?*

Natalie flops onto her back. "Do you have a shovel?"

"What?"

"A shovel. I'm the mole rat of the family, so it's past time I started digging my hole. Where best, do you think? Northumberland feels fitting. Somewhere on the moors."

Right. I'm dealing with my own existential crisis, but if I've learned anything today, it's that changing my style on the surface won't change who I am beneath. And unfortunately, I'm too much of a fifty-five-year-old aunt to leave anyone lying in their misery. I hold out a hand. "I'll start the kettle."

Natalie's head rises slightly, the way Alicia's dogs' sometimes did when I was over for dinner and the smell of fresh cooking wafted out from the oven. If you ever want to cheer up a British person—or apologize to them, or drop some bad news, or let them down gently, or have any form of productive interaction, really—offer to boil some water. I grew up in New York, so the powers of English Breakfast and Earl Grey are diluted on me, but whenever Mom or Aunt Lisa or Benji are down, I've found that the best bandage is tea.

I wiggle my outstretched fingers until Natalie reaches

up and lets me pull her to her feet. Then I walk into the kitchen to cheer up a girl I barely know.

It turns out Natalie is easy to get to know. The biggest obstacle in conversing with her these last few weeks was apparently her door, which I learn was only closed because "I don't have a stopper." Now that the sole barrier between us is two steaming mugs, she's happy to spill her whole history—most of which revolves around her older sister, who is "beautiful and perfect and, worst of all, nice." Natalie got into sculpture because "it's the only thing Nora can't do" but worries "that's not a valid reason to build a career." Her parents support her creative endeavors, but they went to Oxford for biology, and so did her sister. Hence, "I'm the mole rat."

Listening to Natalie makes me think about Eli, in that I've learned more about her in five minutes than I've learned about him in three weeks. Eli and I only stay in the present; our conversations revolve solely around the photography project or his art class. Sure, we had that one productive chess evening, but I don't know why he quit competing or how he got into photography or where he's from or who's in his family. The reverse is true, too—he knows I come from portraits, but not about Calum or Glenna's or how I ended up in London studying art that I hate. Meanwhile, Natalie's laying it all out there, and it's *nice*. I mean, I thought I was the only one questioning my reasons for enrolling in this school. Apparently, I'm not.

"How often do you talk to your sister?" I ask.

She shrugs. "Not often. She's older."

"By how much?"

"Five years. Which is too many, I reckon. She's so far ahead she forgets to look back." Natalie tips her mug toward me. "You have that brother. Is it the same?"

I shake my head. I can see how an age gap like Natalie's might feel like a race, but Calum is *ten* years older than me. He was a teenager before I was in kindergarten. And then I was six, and he was gone. If we were running, it was in two separate decades. Sometimes I wonder if that's why we get along to the extent we do. Growing is ugly. I wasn't there for his worst years, and he was an adult for mine. Would we be as close now if we'd lived under the same roof then?

My tea is getting cold. I bring the mug to my lips, but just as I do, there's a knock on our front door. Natalie pops up from the table and darts around the corner to open it. "There's a boy," she calls. "Not mine. Yours?"

"It's not my brother?"

"No. This one's dressed like a burglar. I'd be curious as to his strategy, because he's also got a broken leg. And possibly heatstroke."

Oh.

My mug drops too hard on the table; lukewarm tea spills over my hand. Eli can't be here. If he's here, he's going to ask why I ran off, which means I'm going to have to *explain* why I ran off—and sure, I just said I liked getting to know Natalie, but I don't want anyone to know *me* because then they'll see I'm just a siren wailing around without anything to say, and—

"About that heatstroke?" Natalie says. "I wasn't joking."

I peer out from the kitchen. Eli's standing in the threshold of our flat, and he looks . . . not how I expected. As I ran away from the bridge, I kept picturing his face: annoyed, confused, exasperated. That's how I would have felt, at least, if someone ditched me with no explanation and then didn't answer my texts. But right now, he doesn't look pissed. He just looks hot.

Sweaty hot. Shut up. And of course he is—the air is practically soup and he's in all black and he just climbed five flights of stairs with crutches. Not to mention I've been home less than an hour, which means he must have barreled straight here after wrapping up his class.

Natalie eyes him the way a scientist might scrutinize a suspicious substance. "Are you dying?"

". . . N-no?" Eli's panting. And paler than he should be, considering how much he's sweating. Is he going to vomit? He looks like he might vomit.

I gesture down the hall. "The toilet's there—"

He beelines for it.

"Right," Natalie says after the door slams. "Who is he?"

"Eli." That's not helpful, so I elaborate: "He's here to yell at me." I head back into the kitchen. "Do we have ice? Something colder than ice?"

"No," says Natalie. "Why is he here to yell at you?"

"I left him alone with a bunch of old people on Tower Bridge." I fill a glass with water; it feels lighter than it should. "Is this an emergency? Does he need more than . . . hydration?"

"I'm fine!" Eli calls from the bathroom. His voice makes both me and Natalie jump. I knew our walls were thin, but not *that* thin.

"Are you sure?" I shout back. "Because the last time you said you were fine, your ankle was broken!"

Natalie tilts her head. "I have questions."

Glass in hand, I storm back into the hall. "Eli? I will be so pissed if you die in there after having had the opportunity to warn us—"

The bathroom door flings open. "I'm *fine*."

He is fine. I can tell immediately—this is not a repeat of the Ankle Situation. For one thing, he's stopped gasping for air. And I'm not sure if he threw up, but his skin is no longer an alarming shade of white. His jacket is sprawled on the ground, and he's splashed water over his face to calm the sweating. He's still a mess, though. And he doesn't smell particularly pleasant. I set the cup of water on the sink and then gesture at his summer-inappropriate cargo pants. "I'll find you other clothes."

Anyway. That's how, instead of yelling at me, Eli ends up in my shower.

Chapter Eleven

In no universe did I imagine this evening concluding with Eli in my room in my clothes, but here we are. I gave him pajamas because there isn't anything else in my wardrobe that would do him justice. The flannel pants are a laughable length on him, but I stole an old Glenna's tee from Dad's closet before I left for London that isn't too egregious. It's weird, though. Eli's wearing my grandmother's namesake across his chest, and to him it has no significance.

I'm staring, probably too much, but it's because I'm trying to gauge where he's at. Eli doesn't look angry at me for ditching him on the bridge. Maybe he is, but exhaustion's outweighing it. I offered him the bed because I figured it'd be more comfortable for his ankle, but he turned pink at the suggestion and stared at the butterflies on my sheets like they were going to swarm until I waved him over to the other side of the room. Now he's curled around the back of my desk chair, his wet hair dripping translucent patches into the worn Glenna's shirt, the dark strap of a binder poking out from one side of the stretched neckline.

"Did I do something?" he asks.

"What?" I'm on the bed since he refused it, in properly fitting pajamas and with my own hair trickling streams down my back. After Eli showered, I was the only one still looking like a red, sweaty mess, so I figured I should wash up, too.

"Was it my directions for taking that photo?" His

thumbs dig into the waxy wooden back of the chair. "I've been told I'm blunt, sometimes. Too blunt. Or was it—"

"Wait—what?" Does he think *I'm* angry at *him*? I replay the final moments on the bridge. Eli made me see how my idea about perspective was a concept without a point, and that made me spiral into realizing *everything* I've made has been a concept without a point, and then I ran off and abandoned him to round up twenty-nine senior citizens on his own. I assumed he was pissed about the outcome of that situation; it did not occur to me that he might also be preoccupied by the cause.

His eyes flit down. "Did I—"

"No, sorry." I shake my head. "No, I ditched you, and not because you did anything. I should have at least explained why."

"Oh." His fingers pause on the chair. "Why, then?"

"Huh?"

He looks up at me. "Why?"

Ah.

I haven't talked to Alicia about my existential art crisis. I haven't talked to my parents. Benji. Calum. But now Eli's asking, and he's wearing a Glenna's shirt without understanding what it means, and yeah, I want to be known as more than our shop, but how can I be known at all without it?

"I'm from this little town. In upstate New York? It's called Crescent Valley." My eyes are on my lap and Eli's shirt and out the window into the dark. "My mom is Scottish, though. She grew up in Edinburgh. My grandma Glenna started a business there. She specialized in portraits. After she died, my parents continued the shop in her name, this time in my dad's hometown, and that's where I was born.

"My childhood was good. Mostly. My brother ran away when I was six, and that sucked, and it sucked more when I found out why, but honestly the most shocking thing that happened to me was finding out Glenna's might go bankrupt when I was twelve. I fell in love with art because of our shop—I even have this old cup where I keep a paintbrush from every year I've held one. The first is from when I was two. Losing Glenna's would have meant . . . I don't know. It's hard to think about." My throat is dry. I force myself to swallow.

"In the end, the shop didn't go under, but in high school, I kind of did. The problem is my portraits look exactly like my dad's. Even when I branched away from oil painting for a bit and started doing digital art to expand the range of products offered at our shop, I couldn't detangle my work from his. So that's why I'm taking photography and a bunch of other classes I don't like. I've been trying to find my own style. But then you asked what point I was making about perspective, and I realized the problem isn't just how my art looks—it's that I also don't have anything to say. I just paint beautiful lines with nothing underneath them. And—so. That was a brick to the face. I needed to run off and cry for a second, but it's—" I want to say *it's all good now,* because that's what you're supposed to say. But isn't that my problem? Saying things for others instead of for myself?

Eli's quiet. It's wild how much words can fill a room. It felt good to release them, but now that they're fading, I don't know what impression he'll be left with. Inside, my problem feels like everything. Out loud, it sounds trivial.

"It wasn't that you didn't have a point," he says finally. "Dr. Lazar mentioned the viewer and the viewed. That could have many interpretations, but you suggested something specific—the subject versus the artist—which implies there's a reason behind your idea. Maybe you haven't figured out what yet, but that's different, isn't it? From not saying anything at all?"

I don't know if he's looking at me; I'm too busy not looking at him. I drop my head to my knees. I did suggest something specific, but why? The difference between a portrait and a self-portrait is the difference between how you are seen and how you want to be seen. That's an idea I think about a lot—not for this project, just on my own—because when I paint, although my goal is to capture my clients objectively, their faces are depicted by my subjective hand. At the end of the day, I hold the power over how they're portrayed. That's a lot of pressure. It also doesn't really seem fair.

"Control." It clicks, suddenly. "With a self-portrait and portrait of the same subject, we can show the disconnect between how someone views themselves versus how they are viewed by others. By analyzing the differences, we can help people take more control of how they're perceived."

Eli taps the back of the chair as if to emphasize my point. "You did have something to say."

I guess I did. It feels like a breath. Like I can finally close my eyes without fumbling in the dark. I don't; I raise my head. Eli's watching me from across the room, and from his slightly amused expression, I think he's seeing something different from what I do when I meet my own gaze behind him in the mirror.

Maybe I need to do this photography experiment on myself. Do other people see me the way I see me? Probably not. I wonder where the disconnect is. I wonder how I can bridge it.

"Why are you smiling?" I ask.

"I'm not." But he is, just slightly, and it looks weird on his face because his lips don't usually bend that way. "Question." Eli drums his knuckles on the desk. "How do you decide which paintbrush to retire into your special cup each year? Is it a lottery system? A democratic vote?"

I scowl. On the one hand, he's making fun of me. On the other, I'm glad to change the subject. "I choose whichever I'm holding closest to the midnight before my birthday."

His smile widens. "Shut up. Artists are nostalgic. Don't you do something sappy with your film cartridges? Or at least have a string of Polaroids on some bedroom wall from your first days of school every year?"

"Hell no. There's nothing from my hometown I wanted to keep."

The air turns staticky. Eli offered up that information on his own, but he doesn't elaborate, so I'm not sure we're in territory he wants to explore. Instead of running onto the path, I prod my foot at a bramble. "What about your camera?" I gesture to where it's perched on the desk. The black leather strap is worn, and some of the buttons don't press properly. Either he got it secondhand, or he's had it for a while.

"Fine," he amends. "There was one thing I wanted to keep."

More prickly air. He shakes his head, and some of it disappears. "Crescent Valley is a nice name. My small town was Landfall, Wyoming. It was just me and Mom growing up, and most of my childhood was her shoving me off to the library for as many hours as she could get away with. I wasn't into the books, not as a kid, but there were also shelves of games. There was chess. A group of old women used to compete in the evenings—they taught me how to play, and I practiced until I was better than them. When Mom realized I had a talent for something . . ." Eli smiles again, but there's no humor in it. "I became interesting, suddenly."

"You don't speak to her anymore." I've known for a while, I think, that he's on his own. Since he hobbled across London on a broken ankle to keep his job.

Eli doesn't nod or shrug or shake his head. He just continues to run his fingers along the back of the chair. "We should meet soon to plan our next steps. For the project."

"I—yeah. Okay."

He slings his camera back over his neck, grabs his crutches from where they're leaning against the desk, and stands. "I'll go now. It's getting late."

"Yeah," I say again. "Okay."

My green pajama pants look even worse when he's at his full height. They stop halfway down his shins, and although the mood in here is low, I can't help it: I snort. He looks like a poorly dressed string bean.

He grimaces and nods down at my clothes. "Thanks for—thanks. I'll return these."

"Actually"—I gesture at the Glenna's shirt—"that's too big on me, but it looks good on you. Or, no—" My cheeks burn. "I just mean, I can only wear it to sleep, but what's the point of wearing a Glenna's shirt to sleep when the whole reason we have them is to advertise? Not that you have to *advertise* for our shop, obviously, you didn't even know it existed until two minutes ago—and that's not why I told you about it, I'm not that desperate—but at least if you wear it in daylight, you won't look like a drowned rat the way I do—"

"I doubt there's ever a situation where you look like a drowned rat," Eli says. And then *his* cheeks are pink, and oh my *God,* why do we keep ending up in conversations where we're both saying the most awkward things to ever come out of human mouths?

I all but shove him from my room and out the front door. Once I'm alone, I expect my face to return to its usual state, but it doesn't. I'm on fire all the way to my ears.

How ridiculous.

It's perfectly acceptable to tell someone they look good in a shirt. That is normal, friendly conversation.

Except I didn't just say Eli looked good in the shirt, I *offered* it to him—all while it was wet and see-through as a result of me having also offered him my *shower*—

Normal, friendly conversation.

Friendly.

Friend.

Urgh.

8:30 p.m.

Alicia Miller: Two of my poems were selected for this semester's literary magazine?!?!

Alicia Miller: Freshmen NEVER get work featured

Me: YOU'RE AMAZING

Alicia Miller: I KNOW

Alicia Miller: Btw the photos you took of that ghost tour looked cool!!!

Alicia Miller: What else have you been up to?

Me: Wait wait

Me: Which poems did you submit to the magazine??

Me: Ones from your portfolio?
Or some I haven't read?
Me: I need the details!!

Alicia Miller: Well
Alicia Miller: IF YOU INSIST

Chapter Twelve

"Piseag!" Mom says when our video call connects. It's her nickname for me—Scottish Gaelic for "kitten." I used to roll my eyes when she called me that, but now it reminds me of home.

It's early, and it's raining. It's October 2, to be exact. Water patters loudly on the roof as I lie on my bed with my phone raised above my head. Mom looks put together as always, in a dress and blazer that look pretty ridiculous in our workshop that was converted from an old barn. Dad waves from behind her in a slightly newer Glenna's tee than the one I stole, paint in his hair and brush in his hand. I haven't spoken to either of them in a while; these first few weeks of school were busy, and I was trying to branch away from everything familiar.

There's a pause. Mom and Dad glance at each other and seem to count under their breath. Then, together, they say, "Happy Birthday!"

My lips turn up in a tight smile. Not because I don't like birthdays, but because this could be any other Thursday. I thought I'd feel different when I woke this morning—more mature or something—but birthdays mean something because they're a ritual, and our family ritual is hiding presents around the house and spending the day giving clues to their locations. Without that ceremony, today doesn't feel like the start of a new year; today doesn't feel like the start of anything.

Mom pans the camera behind her. "Okay, Piseag. It's on the wall but not a part of it."

The sinking in my stomach turns into a clenching. "What?"

Dad smiles softly. "Did you think we would throw away tradition just because you're in another country? It couldn't be as elaborate this year, but we made an attempt . . ."

My eyes sting. I turn my attention to the wooden wall of Glenna's, searching for anything out of place, and—

"Is it that picture?" The only art we stow in the workshop are commissioned portraits, because it's a space we dedicate to our clients; personal decor is kept to the house. But the framed memory behind my parents isn't a painting. It's a photo. Of me. Of us. Of *all* of us.

Mom brings her phone closer so I can more clearly see. It's from a long-ago October, one I don't remember. I can only tell it's October because we're in a pumpkin patch, presumably searching for the perfect one to place on our porch for Halloween. I'm minuscule—two or three, which means Calum is twelve or thirteen. He's trying to pass me a pumpkin that's half my size and seems vaguely annoyed that I can't lift it on my own. Mom and Dad laugh in the background of the picture, and I laugh now, looking at the memory. It's not a moment I recall, but it is one I can relate to, because my wide smile in conversation with Calum's silent frustration is not an interaction confined to the past.

"We wanted to give you something portable, that we could send to London," says Mom. "It's not much, but—"

"Thank you." My eyes are really burning now. Mom and Dad know it's hard for me to get a clear picture of what life was like in our house before Calum left. At the same time, I know it's hard for them to go digging into the past, because my parents broke something that's been stitched back together but will never not hurt. They uncovered this moment anyway, though. For me.

I draw in a breath. Maybe my TRY NEW THINGS list needs an addendum. I make a mental revision:

7. DON'T UNDERESTIMATE PEOPLE.

"How's the shop?" I ask, because I've got to change the subject or I'll start bawling, and anyway, I *do* want to hear about Glenna's. Despite leaving, I miss it. I do. I miss waking before sunrise on chilly winter weekends and painting in my fluffy pajamas. I miss navigating the maze of half-finished canvases that only Dad has a map of. I miss Mom's constant voice on the phone in the back of the workshop, talking in numbers and marketing pitches—languages I'm not fluent in. A part of me wants to hop on a plane tomorrow, but I also know I'm craving home because it's familiar, and that's the whole reason I needed to get away.

Dad gestures for Mom to pan the camera over. She does, and I'm able to see the canvas he's working on. It's stunning. A wedding portrait—but I guess the couple wanted to be painted in a fantasy land, because the background consists of *Alice in Wonderland*–esque plants and a sunset sky. One of the brides wears a white lace dress with a delicate, bejeweled veil. The other has a dress and veil in the same style but in ink black.

Would I have painted it differently? It's hard to know since I don't have the reference photos. Dad does generally go for a darker color palette, but that's not usually enough to tell our work apart.

"How's Calum?" Mom asks suddenly and too casually. She loves him, insufferably, but that was always the problem. Although he talks to her now, more than I ever thought he would, it's still not as much as she'd like.

"Um?" It's been a full month since I've seen my brother, and over two weeks since we've texted, but Benji would have told me if Calum had dropped dead at his desk.

Right??

Right. Benji would have told me.

"He works too much," I say. "But we're hanging out tonight for my birthday."

"That's good." Mom pauses. "Tell him to ring, won't you? A gallery in New York City reached out last week. They're putting on an exhibit and are interested in featuring our work. I want to know what he thinks of the concept."

I nod. If Mom wants Calum's input, it means the gallery likely contacted us because of the message Mom and Dad added to Glenna's site after my brother helped us save the shop from bankruptcy six years ago: *Five percent of all sales at Glenna's Portraits will be donated to LGBTQIA+ homeless youth shelters in upstate New York.* Ever since, we've had a steady stream of collaboration requests from rural queer nonprofits, and Mom often asks for Calum's opinions on the proposed projects before taking them on. It's the main reason why, I think, he's back on speaking terms with her. But a gallery? In New York City? We've never been contacted by an establishment like that. It could be a huge opportunity for the shop.

"I'll tell him to call you."

"Thanks." She sits on a stool next to Dad, who has quietly gone back to his painting, though he still appears to be listening. He's like me: Once elbow-deep in a project, he's not fully present anywhere else until it's finished. "What are your plans for tonight?" Mom asks, turning the conversation again to my birthday. "How are you celebrating?"

I grin. "Calum said we could do whatever I want."

He may live to regret that choice.

I bring Calum to Eli's art class. That emergency lesson I taught at the pub was the most comfortable I've felt in London this semester, so I figured it was a solid place to spend a birthday evening. And yes, we'll be by far the youngest students participating, but when I signed us up, I saw the class isn't actually advertised as "for old people." It's simply listed as "a late-night society of artists, open to all levels." I wonder if the current age demographic happened accidentally; maybe a cohort of seniors initially signed up, and then word got out to the larger community. Either way, I'm confident in my ability to make friends with people of all ages, and Calum is much more likely to have something in common with a cranky old man who yells at kids than a twenty-something who enjoys Tequila Tuesdays.

"Happy birthday."

It's nearly ten p.m., but Calum's still in his work clothes as he approaches me at the entrance to the pub. The circles under his eyes are darker than they were the last time I saw him. They make me want to confront him about his job again, but tonight is supposed to be fun. Instead of causing a scene, I subtly check out his hands. Then I text Benji.

9:53 p.m.

Me: You still haven't proposed???

Benji Saito: You're still wearing that makeup???

I'm not, actually. After my epiphany about style being different from voice, I figured changing my look wasn't going to help me figure out what to say. The foundation was wrong, so it had to go, but glitter is always right. I've stuck with keeping some under my eyes, as well as a few swipes of mascara. I do like *some* makeup—just not the kind that feels like paint on my face. My phone buzzes again.

Benji Saito: Apologies for the city of Paris
Benji Saito: How rude of it to hold an art convention on the momentous day of your birth
Benji Saito: Ruder still that I can't blow it off as my work is being featured
Benji Saito: (It is actually quite cool that my work is being featured but that is beside the point)
Benji Saito: I did send Calum your way with a gift
Benji Saito: He may need reminding to hand it over

As it turns out, Calum doesn't need a gift-giving reminder. When I glance up after pocketing my phone, I see he has pulled two slightly crushed bags from his briefcase. One is lumpy and made of paper. The other is flat and made of dark blue plastic. "Happy birthday," he says again, shoving them both at me.

I go for the plastic one first. Inside it is a second bag, but this one is canvas and clearly the actual present. The hand-painted design matches the jacket I received from Benji last year: Edinburgh Castle amid the cherry blossoms. It's stunning, as is everything Benji creates, but what really takes this to the next level are the scattered bits of embroidered pink flowers and gray stones that lay overtop some of the brushwork. They add texture and fine detail to the piece, and—God. If I didn't personally like him, I would professionally hate him, because *how is his art this good?*

"Oh," says Calum, eyeing Benji's gift. "That's unfortunate."

I frown, but his meaning becomes clear enough when he tries to pluck the second present from my grasp.

"No, no," I say, pulling it away and dipping my hand into the paper. "I'm excited to see what you—"

Socks. For my nineteenth birthday, Calum got me socks. They're black and stretchy and appear to be of nice quality, but none of this negates that they are *socks.*

Calum grimaces. "I realize my gift looks underwhelming compared to . . . that," he says, nodding at Benji's masterpiece, "but people underestimate socks. Without quality protection, your feet will suffer. Especially as you age—"

"As I *age*? I'm nineteen, not ninety!"

"If you don't take proper care of your feet, you will feel ninety more quickly than you expect."

"Right." There's laughter at the tip of my tongue, but I don't let it bubble over because this was a sincere gift. "Thank you. For your concern. Over my feet," I manage, and then I drag him into the pub, because this conversation was only going to go downhill from there.

The space inside is packed. A lot of faces are familiar, but there are also some new ones. Old ones? The class meets three evenings a week, and I've only been twice.

Eli is easy to spot by the bar. Not just because he's not ninety-four, but because he's determined to dress like an abyss even in eighty-degree heat. Truly, my dude, how are you in a black sweatshirt right now?! Despite it being ten p.m., my lavender smock dress sticks to my back with sweat.

He does a double take when he sees me; I didn't tell him I was coming tonight.

Maybe I should have.

I *would* have, but things have been weird since the whole "use my shower and clothes" incident. Okay—not *weird*. Awkward. More awkward than they were before.

Like, the morning after, the first and only thing he said to me was "Laundry not yet but as soon I will."

I either blacked out and missed half his thought, or he did. To be fair, my response of "Yeah cool laundry good" isn't winning Quote of the Year.

When we met in the library on Wednesday to solidify the timeline of tasks we need to get done for our project by the end of October, things started okay but ended with everyone in the vicinity turning to us in alarm because I kicked my fidgety leg into the coffee table and somehow snapped the wood, sending all my books and Eli's backpack thundering to the ground in a heap.

So. Things have been awkward. And maybe that's a little bit why I brought Calum here tonight. Not that my brother's a tension diffuser, but he's . . . you know. A body. Besides, Eli's got a complicated family situation. He's alone in London just like Calum was, so it might not be awful for him to see that my relatively happy brother relatively exists.

Eli's gaze flits from me to Calum to the crumpled gift bags I'm holding in my hands. "Is it"—he frowns—"your birthday?"

"Oh," I say, a little too loudly, "well, yes. To celebrate, I wanted to do some art, and my brother is practically a hundred years old anyway, so I figured we'd join your class. This is Calum." I push him forward. "Meet Eli."

Calum has only just seemed to realize the age demographic of the rest of the pub. His eyebrows raise slightly as he takes in the space, but he looks far more put off by Eli, which I should have anticipated. My brother is not one for small talk—if he had the choice between engaging in a five-minute conversation with a stranger or jumping off a bridge, he would not hesitate in his decision. But it's my birthday. Maybe he'll be more willing to humor me than usual.

Eli tentatively raises a hand in greeting. Calum half-mimics the motion and then gives me a very wary glance. Then there's silence—which, now that I think about it, Eli isn't exactly the Master of Small Talk, either. Maybe this was a huge mistake, actually, because how am I supposed to facilitate a conversation between two people who aren't going to help me in the slightest?

"So!" I clear my throat. "Some introductory fun facts. Eli's teaching this art class! How fun. How nice. We actually know each other from school, because we're working on a photography project together." I gesture at my brother. "Calum also likes art, but instead of studying it, he chose to be boring and go into finance. He got me socks for my birthday. And he ran away from home when he was sixteen—"

"What are you doing?" Calum hisses.

"Nothing?"

Calum stares hard into my face until I grimace slightly, and his eyes narrow in suspicion. Before he can call me out for anything in front of Eli, I grab his wrist and pull him toward an empty table in a far corner of the room.

"Why are we here?" Calum asks as soon as we're seated.

"Art?"

He glowers. "Why are we actually here?"

"Art," I repeat, and then sigh. "And my friend." I nod toward Eli. "He's on his own. I don't know the details, but he cut ties with his mom. And, well, you have experience in that area—"

"*Maisie*." Calum says my name like I'm the reason for all his problems. "I'm not some traumatized rabbit you can pull out of a hat every time you meet another traumatized rabbit."

"I know. Obviously. God, imagine that magic show—how depressing. I just thought—"

"What? Because my teenage years were shit, it's my job to tell some stranger, 'Sorry your teenage years are shit, but don't worry, a decade on and it's only awful occasionally'? I'm no motivational speaker—"

"Clearly." There are watercolors on each table. I point to the palettes on ours. "You don't have to say anything else to him. I just wanted to introduce you. Now that I have, let's focus on art."

Calum stares at me for another moment. Then he shakes his head. "You're frustrating."

"You're worse."

"I'm not."

Instead of replying "you are" and having this go on

forever, I just roll my eyes and pull a blank piece of paper from the pile.

Eli does not attempt to speak to us again before the class starts, which—valid. Instead of quelling the awkwardness between us, I definitely made it worse, but that's a problem for tomorrow. For tonight, I listen as he begins his lesson by explaining the differences between watercolors and other types of paint. Considering he's a photographer, I'm impressed by how much he knows about layering, drying times, and opacity. After his mini lecture, he sends us off with the instruction to paint something we see in this room.

I was too stressed the last time I was here to really take in the vibes, but now that I'm not leading an emergency class, I can appreciate the space. The name of the pub is The Black Cat, and there are cats *everywhere.* Framed portraits of tabbies in old-fashioned clothes. Newspaper clippings mentioning "felines" or "strays" from across the decades. An actual black cat slinks out from behind the bar, and I wonder if she's here because of this pub or if this pub is here because of her.

I decide to paint Calum's hands. When I look over at him to start my outline, I pause. It's been a while since I've seen him do art, but when he picks up a brush, it's like he goes back in time: His eyes are clearer, there are fewer worry lines in his brow, and his lips turn up in this fragile way I only remember seeing when I'd catch him sketching on his bedroom floor in Crescent Valley. Calum never had the problem I did with art because his style looks nothing like Glenna's. It's way more abstract. I know that caused its own pain for him growing up—it can hurt to feel different, just as it can hurt to feel the same. I love his art, though. It's no less precise than mine, even though he blends and blurs more freely. I wish I had the mastery over color theory that he does. I wish I looked so at ease with a brush in my hand.

I wish I could capture him in this moment.

Eli doesn't have his camera tonight, but I have my phone. I raise it quickly, before Calum can notice, and snap a picture. It's blurry in the dim lighting. His features blend into the darkness, just like people do in his paintings.

"Will you help me with a thing after we're done here? It'll be quick."

Calum doesn't look up from his paper. "You're always vague when you want something questionable."

I sigh. "There's this project I'm working on. For school? I need self-portraits of people. Photography self-portraits."

"Find someone else."

"I want one of them to be of you." Calum's lit by soft candlelight, and his gaze is relaxed as he paints a calm scene on his paper. He's a warm person, but he'd never describe himself that way. The contrast makes me think again about perspective. "Come on," I urge. "One photo."

"Maisie. Rocks smile better than me."

"That is objectively untrue. Besides, did I say you have to smile? It's a *self*-portrait. You can look however you want!"

Calum runs a hand through his hair. When he starts doing that, I know he's losing his tolerance for a conversation. "First it was 'come to this art class,' and then it was 'talk to my sad friend,' and now it's 'pose for a portrait.' I know it's your birthday, but I wish you'd be more up front about what you want me for."

"I don't want you *for* anything," I shoot back. "I wanted to do art *with* you. And then I remembered Eli—who isn't sad, by the way, he's just allergic to clothes that aren't black—and then I was watching you paint, and then I was thinking about my project. There's no master plan here. I'd have to be good at math to be calculating like that!"

"You really downplay your skills when it suits you."

I ignore him. "If you cooperate for this photo, then the next time we hang out, you can pick what we do."

Calum raises his eyebrows. The last time I let him choose an activity, he dragged me to some lecture called "The Pre-History of Modern Finance" where some boring dude with a fancy title talked about various monetary systems for eight million hours.

"Fine," he says before I can take the offer back, and honestly? It *is* fine. Calum doesn't talk to me about certain chunks of his past, and that does, I think, sometimes affect my ability to read him. So I'd like to be able to hold my vision of him in one hand and his vision in the other, to see where they diverge. If that means one brutal night of finance lectures or the horrific equivalent, so be it.

Calum takes his picture in the alley out back of the pub. I don't mean he snaps a selfie or uses the delayed timer on his phone—he doesn't need to, because his self-portrait doesn't feature himself at all. He grabs a photo of the brick wall in front of him and then hands the phone back to me.

"It's a self-portrait," I reiterate.

"Yes."

"It's how you see yourself."

"Yes."

"You see yourself as a wall?"

"I can't see myself," says Calum. "I am myself. You can't see yourself if you are yourself. Not properly, anyway."

"Calum—"

"I took a picture of what I'm looking at. Isn't that the closest I can get to representing my perspective?"

I can't argue with him. This is a self-portrait; *"You can look however you want."* And anyway, maybe he has a point: I can't just walk away from my body for a hot second to take a peek at how it looks from the outside. If I could, I'd be spending a lot less time trying to figure out the differences between how I view myself and how everyone else views me.

"Isn't this what you wanted?" Calum asks when I don't immediately respond. His face is neutral, but he sounds slightly distressed, as though I might force him to take more pictures.

"It's perfect." It is. This photo is the perfect example of why he's a good artist. He sees things that other people miss.

I pocket my phone. "Was this really so awful? Tonight, I mean. Doing art. Have I completely scared you off, or would you let me bring you here again?"

Calum looks back at the pub. Then he looks toward me. I'm holding both our paintings: mine of his hands and his of the blotchy shadows on the candlelit walls. His gaze lingers on the candlelight. "Art is never awful."

12:07 a.m.

The Boy Who Doesn't Look Like A Drowned Rat (Eli):
Happy birthday, by the way

Me: Thanks!!!!

Chapter Thirteen

I spend the next week thinking about what Calum said about perspective. The point of our photography project is to show the disconnect between how people view themselves versus how they are viewed by others. But *can* people view themselves? I'm not sure anymore. And if they can't, it means my idea is fundamentally flawed.

There isn't time to start over. We're two weeks into October. In another two weeks, our first draft is due to Dr. Lazar. Eli doesn't want to backpedal. He thinks we should keep moving forward because "we need the entire idea in front of us to see what needs fixing." Sure, but what if *everything* needs fixing?

We can't afford to get stuck on that now, so Eli starts on the essay while I photograph Natalie. I choose her as our third subject because—to be honest, it's because her room is four feet from mine.

"Like this?" she asks, tilting her head down.

"Perfect."

My version of Natalie is a recreation of the first time I saw her. She'd been crouched on her desk, considering dumping Ribena on my brother's head, and after a month and a half of living together, this still feels like a good representation of who she is. I position her in that same pose: face toward the window, hand on the bottle, sharp shadows from the overhead light cutting across the walls and floor. After I snap the photo, I hand the camera to her. It's not Eli's—I borrowed one from school. I kind of wanted to go for a DSLR, but we've only spent a week handling them in class, and I'm not confident enough to configure the settings on my own. So I went back to the Polaroid. Aside from being straightforward, it's also an artsy camera, and Natalie is artsy. I mean, we all are at this school, obviously, but instead of pictures on her dorm room wall, she's strung up chains of CDs. Instead of a laptop on her desk, she's got a record player. And then there's the winged eyeliner, oversized concert T-shirts (today's says "SHINee"), and blue-green hair.

Natalie turns the camera over in her hands. "Can we take it outside?"

I shrug. "Sure. Where?"

"Nature."

Natalie's version of nature is the Joy of Life Fountain in Hyde Park. It's just past eight p.m.—the sky is dark, the grounds are uncrowded, and the sepia lighting from the streetlamps makes me feel like we're in a picture of our own.

"Be quick about it," Natalie says, shoving the camera against my chest and then, before I have time to process, kicking off her shoes and bolting full speed into the fountain.

"Natalie!"

An old man on the opposite side of the cobbled space takes an indignant step forward. Natalie cackles into the air and throws up an armful of water. I snap the photo when her hands are high over her head and droplets are spraying down toward her upturned face. The Polaroid doesn't capture the details, but it does distort the light in a cool way that turns the splash of water into fire.

"Should I retake it?" I ask Natalie when she climbs out

of the fountain. "I didn't bring another camera, but I could use the flash on my phone."

She shakes her head. "I like the chaos."

Clearly. I wonder if that's where the tightness in my throat is coming from. Natalie is not Alicia, but running into a fountain at night and laughing as an old man sputters is familiar territory. I've been here before, at another age in another country.

The streetlamps turn from warm to cold; their light no longer feels nostalgic. I've had other friends besides Alicia, but I've never had friends without her. Being here with Natalie feels like I'm moving on. I *wanted* to move on—from small towns. Tight spaces. Not from the people I love.

Natalie's looking at me. I wish I could see what she sees.

"Jump in the fountain," she says.

"*What?*"

"I'll do it with you."

The temperature started to drop this week. Natalie's shivering in her wet T-shirt in the dark. "Absolutely not."

"Oh, c'mon. There's something about cold, dirty water that really wakes one up."

I don't like waking up. I like being *awake,* but not the jolt into it. Whenever Alicia would do things like this—climbing the statues in our town square, running through Mrs. Thompson's cornfield at night—I never partook. I was the lookout, because Alicia was daring and loud and outgoing, and I—well, I was, too. But I let her have those titles in our friendship. Just like she let me be the talented artistic one, even though she was also talented and artistic in her own right.

The fountain looks muddy and uninviting, but Natalie holds out her hand. She's grinning. My chest hurts—I'm homesick, I'm guilty—but I came here for a reason, and that reason wasn't to be who I was in Crescent Valley.

I let Natalie pull me forward. Her fingers are sticks of ice. The impact of the water is worse: My whole body clenches with the shock of it, and then I'm soaking wet in a fountain in London and people are staring and Natalie's laughing and I stand there and shriek.

TRY NEW THINGS

1. STOP HELPING OUT AT GLENNA'S.

2. GO TO AN ART SCHOOL FAR FROM HOME. MAYBE IN ANOTHER COUNTRY.

3. NO PORTRAITS OR OIL PAINTINGS. ONLY SIGN UP FOR CLASSES IN MEDIUMS YOU HAVE NO EXPERIENCE WITH.

~~4. EXPERIMENT WITH YOUR APPEARANCE AND CLOTHING.~~

5. MAKE NEW FRIENDS ~~(BECAUSE ALICIA IS GOING TO)~~. (BECAUSE YOU WANT TO).

6. ~~ALWAYS SAY YES. EVEN WHEN YOU DON'T WANT TO.~~ SAY YES MORE THAN YOU SAY NO.

7. DON'T UNDERESTIMATE PEOPLE.

8. JUMP INTO THE OCCASIONAL FOUNTAIN TO WAKE UP!

Chapter Fourteen

Our fourth photo subject is a woman from Eli's art class, one I've never met. His version of her is sharp shadows and angles. The self-portrait is also sharp, but in profile and more focused on the scarf she's crocheting. Since he took the photos without me present, I don't know which is more accurate to her person.

"Your turn," says Eli.

"What?" We're in an empty studio, the photos laid out in order on the floor between us. Four subjects down, one to go. Plus the essay, which is just bare bones right now—I'm drafting the intro and conclusion while Eli's outlining the middle. There's less than one week until the deadline, and we can totally finish. If we find our final subject in time.

Eli jabs a crutch at the empty space next to photos seven and eight. He's been moodier than usual this week, and by the absurd way he's hanging off the side of his chair, I think it's because he's restless. Last Friday we couldn't meet because he had a doctor's appointment. When I asked the next day how his ankle's been healing, he'd snarled, "*Slowly.*"

"If I had to pose, so do you," he says now and with zero sympathy. He lunges forward and grabs his camera. "We'll do it here. The lighting's good."

"*What?*" I'm not opposed to a self-portrait. I've been thinking about taking one on my own time, just for fun. But that's very different from agreeing to be a subject for our project, which involves a second photo that's directed by Eli. "Find someone else."

"No." He points toward the studio door. "Change into your worst clothes."

"*What?*"

The pointing turns into shooing. "Quickly. Before the sun moves."

"If this is your way of saying you see me as an ugly troll—"

"Do you really think that's my end game here?"

"I don't know!" Why else would he want to photograph me in the sweatpants with the hole in the butt that I keep at the back of my closet?

Eli drops his arm. "Can you just trust me? My idea won't work if I tell you what it is."

I hesitate. Eli's prickly; he's not sharp. His words cut me on Tower Bridge, but that was because I was leaning into them. He doesn't jab me with his edges—he doesn't touch me at all, actually. When we walk, when we sit next to each other in the library, he keeps a careful distance. Like he's scared of me. Like he doesn't want to scare me. I'm not sure what that's about, but it's coming from somewhere intentional.

Intentional is a good word to describe him. Not just as a person, but as a photographer. The art he makes is art he means. And, well, if Calum's right—if people can't see themselves—then maybe a portrait through Eli's eyes would open mine.

"Okay." The word is drawn out. As in: I have to draw it out of me. Eli will shoot me honestly, and that's good; that's terrible. "I'm going to regret this."

"You won't." He tilts his head. "Well. Maybe."

Great.

When I return to the studio twenty minutes later in my holey gray sweatpants and a sauce-stained T-shirt (thanks, Zizzi's), Eli won't let me through the door.

"Close your eyes," he calls from inside the studio. "Don't open them until I tell you."

I'm really very done with him, but I'm also too nosy to back out at this point. "I don't have a good feeling about this."

"Your feedback is noted. Are your eyes closed?"

My arms wrap around my middle. "Yes."

"Are they actually?"

"*Yes.*"

There's a pause. Then the door hisses open. "Keep them shut," he says. "Take five steps forward."

In the dark, I have no sense of anything. My body forgets it's connected to me. My legs wobble because I can't tell where the floor is. "Am I going to bump into something?"

"You're fine."

The studio was all but empty when I left—just the chairs I pulled in from the hall and our project on the floor. I don't know what Eli did to the space while I was gone, though, and that makes everything louder and more imminent. "You'd tell me if I was about to crash through a window, right?"

"Pretty sure you can answer that for yourself."

It's difficult to roll your eyes when they're closed, but I do my best. Eli either doesn't get what I'm going for or he ignores me.

"One more step. A little to your right." When I'm situated to his apparent satisfaction, there's a pause. "Okay. Open in three, two—"

It happens quickly. My eyelids draw up, and the world is too bright after all that darkness. Eli's sitting a few feet in front of me. His camera's on a tripod. That's all I see before something flies at my face.

I scream and raise my arms. An object smacks into them—no, a substance. It doesn't hurt. It's cold. It's wet.

It's *paint.*

I open my mouth to shriek again, but another glob rushes at my face. This one smacks my cheek and collar. There's purple in my hair and blue on my hands and—

Pink comes out of nowhere to clock me in the chest.

"*Eli!*"

"Got you," he says, and I'm not sure if he's referring to my splattered clothes or my portrait. Now that I'm no longer being attacked, I'm able to take in the scene: Eli's got three cans of paint open next to his chair. His right hand is covered in a mixture of the colors, while his left holds a tiny remote to control the camera. There was an attempt to put a tarp on the floor, but there's pink and purple all over the wall behind me.

Eli raises his dripping fingers. "Can you pass me a paper towel?"

I gesture at my clothes. "You. Threw. *Paint.* At. Me?" It was too fast. Too absurd. It hasn't processed.

"Yes," he says impatiently. "And I want to see how the shots turned out, but I can't with my hand like this."

"You threw paint at me!" This isn't something I'm ready to move past. Purple mats my hair and slithers down my neck. I'm not *mad,* exactly, but I'm not happy! It's a similar feeling to when you turn on a playlist you usually like but didn't check the volume, so the first lyric jolts you into space.

"Sorry," says Eli, but his eyes are on his camera, and he doesn't sound sorry at all.

I think that's why I do it. Instead of going after the paper towels, I stalk forward and flick a glob of paint from my clothes onto his.

"Argh!"

"Annoying, isn't it? And burns, too. Wall paint, funny enough, is meant for *walls.* Were you trying to peel my skin off? Or did you just not think this through?"

"It burns?" He looks up, and the alarm in his expression makes me wince. I may have exaggerated the extent of my discomfort because *Hello??* He threw *paint* in my *face.*

"It's fine," I amend. "Just a little itchy. I'll shower when I get back to the dorm." I grab a handful of paper towels from the sink at the back of the studio. "Here." I shove a few at him.

"Sorry," he says again, and this time it's more sincere. "I've been conceptualizing this for a while, but I don't usually work with paint. It didn't occur to me some types are, you know. Wall-specific."

"It literally says *wall paint* on the cans—" I shoot back, but then the first part of his statement hits me. "Hang on, what do you mean you've been conceptualizing this for a while? I thought it was an on-the-spot idea because we needed a final subject?"

"No, I—" He pauses. "When I think about you, I think about paint. You describe portraits like you're done with them, but your tone doesn't match. You always sound like you want to run to them. I've been trying to figure out how to capture that contradiction, and—" He reaches for his camera with his now clean hands and fiddles with the buttons. The photos fly across the monitor until he pauses on one and holds it out for me to see.

I stop breathing.

Eli somehow caught the precise moment before the second glob of paint hit me. It flies through the air while my arms rise to cover my face. There's indignation in my expression and shock in my squeezed-shut eyes, but it's my mouth that I stare at. It's wide open in a scream, but my lips are turned up at the corners like I'm—not *happy*, but relieved? Paint is my headache; it's also my home. As frustrating as I find it, I can't help but relax when I'm near it.

Eli saw that. He saw me enough to capture that.

Hot pressure builds in my eyes. I don't know why.

Eli stares up at me in this way he sometimes does, like I'm big and he's small. I don't know why.

But I do know why. It's right there when I choose to look. So, I do look. I stop pretending not to. My gaze settles on his mouth. "Can I—?"

"Yes."

And then it's easy. I put a hand on his shoulder and a hand in his hair, and when I lean down, I kiss him.

Chapter Fifteen

So. That happened.

It's cool. It's chill. I mean, I've kissed people before. First, there was Max Fields, who kind of punched his mouth into my mouth at the eighth grade winter dance. It was not enjoyable for either of us, and he never made direct eye contact with me again. After that was Owen Thomas. He asked me out sophomore year, so we went to the movies and kissed in the back row. It was definitely better than clashing teeth with Max. I thought it was the start of something, until a few days later when it became clear he'd only gone after me as a way to get in with Alicia. Not the best tactic, bro. She tied his shoelaces together, and he fell flat on the grass in PE. Then there was Stacy Lee. She kissed me in someone's basement during Truth or Dare. It wasn't bad, but I didn't feel, like, fireworks or anything. I had no burning desire to kiss her again.

I would kiss Eli again. It's been three hours, and I still feel my hand in his hair and both of his in mine. He smelled like the paint that's under my nails, and his tooth scratched my lip in a way that shouldn't still burn but does. We kissed until some very rude person knocked on the studio door because they'd reserved it after us, and then I spent a frantic few minutes taking paper towels to the blue-pink-purple walls while Eli disassembled his tripod.

And that was it. I went in one direction to the dorm, and he went in another to the library.

Now I'm in my room. My feet take me from the window

to the door, the door to the window. Should I text him? I shouldn't text him. Except I should probably text him, because we didn't talk at all after the kiss, and it feels like one of those relevant things, you know, that's worth discussing?

I text Alicia. She doesn't know about Eli. Mentioning him would have been a great way to make my life seem more exciting than it is, but—I don't know. I guess I didn't want to talk about him until I knew what to say.

6:00 p.m.

Me: Hello
Me: So
Me: There's this boy
Me: That I kissed

Alicia Miller: HELLO???
Alicia Miller: BEQUEATH UPONST ME THE DETAILS

Me: Uponst isn't a word??

Alicia Miller: UPONST IS A WORD IF I SAY IT'S A WORD
Alicia Miller: THE DETAILS
Alicia Miller: BEQUEATH THEM
Alicia Miller: UPONST ME

Me: All right!!
Me: The details
Me: Uponst you
Me: I will bequeath!!!

I don't see Eli for another three days. The kiss happened on Monday, and now it's Thursday, and we still haven't talked about it. I know we need to talk about it, but we don't have photography on Tuesdays, and he missed class on Wednesday because of a doctor's appointment. So now the kiss has to go down in priority because our project draft is due by midnight on Friday, and we're still one photo short. My photo, specifically. My self-portrait.

It's not that I haven't tried to take it. For the last three days, it's the *only* thing I've tried to do. First, I took a bunch of selfies in my dorm, because I figured it's the space that looks the most like me in London. But that's when I realized my room doesn't look like me at all. When I bought my bedsheets and posters, I did so with my TRY NEW THINGS list in mind. I'm not a fan of bugs, so the butterfly duvet cover was an attempt to push out of my comfort zone. And because the walls of my room at home are pastel pink, I chose black-and-white prints for my decor here, which brings a sharpness to this space that I'd actually prefer to be soft. I take the prints down after coming to this conclusion and make another addition to my list:

9. NOT EVERYTHING HAS TO BE UNCOMFORTABLE.

Since my decor is in desperate need of renovation, I decide to take my self-portrait elsewhere. My first thought is Calum and Benji's flat, but although I do feel like myself there, it's a place that looks like them, not me. So I try out a variety of other spots across London that have become meaningful to me over the years. After dozens of pictures across different cameras, I have a few that aren't bad. But the problem is, Eli's photo of me was on another level. He looked at me in a way I'm not sure *I've* looked at me, and not that this is a competition, but I do feel pressure. What does it say if someone else can portray me better than I can portray me?

"What are you doing?"

I startle and raise my spatula as Natalie bursts into the kitchen, sniffing the air. "Cooking?"

"Are you actually?" Her gaze is judgmental. "I smelled smoke."

"There's no—" Oh, my quesadilla is on fire. I don't mean it's a bit black around the edges—there's a proper flame crackling over the top. "Argh!" I lunge at the pan and shove it into the sink.

How disappointing. I scrub away the char, dry the pan, and pull the cheese back out from the fridge. Then I turn to Natalie. "Do you want one?"

She balks. "Oh. Er . . ."

"I won't burn it."

She raises her eyebrows.

"You know—again," I add.

"If you say so." Natalie sits. "We need to talk, anyway."

"About what?"

She walks her fingers along the wooden surface of the kitchen table—back, forth, back, forth. "Marcus and I are in a course on Gothic architecture, and we learned recently that our dormitory was built in the 1850s. All that to say, he's convinced we've got a Victorian ghost. I've nearly convinced him, anyway. Tonight, when you do your pacing, can you wail a bit as well? He'll proper piss himself."

My cheeks burn. I've been pretty restless the last few days and have only managed to get to sleep every night after walking approximately a mile around my room. "Sorry," I mutter. "I'll be quieter."

Natalie leans forward on her elbows. "Is it midterms? My history of sculpture exam was a menace. I revised for three straight days but am still fairly certain I missed half the questions. Of course, that could be because I fell asleep a quarter through."

I hesitate. Natalie's cool. I could tell her about Eli, but it feels strange to have this conversation with her instead of Alicia. Not that I haven't talked to Alicia about Eli, but she only knows we kissed. Her life in Iowa is going so well that I didn't want to mention the pacing. I've explained a bit about the photography project, but I haven't shared how I'm worried there's a flaw in our thesis, or that Eli saw me more clearly than I've seen me, or that I'm still not making art that says anything. If I tell her those things, the distance between us will widen, because it's hard to relate to someone's bad, isn't it? When you're going through a lot of good?

I flip the quesadilla. "You remember that guy?" I say slowly. "Eli? With the crutches?"

"Heatstroke?" says Natalie. "How could I forget?"

"Right." I cough. "Well. We kissed."

"Of course," says Natalie. "And it was bad?"

"No, it—what do you mean, 'of course'?"

Natalie raises an eyebrow. "Every time you say his name, you go an alarming shade of scarlet. He wasn't any better. A fair claim could be made he was worse."

"*What?*" My face is not scarlet. It's just hot in this kitchen because I'm standing close to a flame, and—

The only person I'm kidding here is me.

"It wasn't bad." I flip my quesadilla again. "Well, maybe he thought it was bad. We haven't talked about it, but how do you bring up this sort of thing? It's not a conversation for photography class, or while we're working on our project in the library, or—"

Natalie cuts me off. "Marcus's girlfriend is hosting a

fancy dress party tomorrow night. Open invitation. You should come—bring Heatstroke and have your talk there."

A party? My nails dig into my spatula. I have to tell a boy I like him and he might not say it back! How embarrassing. Humans are so embarrassing. My stomach's churning just thinking about all the terrible ways this could go, but if we have our serious talk in an unserious environment, maybe some of the pressure will lift.

"Yeah," I say to Natalie. "Okay. I'll invite him." I grab my phone off the counter to text Eli, but when I turn it over, I realize he's texted me first:

7:48 p.m.

THE BOY WHO THREW PAINT AT ME (Eli): Hello

THE BOY WHO THREW PAINT AT ME (Eli): Are you around?

Me: What's wrong??

THE BOY WHO THREW PAINT AT ME (Eli): My camera just broke

THE BOY WHO THREW PAINT AT ME (Eli): And I didn't back up all our photos

THE BOY WHO THREW PAINT AT ME (Eli): I have the nine we decided on, but the rest are gone

THE BOY WHO THREW PAINT AT ME (Eli): So we won't be able to offer Dr. Lazar alternatives if she hates our draft

THE BOY WHO THREW PAINT AT ME (Eli): I should have been more careful
THE BOY WHO THREW PAINT AT ME (Eli): I'm sorry

Oh. Not his camera.

Eli brings his camera everywhere. Even to photography class, as though to prove to it that it's still his favorite even when he's working with other devices. He should be distraught, but his texts are neutral. Like his voice was when his ankle broke and he didn't want me to know.

The second quesadilla burns. No fire this time, but it's gone past crispy and into an inedible char. I toss it in the bin and then turn back to Natalie. "I'm sorry. I have to go."

Eli's room is three floors down from mine and has the same layout—the bed and wardrobe to the left, the desk on the right, a window across the back wall. Aside from the dark green bedsheets and tripod in the corner, he's done nothing to make the space his. It surprises me, because he's such a thoughtful artist. It doesn't surprise me, because when Calum left home, his room looked barer than this.

When I walk in, I find Eli standing frozen in the center of the narrow space, holding his camera like a dead thing between open palms. It takes a second for my brain to process this—he's *holding* it. With both hands.

"Your crutches are gone." The plaster cast is, too. There's a less bulky brace on his ankle that looks like it would fit in a shoe.

"The doctor said I should start walking." He doesn't

look up from the camera. "My leg's weak, though. I went to the park to take photos. I tripped."

"Are you okay?"

He shrugs. "Probably. But this isn't." He holds out his hands for me to see.

The camera's in pieces. The front lens is cracked, the back monitor shattered. Those bits could probably be fixed, but there are green chunks chipping out from the sides that indicate a more vital injury. "I'm sorry," I say.

He shakes his head. "It's my fault. I should have backed everything up—"

"Don't worry about that. We can take more photos if we have to. And we might not even have to! Dr. Lazar might like the ones we chose." I pause. I watch his very blank face. "I meant I was sorry about your camera. I know it was important to you."

He shrugs again. Neutral, but unnatural. His shoulders are tight. His voice is stiff. "It's fine."

"Eli—"

"It was old, anyway. I wasn't the first owner. Or the fifth."

I don't know what to do. He's obviously not going to cry or yell, but that doesn't mean he's not devastated. I'm good at hugs. I'm less adept at comforting someone who's glaring down at their dead camera with an expression I can only describe as *Call Me Sad and I'll Bite You.*

"When did you get it? Your camera." Maybe reliving its history will cool the fire in his eyes.

"We've been friends for a while, but I've only had him a few months."

"Him?" I guess I fail at saying it casually because Eli turns his hard stare on me.

"Jasper. Shut up," he mutters at whatever's on my face. "You have a cup of special paintbrushes. I can name my camera."

I'm not judging him. Well, I am. But not in a bad way. People name the things that matter to them. This just proves he cares. "What do you mean, you were friends for a while? Did you, like, ogle him in a shop window before buying?"

Eli shakes his head. "I took a photography class in high school. It was an elective—just a semester—but the teacher was kind. After it ended, she let me borrow Jasper whenever I wanted, and on Fridays we'd eat lunch in her classroom while going over my photos. At graduation, she gave me Jasper to keep. Definitely against school policy, but I only got out of that town because she helped me develop a portfolio, and—" He pauses. "I mean, I wasn't sure if I'd finish high school. So it was nice. To know someone cared."

"Why weren't you going to finish?" This is about his camera, so maybe I shouldn't shift the conversation. But his camera is about where he came from, so is it even a shift at all?

Eli hesitates. "I don't know how much you know about chess, but there are two categories of competition: open and women's," he says finally. "When I first started playing, my mom would enter me in the second one, because, sure." He frowns. "I earned a prestigious title in that category—it's why the *ESPN* piece happened. But—I preferred the open events, and for a while, that was fine. As long as my ratings kept improving, my mom didn't care where or when or under what name I competed. But around the time I turned sixteen, FIDE—the International Chess Federation—imposed stricter regulations. It meant if I continued competing as me—as Eli—I would be stripped of that title I won when I was younger. Which—" He pauses. "I didn't want that title. It tied me to a category I didn't belong in. But without it, Mom thought I'd be less valuable to sponsors. And that was always her goal—for me to use chess to make money. Even though there's not much to be earned unless you're a top competitor. And I wasn't. A top competitor, I mean. I was good for my age, but I wasn't the best in the world.

"Anyway. We fought. Things—escalated. When she kicked me out, school got harder. Obviously. Everything got harder. I didn't have time to compete senior year, but that was fine. I liked chess because it was a game. Once it stopped being a game, it wasn't fun anymore."

There's silence. Of course there is—what could I say? This isn't the type of situation with a solution, so I don't pretend to give him one. I just think.

People tell me terrible things more often than you'd expect. I've had strangers in cafés dump their whole lives in my lap. I found myself comforting kids I didn't know behind the bleachers at Crescent Valley High more times than I can count. I think it's my size: I'm too small to be intimidating. Or maybe my eyes: I'm an artist, and people can feel when they're being carefully watched. My point being, Eli said a lot, and it's heavy, but I've got experience with heavy. It's all about figuring out where best to put your hands in order to help hold up the weight.

Except, I don't think Eli wants me to touch this weight. Not the burden of chess or his mom or being kicked out. He mentioned it all very quickly and skipped over the details; these memories are not places he lingers. I don't think they are places on which he wants me to comment, but it feels wrong to just brush over everything he said.

My gaze turns back to the rubble in his hands. His broken camera is a new wound. It's the only one I might be able to mend. I step closer to better see its shattered remains. "Maybe we should show Dr. Lazar. She might know somewhere we can take it for repairs."

Eli shakes his head. "I know cameras. This one's beyond fixing."

He moves, finally, over to the desk, where he dumps Jasper in an unceremonious heap. He's limping. Heavily. Maybe that's normal after two months on crutches, but Eli also mentioned he tripped.

I bite my cheek to keep from turning this conversation into a confrontation. "What will you do with Jasper? If you can't repair him, I mean?"

Eli shrugs. "I don't know how trash works in the UK. Can I use the regular bin? Do I need a special tag for electronics, or—"

"You're going to throw him *out*?"

"What else can I do?"

I pick up the cracked lens and then the damaged body. Jasper has likely lost the ability to take pictures, but we keep talking about perspective. Does a camera have to be a camera? Surely there's a way to look at these parts without seeing garbage. I glance at Eli. "Can I give this to someone to fiddle with? He won't be able to fix it, but he could probably turn it into something new."

"Okay."

Silence again. This time, it's harder to breach. I scratch at my ear. "I can leave," I say. "If you want to be alone."

"Okay."

Fair enough. I gather the camera into my arms. "It'll probably be a while before you get this back. A few weeks."

"Okay."

Eli's not looking at me. He's standing with one hand planted into the desk like it's taken root. If I walk out the door and come back in the morning, I have a wary feeling he won't have moved.

"I'm watching this show," I try. "It's awful? Kind of a mix between *Family Feud* and *Floor Is Lava*, where the contestants balance on this log and get whacked off if they answer too many trivia questions wrong. I could grab my laptop. If you want?"

"Okay." His eyes are somewhere out the window.

"Eli." I don't mean to growl, but actually maybe I do, because sometimes his opinions stay buried unless they're yanked like teeth from his mouth. I stare at the back of his head. "Eli," I try again, quieter. "I can go. I can stay. Either is fine, but I won't know which you want unless you tell me."

His hand twitches on the desk. It looks tired. He looks tired. Of course he's tired. For a moment, I don't think he's going to respond. But then, finally:

"Stay."

A trivia show where contestants get whacked off a log when they get questions wrong, never to be seen again? I lied. This isn't awful—it's fantastic. Come on.

Half of my brain is riveted by this phenomenon that is reality TV. The other half is extremely aware of Eli's head, which has fallen against my shoulder. He's asleep. Which is chill. I'm chill. I've watched plenty of shows on plenty of beds and have on several occasions become a human pillow. Nothing weird about it. Got to love casual friendship things.

Is it a casual friendship thing, though, if a few days ago we kissed?!

I didn't want to complicate tonight with *Hey, remember when I grabbed your face and put it on my face hahahaha should we do that again, or—?* but his hair is soft. It smells like coconut. Casual friendship coconut.

Urgh.

In the quiet dark, I should feel calm, but instead my brain is like static, sparking uncomfortably every time it touches on a different topic. Aside from kisses and coconut-scented hair, my attention keeps flipping to the fire that's brewing in my gut and threatening to spew out of my eyes.

I'm angry. It didn't hit me as Eli was speaking about home or even in the immediate aftermath; I was too focused on figuring out what I could say that wouldn't make things worse. But now he's sleeping, and my laptop is laughing, and it's so quiet that I could scream.

My parents have done messed-up things. They've hurt me—they've hurt Calum more. And at the end of the day, a blow is a blow no matter why it hits you, but Mom and Dad have done what they can to rebuild their relationship with my brother. That doesn't magically fix the past, but it does show they regret the impact of their actions.

Meanwhile, Eli only mattered to his mom when he was useful. I don't understand that. I can't.

My arms are buzzing. I'd punch a wall or at least a pillow if the movement wouldn't disrupt him. Eli should be allowed to sleep. Something should go right for him.

I think I've been making things wrong for him.

I stare hard at the laptop. The voices emitting from it sound softer, suddenly—muffled—as though I reached out and lowered the volume.

Eli's ankle was my fault. I mean, not entirely—I didn't *push* him down those steps—but he tripped because I was in his way. And then he got heatstroke. Well, not *full-blown* heatstroke, but he turned an alarming color and may or may not have thrown up in my toilet because I left him alone on a bridge. And now a draft of our photography project is due in less than twenty-four hours and we're going to have to hand in something incomplete because I couldn't take one decent self-portrait.

Why can't I take a self-portrait? Art used to make sense. Did it ever make sense? This game show doesn't make sense. Everything's blurring together.

A colorful streak in the corner of the screen catches my eye. It's an application in my dock. Photos. I haven't opened it since coming to London. When I click it now, pictures pop up. Of me. Of Alicia and me.

God. In the earliest ones, we're babies. Thirteen, maybe? Yeah, I had that pink in my hair at thirteen. We look young and ridiculous in my backyard, posing like we're going to be on the cover of *Teen Vogue*. I wasn't as concerned, back then, with how people saw me. I just smiled with my hip popped too far to the side, wanting to hold on to the moment.

My fingers inch forward, pressing another application: Photo Booth. It automatically turns on my webcam.

A camera doesn't have to only be a camera, so why does a self-portrait have to only be a self-portrait? I don't think a photo of just myself would be a good representation of who I am. I mean, if those pictures on my laptop didn't also include Alicia, they wouldn't be causing my throat to tighten. Maybe that's why I've been having so much trouble capturing myself for our project. I came to London to learn who I am on my own, but that hasn't meant *being* alone. This city was never a stranger to me because it's my brother's, and photography only means something because of Eli. It would be odd to look back at pictures from this time in my life and not see him in them. So, I angle the laptop to make sure he's in this one.

I snap the photo.

Chapter Sixteen

"Did you chuck this off a cliff?"

It's noon on Friday. Calum's at work. Benji's examining Eli's camera in the afternoon light. I told him I was coming over, but I didn't tell him why. When I plopped the several pieces of Jasper down on the coffee table, Benji gave me his most judgmental look.

"It's my friend's," I say. "He dropped it."

Benji nudges the cracked lens with his iPad pencil. "I can fix a wobbly table. Maybe a bit of flooring. Certainly a tear in fabric. But anything with a circuit board is above my pay grade."

"He knows it's beyond repair. I just thought maybe you could turn it into something so it doesn't have to be thrown out? I know you don't usually work with materials like this, but if anyone can do it . . ."

"Yes, yes. Flattery will get you everywhere." Benji eyes the pieces more carefully. "Tell me about your friend."

"Why?"

"I can't make him something he'll like if I don't know what he's like."

Fair enough. How do I describe Eli? "He's thoughtful," I say. "As in, he thinks a lot. He's stubborn, but that's because he only says things he believes. He doesn't say everything, though. He's terrible about admitting when he's hurt or upset, which is unfortunate because he's had an awful few months. I'm not sure what he'd want his camera turned into, but he always used to wear it around his neck. Maybe earrings? He's got a lot of piercings, and that'd be a way for him to keep it on him . . ."

"Right." Benji scribbles a few notes on his iPad.

"Is that enough information?"

"One more question. How long have you liked him?"

"Only a few—*hey*."

"I know. How dare I? The audacity. The nerve!" Benji raises an eyebrow. "What's his name?"

"It's 'Have You Proposed to Calum? No? Then You Don't Get to Sit There and Judge Me.'"

"Is that a family name?"

"Go *away*."

"Oh, but you'd miss me." Benji sets down the iPad. "How did you meet? Are you dating? Have you—"

"I will not take questions about my love life when you are hopeless with yours!"

"*Hopeless?*" Benji scoffs. "I'll have you know, I've a hike planned for the weekend after next. So long as the weather holds and we run into a bear, I should be engaged by evening."

He says it proudly. Like he expects praise. I have to physically restrain myself from lunging at his shoulders. "Hi. Hello? Repeat that, please. One more time."

"We'll likely be engaged by next—"

"The *bear*, Benji. Why is there a *bear*?"

"Well," he says as though he is the master of all knowledge, "as established, Cal enjoys approximately zero things. The *Shrek* proposal was a mistake, obviously, but you know the film *Brave*? About those people who get turned into bears? It's set in Scotland, and Cal considers your aunt Lisa's flat in Edinburgh home. Discovering we haven't had bears in the UK for over a thousand years was a bit of a snag, but! Did you see the headlines last week? One escaped from the zoo. I figured it was a sign—"

"Benji, this isn't a proposal. It's a murder!"

"No! Bears are memorable. I'm creating a memorable moment—"

"A moment is only memorable if you survive it!" I roll my eyes. "Why are you having the worst time with this? Calum isn't complicated. Tonight, when he comes home from work, just say *Hello. Marriage. Yes?* and he'll go *Oh, okay, sure,* and you'll live happily ever after. It's that simple!"

"You didn't know him when I met him."

Wow. Ouch. I don't think that was supposed to hurt, but my body shrivels in on itself. I *didn't* know Calum when Benji met him. They were eighteen, and that year is part of the chunk of my brother's life I'm not allowed inside. Benji is, because he was there. I'm not, because I wasn't.

"No, sorry." Benji stares at whatever's on my face. I fidget where I'm sitting on the floor. It's so rare for his eyes to not be laughing that I don't know how to look at them when they're firm like this. "I just meant you're right. Calum's not complicated. He wakes up and goes to work and goes to sleep and goes to work. He's happy for life to simply move forward, but that's because, for a while, I don't think he thought it would. So, it's important. That this feels important."

Okay. Now it makes sense why Benji's in a knot. Calum rarely talks about the past, but when I was twelve, he did sit me down and try to explain why I hadn't heard from him in six years. To be honest, I don't remember much of that conversation. It came at me from nowhere, a slap so loud the world narrowed and my ears rang. It was hard to process that the reason my parents never told me why my brother left home was because they were the ones responsible for him leaving. It was even harder to sort through my hurt—which part was from being lied to, and which was indignation at how my brother had been treated? Calum didn't need me to be angry on his behalf. He didn't want me to be. But it took weeks to internalize that my choice to forgive our parents could not be contingent on his.

That was a lot for one summer. Some parts are blurry, but other bits are startlingly clear. During our conversation, Calum said, *"It felt like there wasn't any space in the world for me, like I wasn't allowed to exist."* I remember his words verbatim because the feeling was so unfamiliar to me. I never experienced that in Crescent Valley. Not with Mom and Dad. Not with my friends. But ten years is a long time. Even five years is the difference between Mom telling Calum he couldn't be public about having a boyfriend in high school and her not blinking twice when Alicia asked a girl to our fifth grade dance. I think time is also the difference between Calum being intentional about labels and me not bothering with them for myself. I've never given much thought to who I'm attracted to because I've never needed to. My only criteria is that they are kind. But Calum couldn't be gay in Crescent Valley, so he left our home and made his own. Creating something from nothing is an impossible task, but Calum lives in London now and has a questionable but well-paying job and a questionable but well-meaning boyfriend, and that's much bigger than *Hello. Marriage. Yes?* So I get where Benji's head is at. I do. But I also think he's putting himself under a lot of pressure.

"It's nice that you want to do something nice," I say finally. "But there's got to be a middle ground between murderous bears and *Want this ring, bro?* The next time you have an idea, consult me. I promise to give honest feedback."

"Maisie Clark, do you ever *not* give honest feedback?" Benji says, but then he smiles like that's maybe not a bad thing. "I'll consider keeping you informed—but enough about this. Your camera boy. Explain."

I roll my eyes. "He broke his camera. I gave it to you. The end."

"Are you dating?"

"We're friends."

"But you kissed?"

"We're friends."

"Was that his decision? Or yours?"

"Kissing?" I ask. "Or being friends?"

"Both," says Benji. "Neither. You've confused me."

I've confused myself. "We did kiss," I admit. "But we haven't talked about it, so things are weird now. And before you tell me about this amazing tool humans have called 'communication,' there's a party tonight and I'm going to invite him. We'll have a conversation there."

My phone is on the coffee table. Benji slides it over to me. "Go on, then. Invite him."

I breathe out through my teeth, but not because he's wrong. The clock is ticking; I only have so much time to send this text. I pull up Eli's contact and stare at our messages. I sent him my self-portrait this morning. Instead of saying anything about how he's in it and asleep on my shoulder, he simply sent a thumbs-up and wrote back: *I'll send in our project.* Then, ten minutes later: *Sent.*

And that was that. Our draft flew out of our hands

and into Dr. Lazar's. It'll probably be torn to bits, but we created something. A whole, complete something. If that doesn't call for a celebration, I don't know what does.

12:23 p.m.

Me: Hi!

Me: There's a Halloween party tonight do you want to go??

Me: With me?

Camera Boy (Eli): Okay

Me: Cool!!!

"Was that so difficult?" Benji asks, peering at the screen.

I push him away. "Don't talk to me about romance, Murder Bear."

Chapter Seventeen

When Natalie said Marcus's girlfriend is having a fancy dress party, I should have realized it meant *Marcus's girlfriend* is having a fancy dress party. As in: Marcus's girlfriend is also a student in our dorm. Therefore, thirty-five people will be crammed into a flat built for ten at max.

She's tried her best, though. The narrow halls are draped with cobwebs, pumpkins line the floor, and there's a massive bucket of candy on the kitchen table. I didn't think Halloween was that big in the UK, but we're a bunch of teenagers. Any excuse for a party, I suppose.

"Welcome!" Marcus's girlfriend is in my ceramics class. Her name is Tessa, and she's far more adept in the medium than I am. She likes to sculpt animal figurines—Highland cows are her specialty—and they are the cutest things. She grins at my outfit. "How long did that take you?"

I glance down at myself. By the time I decided to attend this party, it was too late to order a costume. So I got creative. Instead of throwing out my pasta-stained top and holey sweatpants that Eli got pink, purple, and blue paint on, I decided to add to the mess. The colors were a challenge to work with until I realized I could turn them into flowers. So, I did—all over the clothes, and my hair and body as well (with skin-friendly paint this time because *I* am sensible). Anyway, I'm not sure how I feel about the look. It's the most abstract thing I've voluntarily created. But it was fun to experiment with my art without the result hinging on a customer's approval or a grade.

"A few hours." I pinch the shirt. It's heavy and itchy—an okay outfit for one night, but definitely not my style. "You look amazing, by the way."

Tessa's grin widens. She's dressed as a mermaid. The gold eye makeup and false blue lashes are vivid against her dark skin; there's more gold beaded into the braids in her hair, body glitter sparkles off her arms and neck, and—the *tail.* It's a skirt made of sheer fabric, with hand-painted scales that I'm sure she designed herself because they've got the same level of detail as the fur that makes her ceramic cows so stunning.

"You here with anyone?" she asks.

"One of my flatmates. Natalie?" We walked in together, but the second she spotted the candy, she bolted into the kitchen. I tried to elbow after her, but the people in here are starting to feel like a sea. And anyway, I can't help but linger near the front door. "Also this guy. Eli? I hope it's okay I invited another person. It's pretty packed in here."

Tessa waves a hand. "I know Eli. He's good with a camera—the best in Intro to Filmmaking. Quiet lad, though. Can't picture him at a party."

I wouldn't describe Eli as quiet, but now that Tessa says it, I can't exactly imagine him dancing it up to a pop song. He agreed to come, though. Maybe he likes Halloween. Or—you know. Me.

Someone calls to Tessa over her shoulder—something about the drinks. She gives me an apologetic nod and then makes her way toward the kitchen. It's louder once she's gone. There are ten conversations happening within earshot that I now have no choice but to pay attention to, and the music suddenly doubles in volume. This is not the laid-back environment I'd hoped for in order to have a conversation about the kiss. I *like* partying, but I also like breathing. It's so cramped in here that I'm beginning to doubt my ability to do both.

The front door is held slightly ajar by a stopper. It shoves forward suddenly, and I have to push back against it with my shoulder so it doesn't smash into my face. I'm thinking of dodging past the newcomer and into the October air, but when I look up, I see Eli.

He's wearing one of his typical outfits: a black hoodie and cargo pants. I'm about to yell at him for not attempting a costume when I see the piece of paper taped to his chest. He wrote *I'm a Black Hole, in Case You Can't Tell.* He also has his crutches again.

I frown. "Did something happen?"

"What?" he shouts.

Eli's still standing in the open doorway. It's too loud to have a conversation here, so I gesture for him to move into the hall. "Let's talk outside."

He frowns. "*What?*"

"OUT! SIDE!" I point frantically until he gets it and takes a few steps back.

It's nearly as loud in the hall. Music and chatter bleed from the cracks in the door, and there are more people heading up and down the stairs. We're on the second floor—Eli's floor. We could slip into his room, but after the suffocating heat of bodies on top of voices, I'm desperate for fresh air.

"Can we . . . ?" I point down.

He nods. "You'll have to, though . . ." He holds out one of his crutches. It takes me a moment to realize he means for me to grab it so he can hold the stair railing. I do, and we start down. It's slow going—Eli's putting weight on his injured foot, but not very much. When we reach the ground floor, he's breathing harder than I am.

"Did something new happen with your ankle?"

He shakes his head. "It's been bothering me since the cast came off. I went to the doctor again this morning—she said I'm not walking as well as she'd hoped, so it'll be another few weeks with the crutches. It's—you know. Whatever."

Considering the way he's glowering at the ugly gray carpet, I don't get the sense it's "whatever." Then again, this is Eli—the guy who broke his favorite camera and refused to admit it made him sad.

"Fun fact," I say. "You won't be chucked out the window for having feelings."

"Sure, but admitting you feel like crap just makes you feel more crap, because then other people start agreeing with you that things are crap, which in turn confirms to your brain that your feelings of feeling like crap are, in fact, not crap."

He lost me on that last part. This is something, though. An indirect admission. I leave it there because I don't think he'll say more, and the only more *I* can say is something infuriating like *Healing takes time!* So I just nod at his costume. "Considering you're an artist, this is pretty appalling work."

"I'm a photographer, not a fashion designer."

"Still." There's a headband in my hair. I poked some holes in the cardboard-like material and threaded real flowers through to complete my look. Before Eli can blink, I take it off my head and stretch up to shove it onto his. "Black holes eat things, right? You should at least have something caught in your orbit."

"They don't *eat* things. That's not the scientific term."

"What is it, then? Do you know?"

"Do I look like I study astrophysics as a side hobby?"

I give his monochrome outfit a once-over. "You do dress more like an alternative space expert than a genius chess player."

Eli sighs, but he doesn't take off the headband. "Why did we come down here? I thought you wanted to be at that party?"

"It was loud," I say. "And crowded."

"So—a party?"

"Well, *obviously*, but—" I gesture at the stairs. "Do you want to go back up? Is that why you're asking?"

"Hell no. It was loud. And crowded."

Glad we've established that. I scratch at my ear and then pat my hand against the front door of the building. "Maybe we could walk a bit? If that's okay with your ankle? I wanted to talk to you, actually."

His gaze turns wary. "About what?"

Right. This is a delicate topic. I should ease into it, break the ice. Maybe start with a reference to the photography project, and then bring up the studio, and then—

"Remember how, on Monday, I stuck my tongue in your mouth?"

Eli chokes. On his own spit, apparently—neither of us managed to snag drinks from the party. "Tasteful," he says through a cough. "Great grasp of words, you have."

"Thank you."

"Yes, well." He's staring hard ahead. "Funny enough, I do remember. Your tongue. It would be hard to forget, seeing as it was—as you eloquently described—in my mouth."

My ear itches. It's the paint, or maybe it isn't. I pictured this conversation happening under dim party lights or the glow of the moon—not with this backdrop of fluorescents and an ugly hallway. Maybe it's fitting, though. We met on the threshold of the wooden door my back is currently against. Eli toppled over me, and that should have been the end of it, but instead we ended up like this.

"So." My mouth is dry. "Are we . . . friends, who kissed? Or project partners, who sort of went to a party together? Or—I mean—" I wince. "Do you . . . like me? Should we, like, go on a date? Or something?"

God. I can't be doing this right. If I was doing this right, it wouldn't feel like the world is ending, and also like *why isn't the world ending?* and also like *can I fall in a hole now?*

Eli is silent. At first it doesn't worry me, but then it does—it's been a solid thirty seconds and if he's still not responding, I can only assume it's because he's trying not to hurt me.

"I don't know what I'm doing," he says finally. Quietly. His eyes are low, focused on the ground. "Here, I mean. In London. I left home to get away, but I see my mom everywhere. On the tube. In random shop windows. The distance didn't do anything, and now I'm at this school because of a reckless decision I made for a reckless degree. When I graduate, I can't stay in this country. It'll kick me out, and I'll have to start somewhere new. Where, though? Doing what? I don't know. I can't see it—"

"Whoa." It's not like I don't get the existential dread. If I don't find out who I am as an artist this year, my plan is still to stop looking. It's nearly November, and sure, I've had some realizations—namely that having a voice means having a point—but I still don't think that if anyone glanced at my work right now, they'd be able to say *Oh, that's Maisie's.* So, where will I be next fall? London? New York? What will I be studying? Finance? *Math?* I think about it every day, but if I thought about it *all* day, it would consume me. "It's normal to not be able to see where you're going. I mean, I feel that way, and it's fine—"

"It's fine because your brother's in London," Eli counters. "Your family's in New York. You're not alone, and—it's great you have hands to catch you. But if I fall, I stay down. So it's not that I don't like you. I—of course I like you. But I think I need to know where I'm going before I can try to know someone else." He shakes his head. The wilting flowers in his hair shake with it. "We shouldn't have kissed. Not when we did, anyway. Not when I knew it couldn't go anywhere. That's on me."

My back is still pressed against the front door. The wood is like Eli's voice: soft but sturdy. I can see in the way he's not looking at me, in the way his jaw is hard and his brows are low, that there's no argument I can pull out of my pocket to change his mind. He made this decision a while ago. Maybe four days ago, when we were still in that studio, my hands in his hair. That's why it took us so long to reach this conclusion. He knew what I would say, and he knew what he would say, and this week was a trial in avoiding the clash.

"I wish you'd told me sooner."

He flinches. It makes something bitter lodge in my throat. *"I left home to get away. Now I'm at this school because of a reckless decision I made for a reckless degree."* We're in the exact same position, except for the fact that we're not. He's right—if I fail in London, my family won't let me fall. Eli doesn't have that. He has to make different decisions because of that.

"I do like you," he says again, into the silence.

"I like you, too."

But then we both look away, because this is not the start of something; it's where we draw. Stalemate.

Chapter Eighteen

Something's wrong.

It's Saturday morning, and fresh light shines through my window, and my alarms didn't go off.

Something's wrong.

After my talk with Eli, I showered away my flower costume and cried for a while under the water. Then I cried for a while under my covers. When I finally turned off the light, everything went quiet. But it shouldn't still be quiet.

Where is my phone?

It's no longer on my pillow. I check under the covers and on the small nightstand. Then I duck down, and that's when I see it under my bed. It doesn't turn on when I tap it. Maybe it ran out of battery?

I press the power button, and the screen brightens. It's not dead; I must have turned it off. When it comes back to life, the first thing I notice is the time: 10:15 a.m. The studio space I booked to work on my ceramics assignment is reserved for nine. *Was* reserved for nine. My stomach drops. How did this happen? I've never slept through an art commitment before.

My notifications come in. Missed calls. Several—all dating from between two and five in the morning. My stomach twists when I realize the first four are from Mom. Dad tried twice a few hours later. Then I see the texts.

5:15 a.m.

Mom: Something happened with the shop.
Mom: Call me back when you get the chance.
Mom: Would you also check on Calum?

Bile rises in my throat. I call Calum, but it goes straight to voicemail. I try Benji. The phone rings and rings until there's no answer, so I curse and hang up and try Mom.

No answer.

Dad.

Nothing.

Something's *wrong.*

My body carries itself to the door. I'm in pajamas, but that doesn't matter because my thoughts are caught up in ringing and buzzing and *nothing.* My feet move instinctively—down the steps and out of the dorm and over toward the Circle Line. The train comes, and I go with it. At Notting Hill Gate, my feet find the platform and walk up the escalator and down the blocks until I'm facing my brother's flat.

My finger rings the bell. When there's no answer, my hand pulls out two keys. Calum sent them when I was twelve, in an envelope that also included a plane ticket for me to visit over winter break. I've worn the keys on a chain around my neck ever since, which—maybe that's weird, but my brother was lost for so long. Now I can't help but keep him close.

The first key opens the front door. The second unlocks the one at the top of the stairs. When I burst over the threshold, I expect to be alone since no one answered the buzzer. But Benji's on the couch, his head in his hands, staring down at his phone through a web of fingers. "Oh." He looks up. "Hello."

My stomach squirms. "Where's Calum?"

It's Saturday. My brother would typically be at his office, but those ominous texts from Mom combined with Benji's rigid demeanor make me think Calum's not anywhere he's supposed to be.

Benji shrugs. It's a stiff gesture. "He ran off."

The floor dips. Or maybe I do. Instead of standing in the London flat and staring at its brown couch with Benji sitting rigidly atop it, I'm suddenly in Crescent Valley on a sapphire couch with my six-year-old feet knocking slowly against it.

"School starts tomorrow." I looked from Mom to Dad to the empty chair in the corner of our living room where Calum liked to sit. "Why isn't he back from camp yet?"

Mom didn't look at me. She was uncharacteristically quiet. So Dad muttered, "He isn't coming back."

I frowned. Calum said at the start of the summer he'd walk me to my first day of first grade. He promised, because I promised to stop coming into his room and bothering him all the time, and I held up my end of that deal, so why was he bailing on his?

"What do you mean? How much longer will he be at camp?" To make up for his horrendous betrayal, he'd have to walk me to school for a *month*.

Dad paused. For a very long time. Then, again: "Maisie, he isn't coming back."

"Yes, but for how long?" Maybe people could spend extra time at camp if they really liked it. That wasn't something I wanted Calum to do, though, because after months of him shouting at Mom and Mom shouting back, the silence of his absence was too loud. All summer it felt like any noise I made, no matter how small, echoed off the walls and into my parents' ears and made them flinch. "Another few weeks? Another *month?*" The thought of that—another month of just the three of us in this house . . .

Dad closed his eyes. When he opened them, they were watery. The shock of his tears made my stomach drop the way it had the one time I'd braved a rollercoaster. When the world had fallen away, I'd tried to scream, but I couldn't. No sound came out.

"Not next week," Dad reiterated. "Not next month. Calum isn't coming home, Maisie. Not ever."

Not ever.

There's a hand on my arm. It takes me a moment to refocus, to see Benji in front of me.

"Calum—ran off?" I finally manage. "What do you mean? Where—*why*—"

"Whoa," says Benji. "Hang on, calm down—"

"*Don't tell me to calm down.*" I shove his hand away. "Calum's *gone*. You should care. Why don't you *care*—"

"*Maisie.*" Benji looks at me. His eyes are very hard when they meet mine, but they are also very red. He draws in a slow breath. "You truly believe I don't care?"

No. I don't believe that. I said it, but I don't believe it. Instead of opening my mouth again, I open my arms. He lets me hug him, so I squeeze him tightly. We stay that way for several moments. "I'm sorry."

He pulls away and watches me carefully. "This isn't new—Calum disappearing. He does this. He has always done this. So do you really think we'd have gone ten years without finding a compromise?"

"A compromise?"

Benji glances at his phone, which he's now got cupped

in his palm. "He shares his location with me. Whenever he leaves abruptly like this. So long as he does, I don't follow him." He pauses. "It's . . . not particularly enjoyable for me, when he runs off. But I also know he only runs off when things are particularly unenjoyable for him. Maybe it seems strange, from the outside. This understanding between us. But I trust him. I know he would tell me if there were any reason to be concerned. And you can be sure I would also tell you."

The horror lapping at my chest recedes down my body—past my stomach, my hips, my knees. Anger rises in its place. I've been left to wash out to sea while Calum threw Benji a lifeline. Why does Benji get a lifeline when I'm the one my brother stranded for six years? I'm the one who spent elementary school thinking he was dead and that everyone was just too afraid to tell me. I'm the one who had to bury every question I had about him because Mom and Dad flinched if I so much as said his name.

The coffee table's in front of me. I kick it. I yell. I'm too old to be losing it like a child, but I feel as lost as I did as a child. As helpless. As furious that I'm helpless.

Instead of telling me off, Benji wraps his arms around mine. For a moment, I stiffen—Calum is *gone* and I'm *drowning* and *why do you get to know where my brother is when I don't*—but eventually I sink against him, because Calum is gone, and I'm drowning, and Benji knows where my brother is when I don't.

The details come later and in fragments.

Benji says my mom rang late last night. Something happened with Glenna's—something about a collaboration with an art gallery. When Calum heard the news, he bolted. At three in the morning.

I gather this information and sort it into the beginnings of a picture. Then I lay down some additional pieces on the coffee table between us—starting with how, in early October, Mom had mentioned that a gallery in New York City had reached out to Glenna's about an exhibition of queer portraits they're putting on. The curators liked the samples of work they saw on our website and asked if we would be willing to contribute ten paintings. Mom was in talks with Calum about the collaboration. He approved of the idea, and the exhibition announcement went live last week. I know it gained positive and negative traction—more in both directions than we usually get. I *don't* know what happened that caused Calum to run, but I get the answer an hour later, when Mom finally calls me back.

"There was a break-in," she says. I've got my phone on speaker. It's perched between me and Benji on the couch. He's settled into a calm sort of quiet, not moving much except to occasionally check what I assume is my brother's location on his phone. I made tea he didn't drink. I passed him pretzels he didn't eat. Benji said he wasn't concerned about Calum's disappearance, and maybe he's not, but whatever he's feeling, it doesn't look comfortable. His shoulders are as rigid as rocks. At this revelation from Mom, mine join his, bouncing up high by my jaw and freezing there.

"A *break-in?*" My heart pulses. "Was anyone hurt?"

"No, no. We're okay. But the portraits we'd been collecting for that New York City exhibition were destroyed. Nothing else in the workshop was touched or taken, so . . ." Mom pauses. "It appears to have been a targeted attack."

Benji winces, but he doesn't say anything, so I ask,

"What does that mean? For Glenna's? Do you know who broke in? Are you looking into it? Are you—"

"If we open an investigation, we'll lose access to the workshop, as everything inside will be considered evidence. So your dad and I agreed a better use of our time would be to focus on rebuilding. The exhibition is in January. It'll be tight, definitely, to have ten new pieces ready by then, but if we pause for a bit on Glenna's commissions, your dad thinks he can—"

"You can't close Glenna's." It comes out like a whine. "If you close Glenna's, whoever did this will win—"

"If we back out of the exhibition, how is that better?" Mom counters. "Your dad and I are only two people. It's the shop or the gallery, and we can't back out of the gallery. I . . . can't do that to Calum."

I breathe out through my teeth. Mom let Calum down when he was a teenager, and she's been trying to make up for it since. I don't blame her for that, but if Mom and Dad shut down Glenna's, won't it seem like they're conceding to this attack? Like they're agreeing our art is contentious and our shop needs to lie low? That'd be as much of a slap in the face to Calum as backing out of the gallery.

"I'll come home," I say abruptly. "I'll take on new commissions for Glenna's so Dad can focus on the exhibition—"

"No," Mom shoots back sharply. "You are not dropping out of university."

"I won't *drop out.* I'll just—well . . ." I'll probably have to redo this semester if I go home until January, but that's not the same as dropping out. It's not *ideal*, obviously, but—

"Maisie Clark, if you show up on my doorstep, I will

not let you into the house," snaps Mom. "I'm paying your tuition, if you recall—"

"Someone attacked our shop! Am I just supposed to sit here?"

Benji stands. I assume he's had too much of this conversation, but instead of walking out the door, he stops at the kitchen table. He picks something up, heads back to the couch, and places it in my lap.

It's an iPad. His iPad. I run my fingers along the sides and then press the button to turn it on. I got quite familiar with Benji's iPad the summer I spent at this flat when I was twelve. He taught me how to do art in Procreate, and for a few years after, I sold commissionable digital portraits through Glenna's website. I migrated back to oil paintings by the time I was fifteen because I preferred the physicality of them, but our shop could reopen to digital commissions. I could do them from here, without having to go home.

I propose the idea to Mom.

She pushes back. "Your studies—"

"We just turned in midterms. I don't have another big project due for weeks."

A pause. A long one. Finally: "You wanted to get away from portraits."

I did. I do. But our shop is in trouble, and my paintings don't have to look like mine to keep us afloat: They just have to look like Dad's. That's fine. That's easy.

It's what I know best.

Hours pass in Calum and Benji's flat. My head throbs, aching worse each minute. My brother is missing. Someone broke into Glenna's. Every so often Benji glances over at me and attempts a smile, but his hand is glued to his phone, and at some point, his posture veered beyond tense and into looking painful.

I make more tea. It goes cold. So does the light in the flat, until I force myself up to flick on a lamp. Alicia texts *What did you end up doing for Halloween?* but I can't conjure the positivity needed to reply, so I just sit on the couch, and Benji sits on the couch, and it's silent until nine p.m. when a key turns in a lock.

Calum walks in.

For a moment, everything freezes. Time. Sound. My thoughts. The only things moving are my eyes: up and down, back and forth.

Calum's not in his work clothes. He's in sweatpants and a hoodie and the glasses he only wears when he's not planning to leave the house. He doesn't look at me. He looks at Benji, and that's who his words are for when he speaks: "I'm sorry."

"It's all right."

At first I assume it's a meaningless, automatic response, the way *fine* is when someone asks *how are you?* But then Benji slumps against the couch, and I realize the hitch in his voice isn't anger. It's relief.

"Do you need anything?" he asks Calum, which is so horrendously kind after the day my brother put us through that it makes me flinch, like biting too hard into something soft.

Calum shakes his head. "Do you?"

"*Food.* I could eat this entire flat."

"I'll order something." Calum reaches toward the laptop on the coffee table. "Curry? Pizza? Or . . . ?"

I kick my feet back into the couch, and then forward. There's something building in my chest. A humming. A screaming. My brother sits next to Benji, scrolls on the laptop, and says something low that makes them both smile, like everything's fine, like the world wasn't just ending for hours, like they've already moved on—

"Where *were* you?" The words come from deep in my stomach.

There's a pause. Calum's eyes finally flit in my direction. There's no apology in them like there was for Benji. I can't read his expression at all. "Out."

"Oh, thank you. I was thinking you were *in*, so. Glad that's cleared up."

Calum frowns. "Don't yell at me."

"I'm not yelling. I'm talking loudly because you *ran off*!"

"I did not run off. I needed to clear my head—"

"For eighteen hours?"

"I was clearing my head," he repeats slowly, as though I'm being intentionally obtuse. "And then—"

"You *left*."

"I returned—"

"This time. You returned *this time*."

Calum's jaw clenches. "That isn't fair, Maisie. Why should you have any say over when, or for how long, I am away from my own flat? You do not live here. I do not owe you my whereabouts unless we have plans to meet up, which today we did not." He's glaring like I'm the one in the wrong. Like I'm making a scene over nothing.

Unbelievable. I stand from where I've been sitting for too long and walk past my brother. I yank open the door and let my feet lead me into the night.

Chapter Nineteen

On Monday morning, I don't go to class.

I've never skipped a lesson before, but how am I supposed to sit at a desk and take notes on my laptop and act like everything's normal when everything's not?

I do go to ceramics on Tuesday. But why am I here when someone broke into Glenna's and Calum went missing? The clay in my hand is useless. There's nothing I can build with it that would help my family, so why am I bothering to shape it at all?

Tessa's sitting next to me. She asks if I'm okay. I think. I nod emptily. I think. My brain can't keep up with my body, or maybe it's too far ahead. All I know is I somehow stumble through hours of instruction and make it back to my room and open Procreate on Benji's iPad. That's when I come to an unfortunate realization: Muscle memory is like any other kind of memory. The farther you get from the source, the more you forget the details.

My fingers don't recall all the shortcuts that, at fifteen, were second nature to me; the tools I used for my digital art are different now or in different places or have been updated to handle different tasks. Not to mention, shoving myself back into the role of a portrait painter is a tighter squeeze than I expected: I have to twist into the shape I've spent months trying to twist out of. After four hours of badly recreating old work in an effort to regain my technical skills, my heart beats too fast and my hands tingle with urgency and my index finger on the iPad pencil aches from how I'm gripping it wrong. But then my email dings with a notification and it all gets so much worse, because it's a digital commission request. For me. From Glenna's.

Can I handle it?

It doesn't matter if I can handle it.

I draw in a breath.

I draw the first line.

Chapter Twenty

I finished the digital commission late last night. It's . . . not good, but it's also not bad. I don't have much time to stew in its mediocrity, because when I wake Wednesday morning, there are seven new emails in my inbox. Six are forwarded requests from Glenna's. One is from Dr. Lazar. The subject line reads: *See me in my office before class.*

The throbbing in my head is louder than my heart.

Dr. Lazar's office is a small room in the photography building. I expected it to look like her: neat and crisp. It's not. Plants pile on the windowsill, some deep green and others dry and brown. Framed pieces of art hang on every bare inch of wall and overflow in stacks on the floor. The large wooden desk is covered in papers, as are the chairs. I have to lug an armful of essays onto the ground in order to take my seat.

"I'm sorry," I say as Dr. Lazar searches her apparently organized chaos for, I'm assuming, some sort of disciplinary slip to hand me for not showing up to class on Monday. "I missed our lesson because of a family situation. It won't happen again."

Dr. Lazar plucks a folder from the depths of nowhere and sets it in front of me. It's not a punishment. It's my project.

"I had a few comments about your draft," she says, "and wanted to discuss them in person." Her sharp eyes scan me thoroughly. I'm in sweatpants and a sweatshirt, my unwashed hair hidden beneath the dark hood. No makeup today—not even sparkles under my eyes, which

I'm sure means they look puffy and red from lack of sleep. This isn't how I like to be seen, especially by someone as critical as Dr. Lazar. But it's a feat I managed to roll out of bed at all.

"Is your family all right?" she asks.

I swallow. "My parents own a portrait shop. It was broken into. Everyone's okay, but..."

"We can reschedule," Dr. Lazar says. "I am aware students have lives outside the confines of academia."

I shake my head. I'm already here; I don't want to go through the effort of coming back. "It's fine. What were your comments?"

"Let's wait for your partner before we begin."

Right. Eli. This meeting is about our project, so of course he's coming, too. Clearly, I should have actually read Dr. Lazar's email instead of panicking at the subject line and slapping my laptop closed.

My fingers pick at my chair. The wood is as stiff as this silence.

Dr. Lazar clears her throat. "I'm not surprised by your background in portraits." She taps the folder we're not looking at. "Your photos are quite different from Eli's."

Great. That's just what I need right now—digs at my photography skills while my entire life is crashing down.

"This is an intro course," I say, probably harsher than I should, considering Dr. Lazar holds the fate of my grade in her hands. "I've never worked with cameras in any real way before. If I'd known I was supposed to be an expert, I wouldn't have signed up for this class—"

"You misunderstand," Dr. Lazar replies in an even tone. "Eli is an accomplished photographer. His shots are more technical than yours, but in other ways, they are less precise."

My brow furrows. I sink back into the chair. Was that . . . a compliment?

"Your focus is on the person without consideration for the background," Dr. Lazar continues, "whilst Eli is concerned with how his subjects interact with their surroundings. You capture rawer images. His are more encompassing. It is a good partnership, in that respect. Especially considering your project is, at its core, a study in portraiture."

I . . . did not expect Dr. Lazar's praise, or her insinuation that my photography looks like it's *mine.* It also never really occurred to me that our project revolves around the type of art I've been trying to avoid, because photography is so different from oil painting. Maybe that's why I don't see Dad in my work when I'm holding a camera instead of a brush, even though Dr. Lazar is right—our thesis is literally an argument about portraits. Before I can fully process these revelations, the door opens. Eli walks in.

My breath hitches. It's fine. This is fine. We can be in the same room and contribute to the same conversation, even though *"I think I need to know where I'm going before I can try to know someone else."*

I'm *fine.*

He sits next to me. I don't look at him, but I can feel the heat of his elbow where it rests next to mine and the heat of my face as it burns. How embarrassing.

Dr. Lazar opens the folder, revealing our ten photos. "As I was explaining before you arrived," she says, glancing at Eli, "I've reviewed your project. But before we get to my comments, I would like to hear from the both of you. What about the draft went well?"

Eli shifts in his chair. I decided on the direction of our project, so I should probably take the lead on its critique.

But Glenna's was attacked and my brother ran away, and how ridiculous it is that we're here discussing an *essay.*

"The subject versus the artist," Eli says when I don't offer anything. "I think our photos capture that concept." His gaze is on me. Mine is on the picture I took of Calum. My brother is warm. He is candlelight and watercolors and small smiles in the dark, but on Saturday when he ran away, he was nothing at all.

"And areas you feel could be improved?" Dr. Lazar asks.

Eli's arm twitches as if he wants to nudge me. I'm being an ass by not contributing to this discussion, and maybe Dr. Lazar will factor my silence into our final grade, but my eyes sting and my throat burns and if I open my mouth, I'm going to cry.

"Well," Eli continues, "the essay needs . . . work. Our intro didn't pull enough background knowledge, and we struggled with the conclusion . . ."

"Yes." Dr. Lazar flips through the stapled paper. "I see the effort, but you need to reconsider your argument, as well as employ more evidence to back up your points. Before we delve further into that, though . . ." She taps the two photographs depicting the woman from Eli's art class. "In your other shots, I feel the desire from both perspectives for the subject to be seen, but these two lack the same depth, as if everyone involved was less invested. I wonder if it's your choice of photos. Do you have other options to pull from for this subject?"

Eli shakes his head. "There—was an incident. With my camera."

"Perhaps that's for the best. It gives you the opportunity to reset. Either with the same subject or another." Dr. Lazar's eyes flit back to the essay. "Most of your issues lie here." She taps the introduction. "There's some direction to your argument, but the thesis needs more consideration." She tilts her head so she can read out our words—*my* words, that I first posed to Eli when he was in my room in my shirt: "'The purpose of a self-portrait and portrait of the same subject is to bridge the disconnect between how people view themselves versus how they are viewed by others.'" She looks up from the folder. "I agree there is a disconnect, but why try to bridge it? If people were to change how they present themselves, it wouldn't necessarily mean they'd be viewed by others in the way they intend. We can't control how we are looked at; we can only control how we look. So why illuminate something unchangeable? In order for your essay to carry weight, it should address this complication."

There are rocks in my stomach. With each passing second, they weigh heavier until I'm waiting for the moment I fall through the floor.

Why illuminate something unchangeable?

Dr. Lazar is right. That's a massive hole in our argument. If we can't explain why our project matters, then our work is pointless. Voiceless.

Why illuminate something unchangeable?

I don't know.

I don't even know why we're talking about this essay when I have so many digital portraits to paint. When there's Glenna's. Someone broke into Glenna's. Calum. Calum and Benji. Eli. His elbow is so undeniably next to mine, but the space it takes up feels like an insurmountable distance. I finally turn to look at him. His eyes narrow like he's seeing the messy spiral in my head, but he shouldn't be seeing my messy spiral because *"I think I need to know where I'm going before I can try to know someone else,"* so I try to shutter my face, but I have been on the verge of a breakdown for five days and there is only so much verge to teeter on before I start to teeter over, and—

I stand. It's rude. But if I stay, it will be worse.

"Maisie!"

Eli's voice echoes off the walls of the narrow hallway. Last week, I would have stopped for him, but my idea for our project sucked and I'm sucking him down with me and if I stop, it'll be obvious I'm crying, so I don't stop. I go until he can't catch me.

Except, he does catch me.

One moment, I'm running down the stairs. The next, something—two somethings—soar through the air. They slide and clatter past me, and I'm startled enough by the disruption that I falter.

I spin around. Eli stands at the top of the landing. His hands are free of crutches, which makes sense, considering there's now a pair lying innocently at my feet. "Did you *throw* those at me?"

"Not at you."

My eyes narrow. Semantics aside, this was an entirely unhinged way to get my attention. "You could have—"

"You wouldn't look at me, or talk to me, and you were in the middle of running out on our project evaluation, so." He nods at the crutches. "My doctor was right—they're more useful than I wanted to admit. Multipurpose."

"That's not *funny*."

He's trying to lighten the mood, I think, because he's staring as though girls sobbing in stairwells induces the same sort of horror in him that clowns with chainsaws induces in me. But I don't want him to lighten the mood when we kissed and then he rejected me; when our project isn't working; when instead of burrowing under my covers, I'm dodging projectiles and glowering up at the last person I want to see.

I sit, suddenly, on a step near the bottom of the landing. It wasn't a conscious decision. One moment I'm upright and glaring; the next my head drops to my knees and I'm drawing in breath after stinging breath.

I'm not sure how much time passes. I just know that one moment I'm alone, inhaling too quickly, and the next I'm staring at Eli's feet, which have materialized next to mine on the step.

"Well," he says into the silence. "I messed up, didn't I?"

It's a bizarre enough statement that I raise my head. Then I grimace, because he's staring at the rawness under my eyes, the red around my nose, and—God. He thinks I'm falling apart because of *him*.

"Don't flatter yourself," I snap. "Something happened with my family. I promise you're not the reason my hair's this bad." I attempt to flatten it under my hood.

"Oh," he says. And then, "What happened?"

I shoot him an incredulous look. Less than a week ago, he wanted nothing to do with me!

"To clarify." His voice is slightly strained as he takes in my expression. "On Friday. When I said I needed to sort out my life. I didn't mean we should stop talking. The problem wasn't the talking. It was just, the tongue thing."

"The—" I blink. "The *tongue* thing?"

He flushes. "The kissing. The kissing was distracting. It was highly distracting, and—I can't be distracted right now. But we can talk. Or, you know. You can keep thinking about how you'd like to punch me in the face. I can tell." He gestures at my eyes. "You're considering it."

I draw in a long breath. I expect to find disappointment

at the end of it, but instead I find relief. Friends. He's indicating we can be friends.

It's not what I thought we'd be. It's not what I wanted to be, but I spent the last few days thinking we were nothing, and for some absurd reason, I actually do enjoy talking with him. Even though we keep having conversations that make me feel like *I'm* being punched in the face. I like that talking with him is never boring. I like that he's smart. I like that he pushes against my perspectives on art. I like that he *cares* so much about art. At the end of the day, we do make a good team, so I hold out my fist. "This isn't for your face," I clarify. "It's for a fist bump. A . . . casual friendship fist bump."

Eli stares. Then he does something strange. He smiles. Not a small one—a full one, with his eyes and all his teeth. I've never seen him give in so completely to an expression before. It sharpens the lines of his face in a sudden, searing way—a shock of light in this dim stairwell.

"Thank you," he says for some bizarre reason that I don't have the capacity to comprehend right now.

He taps his knuckles against mine.

Chapter Twenty-One

Apparently, all my problems were caused by the fact that Eli and I weren't talking. Okay, not really. But within twenty minutes of our casual friendship fist bump, several issues are resolved.

First, photography. Eli suggests we head back into our meeting with Dr. Lazar, and now that projectile crutches have broken the silence between us, the idea of my elbow next to his on those wooden chairs feels significantly more bearable. So we go back in, and maybe Dr. Lazar isn't as awful as I've been making her out to be, because instead of asking why I ran out of her office or why there are new tear tracks on my cheeks, she simply picks up our conversation where we left off.

When we walk outside fifteen minutes later, horror is clawing at my throat because we've got to scrap two of our photos and rework the essay from scratch. But then Eli says the thesis might come together once we retake the pictures, which reminds me not everything needs to be fixed tomorrow. We have half a semester to work out what our project's trying to say. So, I pause on that problem and explain my more imminent one: Glenna's. After hearing the details, Eli's singular recommendation is "Talk to your brother," which—yes. Solid advice. But I don't like facing Calum when I'm angry. He shuts down when I confront him, which just infuriates me more, and since my annoyance plus his refusal to engage is not the formula for a productive conversation, I was hoping my feelings would level out on their own. They haven't, though. And at this point, I'm not sure they're going to. So, in the evening, after steeling myself for a fight, I take the tube to Calum's office.

My brother works at Knightley Corporations, a large fancy firm in a large fancy building in the large fancy financial district surrounding Liverpool Street Station. I've been here a few times over the years—never to his cubicle upstairs, but I've waited for him in the polished lobby with the expensive black chairs that look comfortable but aren't.

It's easier than expected to gain elevator access—I simply walk to the front desk and say I'm here for Calum Clark. The suited security man doesn't call up to his office; he just holds out a hand for my passport, which I carry on me because most places in the UK don't accept my US driver's license as a form of ID. After scanning it, he gives me a little slip of paper with a barcode that presumably works on the turnstile and elevator, tells me "Floor 34," and sends me on my way.

The elevator ride is smooth and too fast. My ears pop and my stomach drops, and then the doors open and I'm in a large office full of row after row of uniform desks. I'm conscious of my baggy sweatpants and hoodie, but most of the overhead fluorescents are off and when I start walking, I realize it's because they're motion-detecting. No one's here. Well, one person's here. In the corner. I make my footsteps loud so Calum will hear me approaching, but two desktop monitors take up his attention. He's typing numbers rapidly into an Excel spreadsheet that could be anything from inventory calculations for a national bank to the amount of money the United Kingdom spends on gummy bears every year. Every time he tries to tell me what he does for work, my ears turn off. Not on purpose.

I *want* to listen, but then he says words like *financial* and *analyst* and *statistical computations* and suddenly I'm asleep.

Now that I'm in the thick of the desks, I realize most have little personal touches to them. Calum's right-hand neighbor has an absurd number of pens, from bejeweled to neon to feathery quills. Whoever sits to his left must have just had a baby, because photos of a newborn are tacked over the small corkboard behind the computers, and there's a deflated balloon under the chair that reads *Congratulations!* I expect Calum's space to be bare, but it's not. There's a framed photo of him and Benji and their good friend Rose. They look younger than they are now—probably around my age. Calum appears disgruntled to have been pulled in for a picture, Rose is grinning at him in a way that makes me think it was her idea, and Benji has his arms around both their shoulders and is smiling carelessly up at the sun. There's one more frame on Calum's desk, but instead of a photo, it houses a drawing. One that takes me a second to recognize. When I do, my throat goes dry.

It's mine. A little sketch I did in Kensington Gardens when I was twelve. It's of Calum and me, sitting on a bench in the park. I'd been upset, so he brought me outside to draw with him. I'd never drawn with him before.

"Calum."

At the sound of my voice, he jumps a few inches in the air, smacking his knees hard against the desk. "*Maisie.*"

He's breathing too fast, the way someone might after an intense workout. Or if they've been scared senseless. I take a step back. "I thought you'd noticed me."

He runs a hand through his hair. "Why are you here?"

"To take a tour of these ugly desks. Why are *you* here? The lights are off. Go home."

"I'm working." He is. Even after jumping out of his chair, his fingers continue to type away at his spreadsheet like they have a mind of their own.

I chew on my lip. The truth is, I came here to yell at him. For running. For getting mad when I asked where he ran. *"Talk to your brother,"* Eli suggested, which, in my furious state, was going to involve a level of screaming. But now I'm staring at Calum's framed pictures and slumped posture, and instead of shouting *I HATE YOU!* my mouth blurts, "I promised you could choose what we do the next time we hung out, so. Choose. Take me to that awful finance museum again. Or, there's a coin fair in London right now—I saw posters for it on the tube. Or you could force me to watch *Shrek*—"

"I'm working." He still hasn't turned to face me, but I'm not so easily deterred. Pen Collector's chair is only a few steps away. I grab the back and roll it next to Calum's. Then I plop myself down.

He sighs. "Go *home*."

"Only if you do."

"I can't."

"Because you're drowning in spreadsheets, or because you're trying to avoid thinking about Glenna's?"

Calum's fingers pause. Just for a moment, but a moment's enough. I push the keyboard up and away from his hands. Without something to do, his fingers twitch until he pulls them into fists. "I am not avoiding anything. I'm doing my job."

"Why is no one else doing their job?" I gesture widely at the empty office. "Remember when I was twelve and you didn't want to tell me why you left home so you took on extra work? Intentionally taking on extra work isn't the same as *I'm doing my job*—"

"My boss needs two assistants," he interrupts. "That's why I have been staying late the last few months. I am good at what I do, so the company has been dragging its feet at hiring another person. Why pay someone else a full salary when they can give me a bit extra for overtime instead? Not to mention, there's a project I'm hoping to turn in a few weeks early, which means I need to accommodate by putting in more hours now." Calum draws in a breath. "I am not avoiding Glenna's. I am not avoiding you. I am just"—he nods at his screens—"*working*."

He sounds sincere. It makes me want to believe him because, for someone who is very private, Calum is an astonishingly bad liar. Case in point: I'd asked if he enjoyed some cookies I'd made over the summer, and he couldn't say yes without turning bright red and mumbling that the taste of burnt dough is usually unappealing but was marginally palatable this time, actually. Maybe he *thinks* he's sincere about why he keeps staying so late at his office, but he just ran off for eighteen hours because someone broke into our shop. Forgive me for being skeptical.

Calum resumes typing into his spreadsheet. "I'll be here a while longer. You should go."

"*You* should go."

Pen Collector's chair is comfortable. So is the room temperature of this office. The clacking of Calum's fingers on the keyboard is methodical and practiced: a constant rhythm—a song. It lulls my head to my arms and my lashes to my cheeks. The overhead light clicks off again, and without my hands to wave frantically, it doesn't turn back on.

I listen to the playlist of Calum's typing until I'm not listening to anything at all.

Chapter Twenty-Two

For the next week, I go to Calum's office every evening. At first, I try bribery to get him to leave.

I got tickets for that awful coin festival! Come with me!

There's a spreadsheet convention downstairs! Or there could be! If you initiate it!

Nothing works. Calum is stubborn on a good day, and these have not been good days—they have been long days. Most nights, we stay at his desk past ten p.m. As time drags on, Calum stops responding to my nudges. He stops saying much at all. His fingers go *clack, clack, clack,* and the motion-sensor lights go *click, click, click,* and if he doesn't stop lulling himself to sleep with this monotony, I'm worried he'll never wake up.

I'm finding it hard to wake these days; my brain is stuck in this office even when my body is not. Part of that might have to do with Eli. We decided to be friends, but we haven't been acting like it. I think the barrier between us is the photography project, because what if we fight again and it affects our work? What if our ideas clash? Considering our history, the likelihood is high, so we haven't hung out outside of class. We also haven't made any concrete efforts to incorporate Dr. Lazar's notes into our revisions. The unproductiveness of it all keeps looping my brain back to Calum, because my art is stalling out the way his life is. And although I'm no closer to finding my voice, maybe I can at least help my brother back to his.

It's a little past nine in the evening. I'm working on a Glenna's commission while Calum muddles through whatever it is that keeps him so late at his desk. I've been whirling through digital portraits in every spare minute: sketching before breakfast, painting on the tube, rendering between classes. It's infuriating, falling back into this medium, because the thing is: I love it. I love it more than photography, more than any of the classes I shoved myself into this semester. Maybe it's because I'm nosy: People are interesting, and I enjoy studying them until I can portray them. And although we're exploring portraits in photography, it's not the same as the work I did at Glenna's because photos are instant. There's setup before and editing after, but the *during* is over in one bright flash. I've missed the during of painting. I've missed being stuck for weeks inside a messy canvas and having to carve my own path out.

Still, the second I start in on a new base sketch, even for a digital painting, the techniques I learned from my dad take over, and I can't see me under all of him. So when I shove my current piece at Calum, it's partly because I'm hoping art will pull him out of his infinite cycle of work, but it's also because I can't stand looking at Dad's reflection in my lines anymore.

"Can you help?"

This current commission is of a pet; we've been getting more of those lately. Someone named Anaya has a turtle she wants painted, and I don't know where to start with coloring the scales. Calum is more adept at digital art than me—especially when it comes to animals. His web comic centered around a green giraffe named Dottie, which sounds awful but was surprisingly poignant.

My brother is quiet. From the way his fingers stalled for

a moment on his keyboard, I know he heard my question, but he's been ignoring my presence all week. I tap him with the iPad pencil, and then again, and finally he takes it from my hand.

"This is Benji's," he says.

"What?"

Calum holds up the pencil and then nods at the screen on my lap. "You think I haven't asked him why you've been borrowing it?"

"I took on some work for Glenna's." It isn't a secret—not one I could have kept, anyway. A quick look at our website shows we've temporarily shut down regular shop production and are only taking on digital portraits. Plus, Mom and Dad assured Calum they're not backing out of the art exhibition, which means *they* don't have time to work on new commissions.

Calum stares at me for another moment. Then he says, "You came to London to get away from Glenna's."

I shrug. "It's fine. I mean, it's temporary, and it's not that I don't *like* portraits—"

"From a business standpoint, the right move after an economic loss is to drop unnecessary obligations and focus on regaining profit. From a personal standpoint—" His jaw clenches. "I didn't ask Mom and Dad to prioritize the exhibition. I specifically asked them *not* to, but no one seems to care—"

"They just want to help! We all do! Why does that bother you?"

Calum runs a hand through his hair. "I'm not bothered. Well, I am. But it's not the motivation, it's—" He shakes his head. "It's not the sentiment—except, it is, even though—that's not . . . but . . ." He shuts his mouth. He doesn't reopen it.

"You're not bothered we're trying to help with the exhibition," I clarify. "You're bothered by something else. Is that... right?"

Calum stares at his desk. He doesn't agree with me. He also doesn't disagree.

"Okay," I say. "Well... I'm going to keep working on these commissions. Because I'm doing them to help. I'm doing them for Glenna's."

Calum presses his palms to his eyes. I'm frustrating him, but I'm not sure why, and I don't think he knows, either. This happens, sometimes, when we fight. It means there's no use continuing this conversation, at least for now, because a problem can't be solved if it can't be articulated.

The silence settles as I turn again to my turtle. I haven't even painted one line, however, when a hand is tugging the iPad pencil away. At first, I think this is some convoluted attempt to fight with me, and I almost yank it back, but Calum's eyes are on my commission. I tilt the screen toward him, and this time, he takes it.

For the next hour, Calum watches the iPad, and I watch him. I see the moment—about fifteen minutes in—when he relaxes into the activity. His eyes get softer. His jaw becomes less rigid. I'm not sure if he took on my painting as a peace offering, or as a way to escape his tangle of thoughts, or for some other reason I can't make sense of. Whatever the cause, I'm glad for it, because as he layers brown over yellow over green, the turtle takes on an abstract quality that I could never have achieved.

"You're a great artist," I say, because it's so true that I can't help it. Calum didn't grow up in Glenna's workshop the way I did. He didn't spend his childhood studying portraiture. But technical details don't matter as much as a strong vision, and although my brother can get stuck in his head, he's never unsure on paper.

He doesn't respond to my compliment, but he heard me. He smiles.

Chapter Twenty-Three

On Sunday, Eli and I meet on the steps of the dorm to discuss our project. Neither of us was forthcoming with revision ideas over text, so eventually he messaged *Let's talk in person,* and now here we are.

He looks up as I approach. Instead of his usual black hoodie and cargo pants, he's changed it up for a black hoodie and sweatpants. The clothes suit him, even though they would bog most people down. The secret, I've realized, to making unfashionable clothes fashionable, is to be hot. When you're hot, you can make a garbage bag look like a designer outfit.

Not that I'm saying Eli's *hot.* Or that his clothes look like garbage. He just doesn't look ugly. In clothes that could be ugly.

Shut up.

I gesture in his general direction. "Oh no. What will you throw at me today if you need to get my attention?" His crutches are gone; he's standing steadily without them.

"Maybe you'll break my other ankle and that problem will resolve itself," he says without missing a beat. "If you do, could you choose a more interesting method this time? At least trip me on purpose."

"Ha," I say, which makes his eyebrows quirk up, which is not hot, because he is not hot, because it will be really awkward if my friend who I kissed is hot.

"Photography!" I cough. "That is—yes?"

"Yes." Eli seems unfazed by my sudden change in

topic, or maybe he's simply as ready as I am to move on to something more productive. "I think I figured out the problem with the two photos Dr. Lazar didn't like. The reason they appear more distant than the others is because they are of a stranger, while the rest of our pictures are of people we know. So to achieve a similar level of depth, our final subject should also be someone we know."

"Oh," I say, because his solution is simple. It's smart. It's smart because it's simple. "You're good. *That's* good. You are good at photography, and therefore you came up with something that is good. Yay! For things. That are good."

Eli gives me a bemused look. I usher him quickly in the direction of the tube. "I've got a subject. Someone I know well, who should be down to participate in our project. I'll text him on our way over."

"Will he be good, though?" Eli asks.

I push his elbow and then firmly shove my hands in my pockets.

It's good. I'm good.

TRY NEW THINGS

1. ~~STOP HELPING OUT AT GLENNA'S~~ ONLY HELP OUT WITH DIGITAL GLENNA'S COMMISSIONS.

2. GO TO AN ART SCHOOL FAR FROM HOME. MAYBE IN ANOTHER COUNTRY.

3. NO PORTRAITS OR OIL PAINTINGS. ONLY SIGN UP FOR CLASSES IN MEDIUMS YOU HAVE NO EXPERIENCE WITH.

~~4. EXPERIMENT WITH YOUR APPEARANCE AND CLOTHING.~~

5. MAKE NEW FRIENDS ~~(BECAUSE ALICIA IS GOING TO).~~ (BECAUSE YOU WANT TO).

6. ~~ALWAYS SAY YES. EVEN WHEN YOU DON'T WANT TO.~~ SAY YES MORE THAN YOU SAY NO.

7. DON'T UNDERESTIMATE PEOPLE.

8. JUMP INTO THE OCCASIONAL FOUNTAIN TO WAKE UP!

9. NOT EVERYTHING HAS TO BE UNCOMFORTABLE.

10. BE FRIENDS WITH ELI WITHOUT BEING WEIRD!

The first ten minutes on the tube are silent. I'm trying to not be weird around Eli, so instead of forcing a conversation, my plan is to go with the flow. But Eli and I are in a strange flow. He wanted to be friends, and when I think of friends, I think of Alicia. I think of how I know random, inconsequential details about her. I think of how I know nothing inconsequential about Eli.

"What's your favorite color?"

He raises an eyebrow.

"I'm just curious."

"Green."

"Oh, cool." I pause. "What's your favorite dessert?"

"What is this? A job interview?"

"Obviously not. What job would ask for your favorite dessert?"

"A sweet shop," he says. "A restaurant, a patisserie—"

"We don't know all that much about each other," I interrupt before he can go on countering my point. "Aside from art, I mean. We don't really talk about anything else, so—I thought I'd change it up."

He pauses. "Waffles."

"For *dessert*?"

"Yes, for dessert. With blueberries, lemon, honey, and whipped cream."

"That's . . . very specific."

"You're very judgmental," Eli says, matching my tone. "What's *your* favorite dessert?"

"Ice cream. From my aunt's shop. All her flavors are unique, and she's always updating the menu with new combinations."

"Which is the most unique?"

I think for a moment. "She did wine and cheese, once. It was good—if you could get over the mental hurdle of having brie in your ice cream."

Eli bites down on his lip.

"*What?*"

"You criticized my waffles."

"I didn't *criticize*—"

He's laughing. At me. I don't generally like when people laugh at me, but the problem is, this time, I'm laughing, too.

When Benji lets us into the flat, he stares Eli up and down. Then he snaps his fingers and says, "Camera Boy."

Eli blinks. "Excuse me?"

"I've got your camera. Haven't I?" Benji glances at me.

Eli glances at me. Although I've done nothing wrong, I suddenly feel like I'm on trial.

"Um." I gesture between the two of them. "Yes, this is—Eli. Eli, I gave Benji your camera after it broke." I look at Benji and try to express with my eyes that *if you mention I told you Eli and I kissed, I will never speak to you again.*

In response, Benji waves a dismissive hand and says, "I haven't got round to the camera yet, but I should have time next week."

"You don't have to," says Eli. His hands are deep in his pockets, and his eyes are wandering around the flat. "Seriously, it's not—"

"I enjoy working with materials outside my usual." Benji nods at the kitchen table, where his supplies are spread. Today he's got a sewing machine set up, as well as squares of fabric he appears to be arranging into a quilted pattern. "Really, you're doing me a favor by breaking up my routine."

Eli doesn't seem to know how to respond to that, which is valid. Benji can be alarmingly kind.

I pull a camera from my backpack. It's a disposable one—the type Eli's students used on Tower Bridge. There's no way to adjust the lighting or focus. It shoots subjects as they are, which is why I chose it for Benji. He doesn't need modification.

"Where should we do this?" Benji asks, eyeing the lens.

"On the floor. By the coffee table." That's generally where I find Benji when I enter the flat. I assume the only reason he's not there now is because he needed access to an outlet for the sewing machine.

It's a quick shoot. Since the camera I chose doesn't give me the ability to review pictures, I can't spend time revising my angles based on the results. For that reason, it's also a risky shoot, but I know Benji. I know I want to capture him smiling, his head thrown back. So I make him laugh. Again and again. And then I tell him to pose for his self-portrait.

Benji considers this, his face settling into something more neutral. In the end, he continues to sit on the floor, but instead of having a spontaneous brightness in his eyes, he looks into the camera contemplatively—like he can see through it. It's an analytical expression, one I might expect from Calum, but not from Benji, who blasts through the world without ever getting stuck in it.

The contrast between the self-portrait and portrait unbalances me. My shots of Benji are carefree. His are careful. And now that I'm thinking about it, *all* our subjects are people I know, and all of them angled themselves differently in their pictures than the way I angled them in mine.

Calum is soft in my photo. In his, he's a brick wall.

Eli is artistically blurred in my photo. In his, he's very precisely aligned with the angles of Tower Bridge.

I posed Natalie mischievously on her desk. She posed joyfully in her fountain.

And even my self-portrait: I took it in the dark. Eli shot me in the light.

Benji's phone buzzes beside me on the coffee table, jerking me out of my head. I don't mean to look, but when he holds out a hand for it, my eyes can't help but flit to the screen:

15:13

Cal: Tried my parents again.
Cal: They still won't pull out of the exhibition.

It doesn't hit, at first. The words. My brain has to swirl them around for a moment to understand. Last week, Calum mentioned he didn't want Mom and Dad to prioritize the art gallery over their work at Glenna's, but that's very different from asking them to *pull out.* Besides, I thought we'd moved on from this. In his office, Calum couldn't articulate why he was bothered by the exhibition. Usually when we have to pause an argument mid-conversation like that, he comes back to me a few days later with a more complete explanation. He hasn't brought the gallery up again, though, and so I thought he'd gotten over whatever his issue was. Not to mention, things have been easier between us this week. He's stopped complaining about me coming to his office. And since the turtle commission, he's been more interested in my digital portraits. Sometimes he holds out his hand for the iPad without me even offering it. So the fact that he's apparently been calling Mom and Dad behind my back...

A match sparks within me, relighting an extinguished flame. I've been taking on more work so my parents can focus on the exhibition. Work I specifically came to London to leave behind. Calum knows that. *Benji* knows that. And, sure, my brother sometimes leaves out key details when informing me of a situation, but Benji is good about relaying the things Calum fails to mention. Why didn't he mention this?

"How long has this been going on?" I ask, waving Calum's texts through the air.

Benji glances at them and then sighs. "I don't love your habit of reading my messages."

"It's not a *habit*."

"There've been too many occurrences for you to really be able to label them as accidents—"

"You're trying to change the subject." I wave the phone again. "How long has Calum wanted to pull out of the exhibition? More than a week? More than *two*?"

Benji doesn't respond, which is answer enough.

I frown. "I've been spending all this time on Glenna's commissions. I wouldn't have done that work if there was no reason for it—"

"You're simplifying an issue that's more complicated.

Cal's been more involved than usual, hasn't he? With your commissions?"

"Well, sure. A little—"

"My understanding is he'd rather your mum and dad spend their efforts on Glenna's than on a side project they're only taking on because they think it benefits him. He also knows *stop doing this thing for me because it's inconveniencing you* isn't a particularly compelling argument, and so instead of having a row, he's been trying to take the burden off you in subtle ways. Helping with commissions, for instance. Asking your parents to refocus on their shop, for another."

"I'm not bothered," Calum had said. *"Well, I am. But it's not the motivation . . ."*

Oh.

"Why didn't you tell me this sooner?" It comes out sharper than I intend. "Calum and I have been fighting for weeks. If I'd known why he was frustrated, it would have . . ." I trail off. It probably wouldn't have fixed things, but it definitely would have eased them.

Benji runs a hand through his hair. It's a gesture reminiscent of Calum, and it makes me realize, with a sudden jolt, that this conversation is probably a mistake. In an argument about my brother, Benji might not take my side.

"When there is reason to be concerned about Cal, I keep you informed," Benji says. "Otherwise, it's not my place to speak for him. I'm only telling you all this now because I know how you get, and I don't want the two of you to fight needlessly."

"How can you say there's no reason to be concerned?" I shoot back. "Calum ran off. He's *clearly* upset about what happened with Glenna's, and you aren't doing anything about it. You just sit here while he works himself to death all day. I've been to his office. I've watched him, and it's different, the way he's burying himself in spreadsheets. He's quieter than usual. He freezes in his typing sometimes, like he can't get out of his head. So maybe I'm annoying him by sitting at his desk every night. But I'd rather be annoying than be *nothing*."

"Maisie." There's an edge to the way Benji says my name. He glances at the camera on the coffee table and then back up at me. His eyes bore sharply into mine, and my breath catches, suddenly, because I've never fought with him—not in any real way. "There's a difference between looking at someone and seeing who they are, and looking at someone and seeing who you want them to be."

"I don't *want* to see Calum like this—"

"You knew him as a teenager, when he was going through something difficult. It's easy for you to still think of him that way, because that version of him is familiar. You don't want to see him as he is now. That person is different. Someone you don't know—"

"I do know Calum. He's *my* family. Not—" I cut myself off, but it's too late. *Not yours.* Benji heard it, even though I didn't say it. It's clear in the abrupt way he turns his face from mine, in the way his shoulders rise as if to block my voice.

My mouth floods with a bitter taste. "I didn't—"

"This conversation isn't productive anymore." Benji's tone isn't angry. It's quiet. It's very careful. "We should pause, don't you think? Before someone gets hurt."

He's already hurt. I already hurt him. "I'm sorry," I mutter, but it sounds hollow even to my ears, and he doesn't turn back around. For the first time in my life, I get the distinct impression he does not want to see me. The realization is an uncomfortable prickle, like a foot falling asleep. It makes me want to jump around in front of him until the feeling eases. But although that might relieve my discomfort, it would probably just amplify his.

"I'll—okay. Do you want me to leave?" I ask.

"That might be for the best," Benji agrees, again in that careful tone. "We can pick this up another time." He's still facing away from me, his shoulders a rounded shield. He does not move while I slip on my shoes. He does not say anything else.

It's only once I'm out the door and slumped against the stair railing that I remember Eli. He's a step behind me, and right now I wish he were anywhere else, because I was just awful to someone I love, and that would have been bad enough without a witness.

"I'm not usually . . ." I start to explain, but I'm not usually what? Someone who speaks without considering the consequences? Someone who lashes out without thinking? I am *always* those things.

My eyes are tearing, and it's pathetic. Why am I crying when I'm the one who caused the pain?

"I'm sorry," I gasp, turning so Eli can't see my face.

He touches my shoulder in a way that makes me think he's about to pull me closer. I flinch back. "Don't hug me. That's not—I'm not trying for sympathy—"

"It's not sympathy. I've got advice." He doesn't go in for the hug; he doesn't take his hand away, either. I can't look at him right now, but his voice isn't cruel. It's low and level, the way it usually is—so different from my loud and wild cadence. "Something horrible happened to your family's shop," he continues when I don't stop him. "It's affecting you. It's affecting people you care about. That's—a lot. You're dealing with a lot, so—is there anyone you can speak with? Someone who knows your family, whose opinions you trust, but who is . . . more neutral to this situation?" He pauses. "When I—when things were difficult, in my house. I have a cousin. It was helpful, talking with him. It always cleared my head."

That . . . wouldn't be terrible. Talking to someone who has distance, but who also understands the intricacies of my family. My first instinct is Alicia. She's not neutral, though. She's always on my side. And anyway, if I call her crying after months of acting like my semester's been fine, she'll be confused. Upset. Angry I've kept so much from her. And while that's a situation that needs addressing, I'm not in the state to do it now. So . . .

I wipe at my face again. Then I look up at Eli. His eyes aren't full of disgust. They're not full of pity, either. His hand is still on my shoulder.

I place my fingers over his—just for a moment—and then drop them back to my side. "There is someone I can talk to. I'll call her when I'm back at the dorm."

Chapter Twenty-Four

"Hon," Aunt Lisa says on the phone—after I stumble through my explanation of what happened at Glenna's and what happened with Calum and how he and Benji are acting like everything's fine when everything's *not*—"take a breath."

Something bright bursts in my stomach. "How can I breathe when Calum's been going behind my back? The more he's hiding, the more likely he'll run away again, and if he runs away again—"

"Maisie Clark, take a breath."

I don't want to, but I have to in order to fuel my rampage. When I do, it forces me to pause. When I pause, I realize my chest hurts. I realize everything hurts.

"London's stifling," Lisa says into my silence. "Everyone's piled up on each other. There's not enough air. Come visit. I'll book your train ticket."

"Come *here*," I shoot back. "Calum—"

"Calum doesn't need you to make decisions for him. If he wants to see me, he'll ask to see me. He's not helpless, hon. He knows himself better than you do."

"I—" My instinct is to counter her statement, but I don't know why, and the words won't fall all the way out.

"Come visit," Lisa says again. "For the weekend. We'll have a wee chat."

I can't. Calum's been making rash decisions behind my back, trying to get Mom and Dad to back out of the exhibition for a ridiculous reason. What if I go and he runs off? What if this time he doesn't come back?

"Calum left Crescent Valley for a reason," Aunt Lisa says like she can hear my thoughts. "But he has no reason to leave London. He's built a life for himself. Why would he knock it down?"

My thoughts stutter. Why *would* Calum not come back? My brother is happy in London. He's happy with Benji. I think he's even happy in his job, despite the fact that he's horribly overworked. But—what if Benji was right in the flat, and I'm seeing Calum wrong? What if I'm missing something huge again, and that huge thing messes life up again, and, and—

I let out a shaky breath, and then another. Maybe I do need some air. Maybe I *should* leave London for a bit to see if that can break me out of this spiral.

I guess I'm going to Edinburgh.

The train ride to Scotland feels like a long breath. Sharp buildings turn to softer houses turn to grassy hills, and the more I inhale, the dizzier I get.

Calum has no reason to run away. I *know* that, and yet I can't stop thinking about twelve years ago, the last time I saw him in Crescent Valley.

It was an entirely ordinary interaction between us. He was boarding the bus for summer camp. I tried to hug him, but he flinched away like he usually did, so I hugged myself instead and said, "Bye."

"Bye," he repeated, and off he went. I don't even think he glanced back at me, but it would have been stranger if he had. He generally didn't look at me when we were that age unless I was doing something particularly annoying.

That's the problem with this whole situation. In Crescent Valley, nothing seemed wrong, but everything was. I couldn't tell my brother was about to not come back, and if I couldn't see something that massive then, how can I trust myself now to see anything at all?

For the rest of the ride, I try not to think about Calum. At first, I scroll through my Glenna's commissions, but it's very hard to look at Benji's iPad after I said horrible things to him. I'm about to shove it back in my bag when I pause.

The summer we met, Benji let me borrow this same iPad so I could try out digital art for the first time. That was six years ago, but I know, even before I look for them now, that my old drawings will still be stored away where I left them. Yes—there they are. Benji kept my mediocre, unpracticed art all this time, letting it take up space in Procreate even though he's running low on storage. I scroll up from my scribbles and over to his sketches, of which there are dozens upon dozens. It looks like he digitally maps out most of his designs for his shop before turning them into fabric and thread. The most recent image is of a forked road, one branch marked with the sort of highway road signs you see in England, the other with signs in Japanese. I recognize the design from the batch of items he dropped in October; he ended up embroidering the pattern onto shoes—one branch of the road on the right foot, the other on the left.

Since that sketch is on here, it means he was still using the iPad regularly for his own work up until a few weeks ago. But when Glenna's fell apart, he dropped it into my lap without a word. He never hesitates to help me, even though he's busy with his own art; even though I'm just his boyfriend's little sister; even though one random day I burst into his life without warning and haven't left him alone since.

"I do know Calum. He's my *family. Not yours."*

I didn't mean it, but it doesn't matter. I let my anger spark into a fire that I made no effort to control.

It's not something I ever want to happen again.

TRY NEW THINGS

1. ~~STOP HELPING OUT AT GLENNA'S~~ ONLY HELP OUT WITH DIGITAL GLENNA'S COMMISSIONS.
2. GO TO AN ART SCHOOL FAR FROM HOME. MAYBE IN ANOTHER COUNTRY.
3. NO PORTRAITS OR OIL PAINTINGS. ONLY SIGN UP FOR CLASSES IN MEDIUMS YOU HAVE NO EXPERIENCE WITH.
4. ~~EXPERIMENT WITH YOUR APPEARANCE AND CLOTHING.~~
5. MAKE NEW FRIENDS ~~(BECAUSE ALICIA IS GOING TO).~~ (BECAUSE YOU WANT TO).
6. ~~ALWAYS SAY YES. EVEN WHEN YOU DON'T WANT TO.~~ SAY YES MORE THAN YOU SAY NO.
7. DON'T UNDERESTIMATE PEOPLE.
8. JUMP INTO THE OCCASIONAL FOUNTAIN TO WAKE UP!
9. NOT EVERYTHING HAS TO BE UNCOMFORTABLE.
10. BE FRIENDS WITH ELI WITHOUT BEING WEIRD!
11. CONTROL YOUR EMOTIONS.

Edinburgh glows at night. It shines even brighter in the winter. The cobbled streets and stone buildings look like a gingerbread village, and there's a fine dusting of snow across the ground like powdered sugar.

Aunt Lisa lives in the Old Town, up several steep, narrow streets from Waverley Station. As soon as I step outside, I slip forward. Snow on cobbled stones is beautiful, but it's also no joke. I was here over winter break when I was thirteen, and three inches shut down the whole city. Coming from upstate New York, I thought the buses halting and the shops closing was ridiculous. But then Aunt Lisa sent me out with Calum to buy groceries, and the only feasible way to make it down the slope of her block was to slide on my butt.

Tonight, instead of butt-sliding, I take a taxi. It's late and it's cold and I've recently become more attuned to the fragility of ankles. The ride is about as terrifying as the walk would have been. The streets, built before cars, are so narrow here. Every few feet up the steep incline the wheels slip, and I'm fully nauseous by the end of the trip. But after I pay and waddle onto the street, my lips twitch into a smile.

Lisa lives above her ice cream shop, *Unique Sweets.* The front window is over-the-top and gaudy: all swirling letters and pink and purple butterflies and graceful strokes of green grass. Calum painted it when he was sixteen. The artistry isn't bad and matches Aunt Lisa's aesthetic, but every time I come here with him, his nose wrinkles at the design.

The shop is dark. It takes a moment of fumbling for me to pull out my phone. When I call up, a light blooms on, and a minute later, Aunt Lisa appears. She looks the same as ever: tall, broad-shouldered, and covered in animal print. Today, it's elephant-patterned pajamas. My aunt loves animals—most of her ice cream flavors are themed around them. Her bestseller is Chocolate Sheep, which tastes like hot chocolate and is covered in tiny marshmallows that are topped with little frosting eyes. My personal favorite is Snow Rabbit, which is a peppermint ice cream with white chocolate ears and a tail made of circular hard candy.

"Maisie!" She barrels into me with a hug, and it makes me forget I haven't seen her in over a year. Aunt Lisa has the kind of heart that doesn't care about time or distance. It's the only heart that got through to my brother when he was sixteen, and being so close to it now—hearing it beat—I kind of understand how one note can calm down the world.

"I'm sorry it took me so long," I mutter into her chest, and I'm not talking about the train ride. I've been in London since June, and we're nearing December. Edinburgh isn't far; it shouldn't have taken a crisis to get me up north.

"You're here now." Aunt Lisa squeezes me tighter. "Come out of the cold."

She leads the way into the shop, then up the spiral staircase at the back that connects to her flat. I love Lisa's place. It's small but cozy, and she's decorated every inch—mostly with loud animal prints and animal figurines and animal signs with cringy expressions like "Fish Out of Water." Mom was devastated when Lisa branched away from Glenna's to start her own business; it created a chasm in their relationship that never fully closed. But I honestly can't imagine them working together. Their styles are so different; they'd be at each other's throats.

"Here." Lisa pushes open the door to the guest room. I freeze.

There's nothing noteworthy about this space, just a single bed with a bear-patterned duvet and a wardrobe shoved against a desk. It's only a room, but it's also a memory: Calum chose to reconnect with me here. Six years ago. In Edinburgh. Mom and Dad sent me to spend a summer with Aunt Lisa, and Calum tracked me down to her flat. I didn't know, at the time, that he'd lived with her. I didn't know I was sleeping where he'd slept. When he barged back into my life, I was furious, because how would *you* feel if you were six years old and Mom and Dad sat you down on the sapphire couch in the living room and said *"Calum isn't coming home"*?

It's getting old, this anger. It's getting old that I can't control it. My heart is beating too hard again, and I should have built up a tolerance to the pounding, but endurance doesn't always mean strength. Sometimes it's just exhaustion.

I look at Aunt Lisa.

I burst into tears.

Chapter Twenty-Five

Aunt Lisa's couch is big and squishy. Sinking into it feels like a hug. So does the mug of tea she makes me. The steam is warm while the world is cold, and after showering and changing into pajamas, I don't feel better, exactly, but I feel less like I'm going to overflow.

"Talk to me." Aunt Lisa sits next to me on the couch, coddling her own mug of tea. It's late—too late for us to be having this conversation—but she doesn't give any indication that I'm a nuisance. Her eyes are firm but kind.

My gaze finds a framed drawing over the fireplace. It's a sketch of a living room with an armchair and a wall of books and an elephant in the center. "When we found out about the break-in at Glenna's," I say quietly, "Calum ran off. I didn't know where he went. And I—I do agree with what you said over the phone. About how he's got a life in London that he's got no reason not to come back to. But even though I know that—even though I know he wouldn't just... leave me again—it doesn't change the fact that he *could*."

"Have you told him you feel this way?"

I shake my head. When my emotions build up, they burst out of me. When Calum's build up, they weigh him into the ground. He's already burying too much in his work. It feels wrong to dump more on him, especially when my fear has no substance.

"Calum is your brother who ran away," Aunt Lisa says, "but he's also your brother who came back. You need to trust he's not the person he was twelve years ago. A good place to start would be remembering he chose to reconnect with you. He found you because he didn't want to lose you. And you let him back into your life because you didn't want to lose him." Aunt Lisa squeezes my arm. "You are both people who care deeply—it's what gets you into trouble, but it's also why you should be honest about how you're feeling. He deserves that. So do you."

I stare into my mug; my warped reflection stares back. Maybe I do need to talk to Calum. Properly. Honestly. But in order to have an open conversation, I can't be tight with emotions like I am now, like I was with Benji. I need to collect myself. I need to breathe.

Saturdays are big for Aunt Lisa's shop. Despite it being winter and her specialty being ice cream, she gets customers year-round. Things really exploded a few years ago when she started doing hot chocolate and flavored lattes during the cold months. When I first visited her, she worked alone. Now, she has two employees. Even so, she has to prep ingredients all morning before Unique Sweets opens in the afternoon.

I help. It's good to keep my hands busy: It keeps them away from my phone. I want to call Calum, to double-check he's where he's supposed to be. I don't, because I haven't gotten a strong enough handle on my emotions to ensure they won't burst out of me the next time we talk.

So I set down my phone and set about chopping peppermints, and I try to laugh at Lisa's jokes and try to breathe out of my mouth.

In the evening, Eli texts.

7:55 p.m.

The Boy Who Is My Friend (Eli): You don't have that camera, do you?

The Boy Who Is My Friend (Eli): The disposable one

The Boy Who Is My Friend (Eli): From the shoot with Benji

Me: No??

Me: I thought you had it???

The Boy Who Is My Friend (Eli): No

Great! All that mess with Benji, and I totally forgot about the camera. It's probably still on the coffee table, which means I'm going to have to ask him for it, which means I'm going to have to *talk* to him, and I'd rather roll around on broken glass than look him in the eyes right now.

The Boy Who Is My Friend (Eli): I went back to the apartment to look for it

The Boy Who Is My Friend (Eli): The living room was a mess because of all the packing

The Boy Who Is My Friend (Eli): But Benji said he'll text you if it turns up

Me: Packing??

Calum goes on work trips, sometimes. So does Benji. But never for more than a few days at a time. If the living room is such a disaster that the camera got lost in the mess...

Me: How much packing?
Me: Like a few items in a carry-on bag?

The Boy Who Is My Friend (Eli): Like half the apartment in several suitcases

Me: WHAT???
Me: Is it Benji who's going somewhere??
Me: Or Calum??

The Boy Who Is My Friend (Eli): I only asked about the camera
The Boy Who Is My Friend (Eli): But I have to film in that area again tomorrow
The Boy Who Is My Friend (Eli): I could stop by
The Boy Who Is My Friend (Eli): If you want?

My first instinct is to run to the train station, but that wouldn't exactly be controlling my emotions. And I *just* hurt Benji because I let my anger get the better of me.

I drop my head into my hands.

Maybe there isn't anything suspicious happening. Maybe there's an extremely reasonable explanation for the packing. When Benji travels to art conventions, he brings products to sell from his shop. That requires a lot of suitcases, and wrangling his stuff together would definitely make a mess of the flat. It isn't strange that the camera got lost in the chaos. It isn't cause for concern.

I breathe in and then out. I look back down at my phone.

Me: No it's fine
Me: Thanks though

It's fine it's fine it's fine it's fine.

The words echo in my head for the rest of the night. After a few hours, I expect the repetition to lull me to sleep.

It doesn't.

12:06 a.m.

Alicia Miller: How are things?
Alicia Miller: Haven't heard from you in a while…

Chapter Twenty-Six

The rest of my time in Edinburgh passes in stilted chunks. Sunday morning, I take a walk through Princes Street Gardens with Aunt Lisa. After, we get breakfast at a cozy café. By noon, I'm on a train back to London. By five p.m., I'm walking up to my brother's flat.

When I push in the door, I pause. Eli wasn't exaggerating. There's stuff *everywhere*. Shoes piled by the threshold. Coats thrown over the couch. I'd think there'd been a break-in if not for the suitcases sprawled under the coffee table.

"Hello?" I call.

Benji pops his head out of the bedroom. "Oh. Hi, Maisie."

I freeze. This is his flat as much as Calum's, and I already concluded he's likely the one packing for a trip. And it's too early in the day—even on a Sunday—for my brother to be home from work. Even so, I guess I was dreading seeing him to such an extent that my brain convinced itself he'd be out when I arrived.

Benji doesn't look at me like I stamped all over his heart the last time we spoke. He gives me an effortless smile, as though there's nothing wrong at all. I want to buy into it, because maybe I *didn't* hurt him, and I've been feeling guilty over nothing, and we can pretend I never said anything terrible. But the more I watch him, the more his expression reminds me of my portraits.

That looks so real, people often say, or *You make art look so easy*. And, yes. I might not have my own voice, but I've been painting since I could hold a brush. I can capture figures and emotions accurately and quickly, without breaking a sweat. My art only looks easy, though, because I've worked very hard at it.

I think Benji looks effortless because he's worked very hard at it. There isn't anything in his smile that suggests it's fake, but it has to be, because I saw the sharp way he turned from me when I implied we weren't family. And then there's the way he posed for his self-portrait. There's something deliberate in how he expresses himself. More so than I realized.

"You're here about the camera?" He gestures behind me. "I found it a bit ago—it's on the kitchen table."

"Oh! Thanks." I glance back to grab it. When I turn around again, Benji's disappeared. "Are you . . . is it for a business trip? All these suitcases?" I call into the empty space he left behind.

"Not exactly." Benji walks back into the hallway, a sewing machine cradled in his arms. He sets it gingerly down on the couch and pats it once. Instead of looking at me, he becomes very interested in a side zipper on the suitcase below him, pulling it back and forth.

"A vacation, then?" It sounds ridiculous even as I say it; Benji's almost always at the flat when I visit, but he's never just hanging around. Now that I think about it, he probably works as many hours at home as Calum does in the office. I can't imagine *either* of them just up and going on a leisurely trip right now, and if Benji were to take time off, surely he wouldn't do so alone . . .

One of Calum's coats is draped haphazardly over the back of the couch. A pair of shoes too plain for Benji's taste peek out from the suitcase under the coffee table. My stomach squeezes.

"That's too many bags for a weekend trip. And it's not just your stuff inside." Despite an effort to contain it, anger boils up my throat. Aunt Lisa was wrong. Calum hasn't changed. He's *leaving* again. Without telling me. The second I decide to trust him, he strands me in the dust.

As if summoned by my fury, my brother suddenly shoves the front door open, a box of toothpaste in one hand, floss in the other.

I freeze. Calum freezes. Then his shoulders slump forward, as though resigned to my presence. Mine rise in anticipation of a fight.

"Where are you going?" I gesture at the bags.

"Crescent Valley." He states it simply. Easily. Like it isn't the most disorienting thing I've ever heard come out of his mouth.

Crescent Valley.

Calum's going to Crescent Valley.

With Benji.

Without telling me.

For a moment, I try to say something that might express the roaring in my ears, but no words will do it justice. So I pick up one of the couch pillows and hurl it at my brother's feet. "What the *hell,* Calum?"

He sidesteps my anger; the pillow lands quietly on the ground. Then he ducks past me and toward the bedroom. I follow, hard on his heels. When I see the state of it, I pause.

Under his careful attire and meticulous schedule, my brother is quietly a mess. The last time I was in here, his work papers littered the floor, the desk. There was an attempt to keep all his crap on one side of the room, but some of it still spilled into Benji's considerably less cluttered space. Today, though, there are no papers. There is no mess. Calum left objects that are important to him—a framed painting of a green giraffe, a battered snow globe of the Statue of Liberty—but the practical items are gone. He's packed like he plans to travel for weeks. The fire in my ears turns from burning to pulsing, from anger to panic.

"When's your flight?" I ask. "When's your flight *back*?"

Calum grabs a bundle of socks from an otherwise empty drawer. "We leave in a few hours. I'll have a better sense of how long this'll take once we arrive."

My hands are fists at my sides. "You weren't going to tell me. I was going to have to come here, and see all your stuff gone, and realize *you* were gone—"

"I was going to tell you."

"*When?*"

"Tomorrow."

I blink at him. "You'll be in New York tomorrow! You're supposed to say goodbye *before* you leave. It's common courtesy—"

"I've no use for courtesy if it means you breathing down my neck while I pack, threatening to follow me—"

"Why are you assuming I'll follow you?"

"Because you have no boundaries!" Calum's eyes finally meet mine. Then they flit away again, landing somewhere past my shoulder. "For weeks, you have sat in my office, acting like I am not fine while I've assured you I am. For weeks, you've prioritized Glenna's over your own art, even though I never asked you to. I understand you are doing what you think is right. But why should your opinions of me matter more than mine? Why do you keep trying to control my life?"

"Because if I don't, you'll just leave again! You keep

leaving without telling me when you'll be back, which means I never know *if* you'll be back—"

"Maisie, of course I'll be back. I'm no longer a teenager. There's no need now to make the choices I did then. Besides, I've grown—"

"If you'd grown, you wouldn't keep running away!" I squeeze my ribs. "I thought I'd never see you again. Did you know that? The first time you left, I thought you were *dead*, because for months Mom cried every time I said your name. And then, six years later, you reappeared. You wanted to get to know me, but that meant I also got to know you. You made me care about you, and—do you know how that feels? To care about someone who's always leaving? Who for years did not come back?"

I look away. "I don't know how to get over something like this when we don't ever talk about it. When Mom and Dad don't talk about it. One day you were here, and the next you were gone, and for years I was furious, because—don't you understand? You were my older brother. You could do all these things I couldn't; you knew all these things I didn't. All I wanted was for you to like me, because—" I glower at the ground. "I *loved* you."

God. This isn't the level-headed conversation Aunt Lisa told me to have with my brother. I'd wanted to bring up my concerns in a mature, professional manner, but when I fight with Calum about home, suddenly I'm six years old again, tugging on Mom's shirt and asking where my brother went, only for hands to push me away and eyes to avoid meeting mine.

Calum stares down at his bundle of socks. Then he turns slightly, so he's not quite facing me. "I did like you," he says quietly. "When we were younger. I know I did not spend much time with you, but I . . . appreciated you being in that house with me. I—I wouldn't have lasted as long as I did. If I'd been there alone."

Something inside me deflates. I sink onto the bed.

"It wasn't personal, when I left," Calum continues from somewhere to my right. "And I won't apologize for it. I will not blame myself for taking the only path I could see. But I—am sorry. For not considering your feelings. And for not always being clear. About when I intend to leave and when I intend to stay." He shakes his head. "It's difficult, sometimes—no longer being on my own. That sounds—strange, maybe. But for a while, I didn't have to explain myself. Now there is more I'm expected to say. That's—hard for me. That has always been hard for me. Which is why I want to go to New York. I can't reason with Mom and Dad over the phone. I'll have a better chance of it in person, when they're not just voices an ocean away."

I press my eyes into my palms. Yeah, Calum doesn't always explain himself, but he's not the only one. All these years, I've kept how I felt about him leaving deep inside, boiling internally because he didn't acknowledge my emotions. That wasn't fair to him. It wasn't fair to me.

"I understand," I say finally. Not all of it—I still don't fully get why he's so insistent that Mom and Dad give up on the art exhibition, but I do get that phones and time zones and miles of separation make communication more difficult.

"Maybe you should come."

My head jerks up.

Calum's still standing on the other side of the room, half turned away from me, socks in his hands. "You said I haven't grown, and I—I don't think that's true. I don't think that's fair. But you're right that we don't talk about home, which probably makes it more difficult. To observe the differences between then and now. So, it could be beneficial. To go to Crescent Valley. Together. You'd be able to compare the present to the past—see how they diverge."

His phrasing catches me off guard. Isn't that why I wanted Calum to participate in the photography project? So I could hold up both our versions of him to see where they diverge?

"Yeah," I say. "I'll—yes. Of course I'll come."

My brother nods very slightly, and just like that, it seems I'm going to New York.

Chapter Twenty-Seven

Calum delays his flight. He reschedules for Tuesday morning so he can rebook with a ticket for me with a return date of next Sunday. I'm not sure if that will be enough time to really see if he's grown, but it's the maximum I can take off from school without facing significant consequences.

I offer to cover the cost of my ticket—I've got money saved from years of working at Glenna's—but Calum hits me with "my job pays better than yours ever did" and, well. I'm not about to argue with that. So, the flight is confirmed, which leaves me free to go to my morning class. Photography.

Today Dr. Lazar wants us to work individually, which is not something we've done much of this semester. She assigns us each a different spot on campus to go off and take pictures of, and it's actually nice to spend time on my own, not worrying about talking to or collaborating with others, just taking in the crisp November air and the stone administration building in front of me. But the nature of the lesson means I'm not able to approach Eli until the very end, when we're back together in our usual classroom and packing up to leave.

"Hey."

He jumps slightly. My cheeks heat as I hold out the disposable camera, because when I look at Eli now, all I can see is him looking at me while I yelled at Benji. "I got this back. Would you mind developing the photos? I'm actually going home for a few days. To New York.

I can keep working on the essay while I'm there, but it probably doesn't make sense for me to bring the camera. Considering, you know. I already lost it once."

Eli's eyebrows crease. "Did something new happen? With your family?"

"Not really. We've just got to figure a few things out with the shop." I stretch the camera out farther until Eli takes it, swinging his backpack off his shoulder and opening the main pocket. Inside is an assortment of clear folders filled with information on UK visas. The top one catches my attention, and I gesture at it without thinking. "Oh, that's good. That's the one I thought you should go for."

Eli does a double take. "You've been researching my career prospects?"

The document I locked eyes on summarizes the qualifications needed for a graduate visa. After Eli's confession on Halloween about how he'd made a reckless decision for a reckless degree, I spent a marginal amount of time looking up how noncitizens might remain in the UK after university. The graduate visa seemed like the best first step because it lets you stay without a job—no strings attached—for two years. That could be a stepping stone to a skilled worker visa, which, from the forums I lightly scoured, seems difficult to obtain. But there are so many sectors Eli could potentially work his way into with a photography degree. From what I briefly researched, he could go into journalism, or do marketing for a company, or—scientists need quality pictures of their findings, right? And after he's gotten that visa and been on it for five years, he could apply for Indefinite Leave to Remain, which would allow him to live here permanently . . .

Eli's staring at me with an expression somewhere in

the realm of bewildered, and—God. Calum was right, wasn't he? I have no sense of boundaries.

"Sorry." My arms wrap around my chest like a barricade. "That was super weird of me. I'll just—I'll see you next week."

I turn on my heel. Eli doesn't follow.

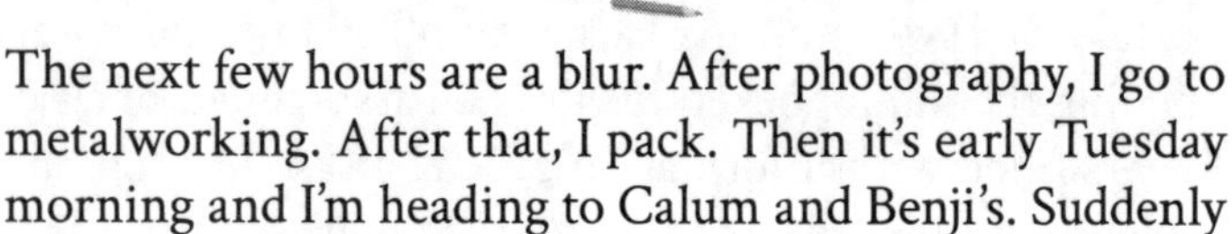

The next few hours are a blur. After photography, I go to metalworking. After that, I pack. Then it's early Tuesday morning and I'm heading to Calum and Benji's. Suddenly we're on a plane, and then it's noon in New York and Calum's renting a car to drive us the three hours upstate from the airport, and then I'm passing out in the back seat. When I wake, we're home.

My eyes open to snow. It blankets the trees next to us and the road behind us and our house in front of us. The rocking chairs on the porch look like marshmallows. The barn-turned-workshop out back is so muffled by flakes that the *Glenna's* sign nailed to the roof would be incomprehensible to anyone who didn't already know what it says.

I'm smiling. Over there is the hollow trunk I used to fill with birdseed, and across the way is the rock that looks like a bear. We're still in the car, but I can smell the sharp air of winter and pine and burning wood, and if I squint to the right, I see the footpath through the trees that takes me to Alicia's . . .

My stomach squirms. Alicia. I owe her so many messages, but everything has been so bad lately that I haven't been able to spin my life into something good. I do text her now—a quick photo of all the snow—because *home* is good. Especially after being away. I missed

Crescent Valley, but I didn't realize how much until it was fresh in my nose.

The car is off, but Calum still has one hand tight on the steering wheel. Benji gives him a small smile. "Back to London, then?"

Calum closes his eyes. Then he kicks open the driver's-side door and steps into the sun.

Chapter Twenty-Eight

My brother is a menace.

What I mean is we trudge up to the front door of our house and knock, and Dad opens it. And then he flinches like he's staring at three ghosts. That's when I realize I should have known better than to assume Calum warned our parents we were coming.

"Seriously?" I hiss after Dad pretends to pull himself together and invites us in and then runs away to find Mom. "You didn't *tell* them?"

"They would have disagreed with my reason for this trip." Calum draws in a breath. "They would have convinced me to stay in London."

I roll my eyes, but then I notice his hand. It's gripping the doorknob, and it's trembling. It's freezing out—I shivered on the short walk up to the porch—but the second we stepped through the entryway, we were blasted by heat. Calum's not shaking because he's cold.

"You've not slept," says Benji. It's true: Calum sat rigidly the whole plane ride, staring at the map as we inched closer and closer to New York. "Why don't you lie down for a bit? It'll be dark soon, anyway."

Calum's eyes flick up the stairs, toward the bedrooms at the top. Then he takes an abrupt step back.

"Take my room," I say before he can bolt into the snow. "I like yours better, anyway. It's bigger."

Calum's jaw unclenches slightly, but he still doesn't respond. His grip on the doorknob looks painful.

Benji puts his hand over Calum's and tugs gently until

his fingers loosen. "I, for one, am dying to see Maisie's room. Will it be bright pink? Emo black? Covered in portraits? Covered in limes? You're a bit of a wild card, Maisie Clark. I never know what I'm walking into with you." He manages to pull Calum a few paces forward.

"Why would there be *limes* in my room?"

Benji gets Calum to the foot of the stairs. "You eat them regularly. Like apples. Not to judge your preferences, but—"

"I don't eat them like *apples.*" I start forward. Benji shakes his head. It's slight, but the meaning is clear. I pull my foot back. "The skin is way too bitter. I peel them—"

"Like oranges, then." Benji tugs Calum up the first three steps. "Your poor dentist—"

"My teeth are fine, thank you. But while we're on the topic of questionable food choices, the amount of garlic you cook with is alarming. Remember that jar of tomato sauce you gifted me? When I tasted it, my nose burned. My *nose.*"

"Please. You can't ever have too much garlic." Benji reaches the top of the stairs. Without looking back, he pulls Calum up with him and into the dark.

As soon as they're out of sight, I inhale sharply. Clearly Calum hasn't changed as much as he thought he had—it's just as hard for him to be in this house now as it was for him back then. And, I mean, that's not very surprising. I've spent all semester trying to change, and sure, maybe I'm more aware of my flaws now, but that awareness hasn't gotten rid of them. I still lash out with my emotions before thinking through the consequences. I still don't know who I am as an artist. I'm still *me.*

"Piseag," Mom says breathlessly, striding through the living room and into the entryway with Dad in tow.

There's snow in their hair; Dad must have run out the back door to grab her from the workshop. Mom's eyes are on the shoes and suitcases crowded like a cage around me. "What—?"

"It's a whole thing." I kick off my boots and step forward to hug her. "I missed you."

Mom and Dad settle on the couch, and I tell them the basics: Calum wants us to back out of the gallery exhibition and reopen Glenna's; Benji and I tagged along; I'm missing a few days of school but don't worry, I got clearance to come home for a family emergency and am in a good spot for finals; I don't know how long Calum plans to stay, but hopefully it's fine that he's here—

"Of course it's fine," says Mom. "It's more than fine." She stands. I grab her wrist.

"Don't go up there." I don't mean for it to come out as forcefully as it does, but at least it makes Mom pause.

She looks at me, then at Dad. He nods. "Let him come to you, Fiona."

I see the effort it takes for Mom to sit back down. She's like me—nosy—but she's been trying these past few years. She's been giving Calum more space.

I frown at my knees. Mom's instincts are as overbearing as ever, but a few years ago, she would not have sat down. She'd already be upstairs with Calum, making a bad situation worse. People can't change at their core, I don't think. Calum will always be Calum; I will always be me. But Mom is not the same as she was—not entirely.

It's only six p.m., but I'm jetlagged and ready for sleep. The problem is I'm in Calum's room. There are old, untouched textbooks piled on the desk—Biology and World History and Algebra II. Dusty graphic novels line a shelf in the corner. A stuffed green giraffe sits atop the pillow; the last time I was home, I saw it on Mom's nightstand, but I guess she decided to put it back in its proper place. This room belongs to a Calum I remember, and he looks very similar to the Calum I know. His flat in London may not be filled with high school work, but it is filled with finance work. Instead of one shelf of graphic novels, he's got a whole bookcase dedicated to them. There are no stuffed animals in his room across the ocean, but he has held on to other sentimental objects: a Statue of Liberty snow globe, the drawing I made for him six years ago that he's got framed in his office. Different items in name, but not in meaning.

My phone buzzes, pulling me from my head and back to the present.

6:03 p.m.

Alicia Miller: You're home???
Alicia Miller: Why???
Alicia Miller: Are you ok?

When I texted Alicia a photo of my front porch, obviously she was going to question why I was randomly in Crescent Valley. I all but asked for her concern. And yet, even though I initiated this conversation, staring at her messages makes my jaw ache. Telling her why I'm home will mean admitting I've been keeping massive bits of my life from her, and if I do that, we're going to fight. At the same time, the thought of brushing off her texts with "No worries, I'm fine!" makes me want to cry.

I stare at my phone. Typing bubbles appear on Alicia's

end and then disappear. She's hesitating. I'm hesitating. We've never been tentative around each other before.

There's a sudden, soft knock at the door. I let my phone drop to the bed and shuffle forward to open it.

"Pink," Benji says. "Your bedroom is pink."

"Are you disappointed?"

He shrugs. "Posters of clowns would have been more of a conversation starter, but pink is a solid choice." He nods at Calum's room. "Can I?"

I step aside to let him through.

At some point in the last few hours, Benji showered and changed into pajamas. He looks fine from afar, but up close, I see creases in his University of London T-shirt from where his muscles are too tense. "Is Calum okay?" I ask.

"He will be." Benji's examining the room, scanning it inch by inch. He raises his eyebrows at the soccer trophies lining the top of the bookshelf. "Didn't know about those."

"Yeah." It's hard to imagine my brother kicking a ball, mainly because I can only picture him doing so in a suit, but fourteen-year-old Calum did not dress as he does now. He had to have been good, too, because more than one of the trophies says MVP. I have no memories of watching a game, but that makes sense. From the dates on the awards, he stopped playing before I turned five.

Benji pokes the Algebra II textbook and then crouches to study the graphic novel collection. There's something soft about his presence. He doesn't disturb any of the objects. He doesn't make loud, sudden movements or sprawl ridiculously on the floor like he usually does when we're hanging out.

I think of his bright voice in the entryway as he coaxed Calum up the stairs. Of the easy conversations he's led me through the past few days, despite the terrible things I said to him.

"I thought nothing ever really bothered you. But that's not true, is it?"

Benji touches his fingers to the desk. "Of course things bother me."

"Then why do you act like they don't?"

He looks over at me, and his eyes are contemplative. Like they were in his self-portrait. Like they weren't in mine. "Cal and I are similar, you know. I also live far from my parents. I also have people close to me, related to me, who have not always understood every part of me. But we all deal with things in our own way, and I'd rather defuse a bad situation than sit in it."

Fair enough. Benji's never said it so plainly, but he doesn't often get to visit his family. When he does, he's always excited beforehand and quiet when he returns. He speaks fondly of his grandparents. I hear him on the phone, sometimes, with his mom. He never mentions his dad.

If you're already lugging around heavy things, it makes sense to not want to add more. I get not wanting to linger in anger, but it isn't easy to let go of a fight for your own sake.

Benji's still watching me with that quiet expression. It's vaguely uncomfortable—kind of like how it felt that time in ninth grade when I turned in a math test without realizing there were more problems on the back. Benji isn't any different than he was five minutes ago, but I'm seeing more to him that I missed before.

"I . . ." It's always been easy, speaking with Benji. He's always made it easy. Even though I can be hard. "I'm sorry," I mutter stiltedly, and then look firmly away. "For what I said. At the flat. I was just upset because there were things Calum was telling you that he wasn't telling me and I . . . I think I've always been a little jealous. That he let you get to know him before he let me get to know him. But like you said, it's not your place to speak for him, and it wasn't fair of me to ask you to." I scratch at my ear. "I just—you *are* family, and you always have been, and I—I just think you're the best. You're, like, my favorite person on the entire planet. So I—thought you should know that."

Benji blinks. Then he smiles. It starts small and quiet, but quickly grows into something more familiar, more free. "Maisie Clark, one thing you are not is subtle. I am well aware you think I'm the most magnificent being to walk this earth—"

"The most humble, you mean."

Benji scoffs, but it turns into a laugh. I roll my eyes, but it turns into a smile. "I'm sorry," I say again. "I know I've got problems with my temper. With boundaries in general. I want to change. I want to be less . . . overbearing—"

"No, don't be less," says Benji. "If you give yourself less space, you'll just burst out of it faster. What you need is *more* space."

Benji is good at a lot of things, but giving advice has never been one of them. You can't be less by being more. Where is the logic in that?

"You've gone quite pale," Benji observes. "I have been told my wisdom is generally awe-inspiring and occasionally upsetting. Which was it this time?"

I toss a pillow at him. He catches it.

"Upsetting, then," he concludes. "Unfortunately, that means the problem is on your end, not mine—"

I toss another pillow at him. He catches this one, too.

"I'm keeping these," he says, holding them up. "Your

bed is horribly firm." Before I can retort, he gives me a final smile and slips out the door.

It's like all my exhaustion was waiting outside the room. As soon as Benji leaves, it floods in, and I barely get the lights off before heaviness washes over me.

Sleep hits my body before the bed does.

8:40 p.m.

The Boy Who Is My Friend
(Eli): Hope you got to New York ok

Chapter Twenty-Nine

I sleep fitfully and wake in a panic, because why am I in Calum's room and why aren't I in London and don't I have photography this morning and shouldn't I be—

Oh.

It's early. Five a.m. Snow falls softly against the window, illuminated by the last of the stars. I close my eyes, but the jet lag is real: I was in bed before seven last night. So I give up, slip on a pair of thick, fluffy socks, and pad downstairs to sniff around the kitchen. Despite the early hour, Dad's at the counter brewing coffee. Mom stands by the stove attempting pancakes. Benji's pulling orange juice from the fridge.

Calum hovers by the window. He looks better than he did yesterday; his hands are steady where they rest on the sill, and the circles under his eyes are less pronounced. This scene—Calum, breakfast, the backdrop of our house—should feel like a resolution. Instead, it feels like a breakdown.

The problem is, when Calum left home, he left a hole. During meals, I'd stare at his chair—he always took the one at the foot of the table—and wonder what food he'd eaten that day. I'd look away every time I walked past his bedroom because I didn't want to see that he wasn't inside. Months passed, and then years, and I still did those things, but they morphed from impulses into habits. I didn't think about them as much. Calum's Not Here-ness took up less space. And then we reconnected in Edinburgh, and that chasm in our house nearly closed completely. I stopped picturing Calum in Crescent Valley because I could picture him somewhere else.

So, there was a hole, and then it shrunk, and now Calum's back, and he's no longer the right shape to fill it. He tries to—he sits down in that chair at the foot of the table—but then Mom does a double take, and Dad stares so hard that his eyes start tearing, and I freeze in the doorway, and the only person who doesn't look like they want to die is Benji.

"Your windows!" Benji gestures at the large ones behind the sink. "How lovely that they look out on the forest. Of course, I'm only assuming—it's too dark to see anything besides . . . more dark, but if I recall from yesterday, there were . . . big trees . . ."

I take it back. Benji seems ready to die, too.

"I asked you to back out of the exhibition," Calum says abruptly, which—I know this conversation is the reason he's here, but I at least expected us to get through breakfast first. "I asked you over and over. It wasn't a necessary commitment, and now Glenna's is suffering for it."

Mom pauses with her coffee halfway to her mouth. Calum is dressed up for this battle, already in a collared shirt despite the early hour, but Mom is all messy hair and flannel pajamas. "As I've explained," she says, her tone more tired than harsh, "the shop's in a good place, and we can afford to take another few weeks off. Besides, we're happy to be working on this project—"

"I'm not happy," says Calum. "Shouldn't my opinion count for anything, considering you're carrying this burden for me?" Instead of looking at Mom and Dad, his eyes stare out into the dark.

"It's not for you." Mom tilts her head as if evaluating her own statement. Then she backtracks. "Well, yes, it is.

But it's also for our town. For our clients whose portraits were destroyed. For the curators who organized this exhibition—"

"The point still stands—you're taking on weight to lift me up. That's never what I wanted. Not now, not when I was sixteen. I just want you to *hear* what I'm saying, and you aren't. You are still not listening."

Mom draws in a long breath. She releases it. "Maybe you're right."

Calum flinches. His arms are braced hard against the table like he was expecting pushback. *I* was expecting pushback—Mom is more stubborn than I am. Or, she was. In the past, once she got in her head that something was right or wrong, there was nothing anyone could say or do to change her mind. But she . . . relented. Just like that.

"We took on the gallery work as a selfless act," Mom continues, "but I suppose it's not selfless if it's unwanted."

"That's not—that isn't what I meant." Calum runs his fingers through his hair. "I would just much rather you protect the shop you worked so hard to build than repaint portraits you didn't destroy." He holds out a hand. Mom stares at it blankly. "Your plans. For the exhibition. I'd like them."

Mom's gaze turns wary. "I understand you're against it, but we've already put a month of work into this reconstruction. Dad's finished repainting one of the portraits, there's another I'm meant to pick up from a client in town today, and we're anticipating the arrival of several other borrowed commissions over the next two weeks. If you'd still like us to pull out of the gallery—"

Calum's hand is still outstretched. "I did not return to Crescent Valley to convince you to throw out what you've done."

He *didn't*? I glance at Benji. He doesn't look fazed by this revelation, so maybe I missed something. What, though? I think back to the confrontation with Calum in his flat. When I asked when he would return to London, he said he wasn't sure. But if his only goal was to convince Mom and Dad to give up on the gallery, then he would have anticipated this trip taking a few days at most. Instead, he packed like he'd be in Crescent Valley for *weeks*.

"I'm here to take over the exhibition so that you can reopen Glenna's," Calum continues. "I'd like your files. As well as email exchanges and addresses of past clients."

"Calum," Dad says quietly. "It's not your job to fix our mess."

"It isn't your mess. You didn't destroy the portraits. But it is *a* mess. And I've got the means to clean it up, considering I put in enough overtime to clear my schedule of commitments through the end of December. Not to mention, thanks to years of never going on holiday, I've an absurd amount of accrued leave."

A light bursts on in my memory. I follow its trail until I realize it looks like the automatic ones in Calum's office. All those extra hours my brother spent at his desk after the Glenna's attack . . . I thought he was curling into his work so he didn't have to think about the shop. Instead, he was curling into his work because he *was* thinking about the shop?

My head hurts. I rub at my temples. "You said your boss needs two assistants. That's why you've been spending more time than usual in the office."

"That's one part of it. This is the other."

Mom and Dad glance at each other. I see the moment they decide to relent. Calum's reasons for why he should take over the exhibition are solid. His plan is also much more logical than *Maisie will single-handedly keep Glenna's open through digital commissions while ten new oil paintings are somehow wrangled together in two months.*

Mom grabs the laptop resting on the kitchen counter. She opens it to a spreadsheet containing a list of names and addresses, then tilts the screen so Calum can see. "The bolded ones are clients who've agreed to let us borrow past commissions. They're being sent through the mail. The highlighted one—Mr. Simmons, Mark—lives in town, so I arranged to pick his up in person today. All together, we have six confirmed to be delivered, plus the one Dad repainted. That means you'll have to figure out the last three. I would recommend focusing your efforts on acquiring existing works, because if the portraits are to be ready for the exhibition by January, it will not be feasible to paint them from scratch."

Calum nods. Then he walks out of the kitchen and toward the front door.

"Um," I say, "where are you going?"

"To pick up Mr. Simmons's portrait."

"Calum," Dad says, following after him, "it's six a.m. You can't go knocking on Mark Simmons's door at six a.m."

Calum pauses in tying his shoe, but remains crouched in the entryway, his whole body tensing as though he's just now realizing that he'll be stuck in this house for at least another few hours.

"Why don't we go for a walk?" Benji suggests. He joins Calum by the front door. "Is there a spot to see the sunrise?"

Mom shakes her head. "You'll freeze to death. The snow hasn't let up in days—"

"Oh, but I love the snow." Benji grabs his coat off the rack. "I haven't seen this much since I was last in Japan."

"You get a lot there?" Mom asks.

Benji nods. "Up north, anyway. My family's near Sapporo."

"Your whole family?"

"Nearly. My parents moved back whilst I was in uni—they wanted to be closer to my grandparents—but my sister lives in London." Benji hands Calum a pair of gloves.

"Millers' Cider Mill is just up the road," Dad says. "They open at seven. If you get too cold—"

"We'll be fine," Calum mutters, and strides out the door.

"Millers' Cider Mill?" Benji calls after him. "Hang on—what is a Millers' Cider Mill? Why isn't it cold? Please enlighten me . . ."

"He has a sister?" Mom asks once they're both out of earshot. "They've been dating for ten years, and I didn't know he had a sister?"

"Her name's Lily." I've met her—she's thirty-three and a doctor and significantly less chaotic than Benji, but despite their differences, he sees her every Wednesday for dinner.

Mom sighs. I can tell she wants to say more, but after a few moments of staring at Calum's and Benji's receding backs, she turns away from the door.

6:10 a.m.

Me: Made it to New York in one piece!!

Me: How's London without me??

The Boy Who Is My Friend (Eli): Quiet

Me: Is that a good thing or a bad thing???
Me: Don't answer that actually
Me: Ahaha

Chapter Thirty

It's too early to do much of anything, so I trudge back to my room. Calum's room. The place where I'm sleeping. Whatever. My texts with Eli stalled, which means while I wait to see if he responds, I'm left staring at notifications of messages from Alicia that I haven't opened yet.

I breathe out slowly through my nose. Last night we were both typing and untyping. We were hesitating in a way that's new, in a way that scared me, because this is *Alicia*. She knows that up through high school graduation, I slept with a stuffed animal every night. I know she's responsible for the "vomit corner" of the PE field, which was christened as such in seventh grade after the mysterious appearance of its namesake during a timed mile run. We've always known everything about each other, and now we don't—all because I created a rule based on a theory that had a huge flaw. Talking about the bad in my semester might have amplified the distance between us, sure, but avoiding the bad *guaranteed* the distance! My rule was wrong. So now, I break it.

I'm not worried about waking Alicia—she likes to get up before the sunrise, to read or do homework while the rest of the world is quiet. I always thought she was unhinged for that, but now, staring out Calum's window into the morning dark, hearing nothing but the chirps of birds and the rustles of leaves, I kind of understand the appeal.

Alicia accepts my video call.

She's in her dorm room. I saw it in October, the last

time we FaceTimed, but it looks different now. More finished. The walls are aggressively covered in posters and pictures, some of which I instantly know are her contribution (an image of a black-and-white typewriter, framed portraits of her dogs painted by me), while others (the musical artists) are definitely her roommate's. There is a larger stack of books on her desk than the last time we spoke; it's almost embarrassing how I can instantly tell which of the poetry collections are her course readings and which were passion purchases. Alicia herself looks more finished than the last time I saw her. She's pierced her cartilage. Her eyeliner is sharper. Instead of the "I don't get haircuts" haircut she's sported for ten years, her ginger waves slice cleanly across her collarbone. The shorter style makes her look older, and it also makes me aware of how little *my* appearance has changed. Sure, I went through those weeks of dressing out of my comfort zone, but I pretty quickly migrated back to my usual sweaters and jeans.

"Hang on," she whispers, slipping from her desk chair and out the door. In the corner of the screen, I get a glimpse of her roommate sprawled across the second bed, mouth open and eyes closed.

The phone bops around as Alicia walks down several flights of stairs. When the movements still and the lighting evens out, her new location reveals itself: some sort of student lounge, with old sofas and battered tables and a vending machine in the corner. Aside from Alicia, it's empty.

"Where are you?" she asks, squinting at me.

I hesitate, then snap on the overhead light. Calum's room flickers into view.

Alicia pauses. She doesn't ask *Isn't that your brother's*

bookshelf behind you? She knows my house too well for that, and she knows I don't make a habit of spending time in this room, and she knows if I'm curled on Calum's bed now, at six thirty in the morning, something alarming has occurred.

I open my mouth to spill everything I haven't shared with her for the past three months, but nothing comes out. It's like a traffic jam in my throat. There are so many things to say, and they all come rushing up at once, and in their frenzy to escape, the exit gets blocked. Finally, something light slips through a crack. "Your roommate snores."

"Yes. But apparently I sleep talk, so. It evens out." Alicia pauses. She waits. I called her, after all.

"Um." My skin itches. "I'm in Crescent Valley."

"I noticed."

I scratch at my ear. I cough, as if that will help my words fall out. And then, finally, some do.

"To be honest, there are things I haven't told you. About the last few months. Not because I didn't want to—I *did*, but . . . it's been kind of . . . it's been difficult. Moving abroad. Branching out from portraits. I had this whole plan and it wasn't working and I . . . if you thought I was failing in London, I thought you'd stop telling me the good things about your semester. I thought it'd make it harder for us to talk if you realized I wasn't having as great a time in college as you. Obviously that was a mistake, though. Because now we're just . . ."

Now, I don't know what we are.

Alicia balances her phone on her knees and lets out a long breath. "I get it," she says, which—*what?* She's not mad?

"I haven't told you everything, either," she continues,

as though I'm not internally malfunctioning. "The poetry society is awful. Everyone's so competitive, and if you can't make friends with the editor-in-chief, then you might as well quit because she'll all but phase you out. I love the literary journal they produce—I've been gushing about wanting to contribute to it since like ninth grade—and it's a big part of the reason I even *chose* this school, so that's all been kind of embarrassing."

Oh. Alicia never had trouble making friends in Crescent Valley. It never once occurred to me that she might struggle socially in college.

"I wish you'd told me that," I lament. "If you'd told me that, maybe I wouldn't have been so embarrassed about my attempt to join the Society of Paranormal Believers, which—I know I sent some cool pictures, but it was *not* a good time."

"What about your roommates?" Alicia asks. "Mine only talks to me when I'm bothering her."

"One of mine is cool. The other two are questionable. How about your classes?"

"*Urgh,*" says Alicia. "I mean, they're fine. But back home I was a good writer, you know? And here, everyone's a good writer. It's a lot harder to stand out."

"I'm not used to being bad at art," I admit. "For like a month at the start of term, I was banned from using the cameras in my photography class because I took too many pictures on the first day."

"*What?*" Alicia shrieks, and she looks so affronted on my behalf that I laugh, and then I want to cry, because all this time we could have been screaming about each other's failures together instead of sitting with them alone.

"Are you going to tell me why the hell you're home?"

Alicia finally asks, lying back on the couch and raising her phone above her head. "Or are you going to make me guess? Because I can guess. The British government tasked you with a secret mission you must complete in New York. The portraits in your workshop woke up one day and started yelling at you for abandoning them. A squirrel—"

"You're ridiculous." I lie down, mimicking her posture, pillowing my head on an arm.

I tell her everything.

After my rant to Alicia, she gave me hers, and by the end of it, I realized I went through this whole semester incomplete. Growing up, Alicia's brain was practically my brain. On any given day, I could tell you what she'd eaten for breakfast and which of her homework assignments was the hardest and where she was in the book she was reading. The reverse was true, too; sometimes it felt like Alicia knew more about me than I knew about me. And then we separated. We spent months apart, and it was almost like I cut myself in half without realizing it. But now I feel back together. I want to stay this way, so before we hang up, I ask if she'd be down to chat more frequently. Obviously we can't talk every moment of every day like we used to, but if we can even set aside an hour a week, it'll be a lot more than nothing. She agrees.

When we hang up, I pull my TRY NEW THINGS list from my backpack. It's scrawled on the blank page at the front of my homework planner—I figured having it there would remind me to look at it every day. As I look at it now, my teeth bite into my lip. The unspoken rule I set for myself with Alicia—don't talk about bad things—was wrong. It was limiting, and it only created more distance between us.

How many other rules have I made for myself that are limiting? With this list, it's like I've been chipping away at myself in the hopes I could be whittled into a new shape. Maybe Benji *was* on to something with his weird advice. All semester, I've been trying to grow out of myself, but instead, maybe I should have been trying to grow into myself.

~~TRY NEW THINGS~~

~~1. STOP HELPING OUT AT GLENNA'S ONLY HELP OUT WITH DIGITAL GLENNA'S COMMISSIONS.~~

~~2. GO TO AN ART SCHOOL FAR FROM HOME. MAYBE IN ANOTHER COUNTRY.~~

~~3. NO PORTRAITS OR OIL PAINTINGS. ONLY SIGN UP FOR CLASSES IN MEDIUMS YOU HAVE NO EXPERIENCE WITH.~~

~~4. EXPERIMENT WITH YOUR APPEARANCE AND CLOTHING.~~

~~5. MAKE NEW FRIENDS (BECAUSE ALICIA IS GOING TO). (BECAUSE YOU WANT TO).~~

~~6. ALWAYS SAY YES. EVEN WHEN YOU DON'T WANT TO. SAY YES MORE THAN YOU SAY NO.~~

~~7. DON'T UNDERESTIMATE PEOPLE.~~

~~8. JUMP INTO THE OCCASIONAL FOUNTAIN TO WAKE UP!~~

~~9. NOT EVERYTHING HAS TO BE UNCOMFORTABLE.~~

~~10. BE FRIENDS WITH ELI WITHOUT BEING WEIRD!~~

~~11. CONTROL YOUR EMOTIONS.~~

I head downstairs feeling lighter than I have in a long time. It's just about seven thirty—too early to do anything in town, and Calum and Benji aren't back yet. So I head to the workshop. I push the door in slowly.

Glenna's was converted from a barn into a studio before I was born, but the skeleton of what it once was still stands: the wooden walls, the high ceilings (now fitted with lamps that simulate daytime for when we work at night), the frame of the metal machine in the corner that I think was once used to milk cows (and that I hide my special paintbrushes behind). Instead of animals, the space is now full of tables and easels. We've got a sketching station covered in graphite pencils and labeled folders of reference photos. Dad spends most of his time at the painting station, but we've also got a drying station and a waiting station, where portraits hang out until they're picked up or shipped off to their customers. Everything looks exactly how I remember it, save for the overflow of paintings piled in the corner of the waiting station. We usually have ten at most, but today there are easily twenty. When I get closer, I realize why: The space is cluttered with the artwork that was destroyed. Some of the canvases are torn in the middle. Others have been splashed with sheets of paint. There are ten ruined pieces total, but it feels like more. They loom over what is supposed to be a comfortable place.

"Why are they still here?" I ask. "Taking up all this space?"

Dad jumps slightly, like he was so engrossed in his current portrait he didn't hear me approach. He follows my gaze and then sighs, turning back to his work. "I can't quite bring myself to throw them out."

I take a seat next to him at the sketching station. He's

got a photograph propped in front of him and a set of pencils to his right. He's drawing for fun, I think—he hasn't been taking on new commissions—and I don't have to ask how he's going to approach this piece. His process is my process—he taught me how to draw. He taught me right here, at this table.

"When did you first get into art?" I ask, gesturing at Glenna's as a whole. Dad studied visual art at Columbia, and I know the story from there, but I don't actually know where it starts.

"Elementary school," he says. "Crescent Valley was even smaller back then. There were fewer students, fewer teachers. Ms. Ryan taught us art from kindergarten through twelfth grade, and she loved what she did, so I loved it, too."

"Does your art look like hers? Since she taught you for so long?" Does *my* art look like hers?

Dad shrugs. "A little, I'm sure. I still use some of her measuring and blending techniques."

"And that doesn't bother you?"

"Why would it bother me?"

It's warm in here, suddenly. My sweatpants are sweaty. My slippers are slippery. Last year, when I told Dad I wanted to branch out from our shop, I didn't explain the reason why. I worried he'd be offended that I didn't want my art to look like his. I worried he'd be disappointed. But now that I'm thinking about it, I didn't just leave Glenna's for London—like my brother, I ran away from home with no intention of ever glancing back. And that's got to be as limiting as my TRY NEW THINGS list was, because how am I supposed to find my voice if I don't even let myself search for it in the place I came from?

"I love your paintings," I say hesitantly. "I'm so glad

I learned art from you, but—I can't really tell our work apart. I thought that meant I should give up portraits to see if I could find another medium that could be more... mine. But I liked working on those digital commissions for Glenna's more than any of my school projects this term. I love our shop, and I love painting, and that should be enough, but—" My voice cracks slightly. "Sometimes I think I'll never have enough substance to look like myself."

Dad is quiet. Of course he is—I've revealed the ugliest part of me, and now that he's seen it, we can't go back to how we were. He'll realize I've seeped through his boundaries like I've done with everyone else, turning his art into mine, twisting his vision into my perspective—

Except, no. I'm speculating. Putting words in his mouth before he's even opened it. I take a slow breath and wait for him to respond.

"When I studied art in college, the biggest lesson drilled into us was that you can't control how people view your work," Dad says. "You might think a drawing in your portfolio is your worst, only for it to win first place in a contest. You might think you created the most important masterpiece on the planet, only for it to be rejected from every gallery. If you look at any era of artists—impressionists, expressionists, surrealists—their work has similarities; that's why they're grouped together. But having similar styles doesn't necessarily mean having similar ideas. What matters more than how your paintings look is what you're trying to express."

I glance back at Dad and the beginnings of his sketch. He's drawn a circle that became a face and a triangle that became the top of a torso. "What are *you* trying to express?"

"Portraits are memories, and memories are delicate," he says. "I want to express care—that's why we cap how many commissions we take on every month. It allows me to give every painting the attention it deserves." He looks up from his drawing. "How about you?"

"I... don't know." Dr. Lazar could distinguish my photos from Eli's—there was something about the way I captured our subjects that she said came from my background in portraits. But that breakthrough hasn't translated into my paintings at all.

"It's okay," Dad says with a small smile. "You've got plenty of time to figure yourself out."

I don't, though. *If I can't find my voice, I'll quit art entirely. I'll transfer to a nonspecialized school and study something broader while I still have time to pivot.* This year revolved around that ultimatum, but... why?

I *like* my school. Even though I'm no closer to figuring out who I am as an artist, I like the people I've met along the way. I like living in London. I like that Calum and Benji are now a tube ride from my door instead of an ocean.

Why do I keep imposing limits on the things that I like?

7:45 a.m.

(Eli): In class today Dr. Lazar made us stand in one spot with one camera for one hour

(Eli): We weren't allowed to move our feet

(Eli): And each photo we took had to be from a different angle

Me: THAT'S RIDICULOUS

(Eli): I think you might have walked out
(Eli): If you were there

Me: AHAHAHA

Chapter Thirty-One

Calum and Benji get back to the house around eight with a variety of goods from Millers' Cider Mill, including the famous Millers' Cider Mill's Cider Donuts and Millers' Cider Mill's Cinnamon Cider (they need a better marketing manager). We all eat a second breakfast, and then, once the sun is firmly in the sky, Calum rises to track down Mr. Simmons. As we're about to walk out the door, though, Mom says to Benji, "You embroider, right? For your shop? I was wondering, we have an old pillow—it was my mother's—and there's a bit that's unraveling at the end . . ."

I attempt to silently warn Benji that this is less about pillows and more about Mom hoping to hurl at him every question she's never gotten to ask, but Benji's either oblivious to my raised brows or humoring hers, because he goes "Well, all right," and Mom goes "Brilliant!" and just like that, Calum and I are picking up this portrait alone.

I don't think anything of it when Calum grabs the car keys. But when he slips into the driver's seat and starts backing out amid all the snow, I'm skeptical. Navigating London traffic and navigating unpaved icy back roads are entirely separate skills. The streets weren't this bad when we arrived yesterday.

"Don't turn the wheel so much." I gesture behind us. "Back out straight. You aren't going to hit that rock if you—oh. Nice."

"I did learn to drive here," Calum says, pulling onto the road, and—yes. I suppose he did.

When we reach 23 Maple Street, Calum pushes out of the car and marches up to the front porch. I have to run to catch up. Despite the snow, my brother's dressed in a suit. He's also holding a clipboard and pen like a solicitor—to record this delivery and take any potential notes, I'm assuming. This behavior is entirely what I'd expect from him, but the fact that he's here, walking up to a stranger's porch, is entirely not.

"Hello?" Mr. Simmons opens his door slowly and with suspicion. I don't know him—I mean, his face looks familiar because everyone's face in Crescent Valley looks familiar, but I don't think we've had a conversation before. He's on the older side—probably late sixties—and is wearing a knitted sweater over pajamas. "Sorry," he says, glancing from me to Calum's clipboard. "I'm not in the market for Girl Scout cookies, but the Wilsons down the road—"

Girl Scout cookies? I know I'm short, but how old does he think I am?

"We're from Glenna's Portraits," says Calum. "You agreed to lend us your commission? For an exhibition in New York City?"

Mr. Simmons's posture relaxes. "Oh, yes. I didn't expect you until later, but no matter. One moment." He dips back inside. When he returns, he's holding a portrait. It's been layered so heavily in bubble wrap that I can't see the details beneath. He holds it out and I take it since Calum's hands are full of his clipboard. The painting is large and bulky, but I'm used to handling portraits. I'm fairly confident I can get this into the car without tripping forward in the snow.

"Thank you," I say.

"Of course. I'm glad you're still going forward with this exhibition—the least I could do was contribute a second piece."

"A second?" Calum asks.

Mr. Simmons nods. "I've commissioned from your shop many times. It's always a pleasure supporting local businesses, and paintings make lovely presents. I've gifted them for birthdays, weddings . . . the one I ordered most recently was for an anniversary. My anniversary, actually. It's a pity it was destroyed—I didn't think there were any photos of Robert and me from before our twenties, but a few months ago, I found an old Crescent Valley High yearbook in the attic. It wasn't in great condition—we had a leak last year, and before that were the bats—so I sent it to your shop. Figured a painting would be a nice way to preserve the memory. We got together that year, in '75. Seemed like a timely present, as this will be our fiftieth."

"You—" Calum's still staring at his clipboard, but the pen is no longer moving. "You were together in 1975? In Crescent Valley?"

"That surprises you?"

"It—well." Calum runs a hand through his hair. "You didn't give us the original photo, did you? When you commissioned that painting?"

"No, no. I sent in a copy." Mr. Simmons watches Calum thoughtfully. "Would you like to see it? The original?"

That's not relevant to why we're here, so I expect Calum to make an excuse to head back to the car now that we have the portrait. But instead he says, "Okay."

I raise my eyebrows as Mr. Simmons patters back into the house. "We don't need that photo. The painting was destroyed, and we've already got the new one . . ."

Calum lets me trail off into silence.

When Mr. Simmons returns, he's holding a battered yearbook. He flips it open to a marked page and holds it out for us to see.

The photo is small—a few inches across and fewer down. It's on a page titled *Debate Club,* and Mr. Simmons and Robert appear to be in a heated argument. If I didn't know they were together, I'd think they hated each other. But on close inspection, there's something in their eyes that looks highly amused. On the wall behind them is a banner that reads *Crescent Valley High,* and out the window is a view of the school's front lawn. I know that classroom—I took geometry there in ninth grade. Calum probably did, too.

My brother stares at the photo from several paces back. I can't read his expression, but his fingers are tight on his clipboard. Suddenly he says, "I'll repaint it for you."

"Calum." The commissions we do in the workshop aren't like the ones I've been doing on the iPad. Oil paintings take weeks, sometimes months, to complete; that's why Mom and Dad have been focused on procuring already finished commissions instead of creating new pieces from scratch. There's no way Calum could have a portrait this elaborate completed by January. Sure, he could paint it without the intention of putting it in the gallery, but this doesn't seem like a great time to be taking on side projects—

"It won't look like the other portraits on our site," Calum continues, ignoring me. "I'm not—I don't paint, usually. My work won't be as polished, but if that doesn't bother you . . ."

"Calum." Mr. Simmons turns the syllables over like a

puzzle. "Calum from Glenna's. I've heard those names together before."

Calum falters. I expect him to turn on his heel and march into the woods, because it's one thing to step back into this town and another to be recognized within it, but although his fingers tighten further on his clipboard, his feet stay firmly planted. "My parents own the shop," he says. "I grew up there."

Mr. Simmons pauses. He tilts his head, as if to consider Calum from another angle. "You didn't stay." It's not a question, and it's specific enough that I'm sure he's worked out that this man is also that kid people still whisper about when my family shows up to community events, that kid who disappeared one summer and never returned.

Calum's staying now. He's enduring this conversation, even though his clipboard has risen up to his chest, as if to block an attack. I don't know what to make of it. I don't know what to make of him, and I'm not sure Mr. Simmons does, either. My heart is beating more than it should, because I know Calum won't run and not return, but depending on what's said next, he might *run*. And if he runs, I'll be—

I'll be *fine.*

I exhale, letting the tension leave my body. If Calum runs, I'll call Benji. Or I'll hang here with Mr. Simmons. Or I'll walk home—it's not that far.

"I read about the break-in," says Mr. Simmons. "In *The Crescent Observer*? It stated which portraits in your shop were destroyed and which weren't. It would be nice if the damaged ones were repainted instead of refunded. It would mean something for them to exist." He holds out the yearbook.

At first, I don't understand the gesture. I don't think

Calum does, either, because he stays frozen on the threshold for several seconds. But eventually, he tucks his clipboard under one arm and reaches out both hands. Mr. Simmons places the yearbook in Calum's grasp, and then my brother leaves the porch without another word, without looking back.

Chapter Thirty-Two

I don't ask Calum where we're going when he puts the car in drive. Well, I do ask. But only after we speed past the turn that would take us home. "Somewhere I'd like to visit" is all he gives me as a response, which short-circuits my brain for a good ten minutes because 1) There is somewhere in Crescent Valley that Calum *likes*? and 2) *What* is this magical place that he likes?!

Crescent Valley is known for its . . . well. The leaves are nice in the fall, and Millers' Cider Mill is a standout. There's not much else, though, besides trees and mountains and cornfields. That doesn't mean it isn't beautiful or there aren't things to love, but it does mean our destinations are limited.

I go through a few possibilities in my head. He won't be driving us to Millers' Cider Mill, because he already went there this morning. Maybe it's the singular coffee shop in our half-hour radius? But no, coffee shops are loud and full of people. Calum's behavior in Crescent Valley might be different from what I anticipated, but I am one hundred percent sure he does not suddenly enjoy places that are loud and full of people. It's only when we turn onto Forest Road that I realize we're heading in the direction of Welcome Home, a family farm with a questionable array of occupants, from cats to snakes to a giant pig named Winnie. It's a newer establishment—I visited for the first time in high school with Alicia—so Calum wouldn't have been there before. I'm about to restart my theory from scratch when I remember his phrasing—"somewhere I'd like to visit," he'd said, not "somewhere I *like*."

"What's your opinion on animals?" I ask into the silence.

"Messy," he responds, which does not sound like a positive, but then we're pulling into the drive of Welcome Home, and I'm confused all over again.

Before I can make sense of why we're here, we are greeted by the biggest dog I've ever seen. It's a Bernese mountain dog. Brown and black and white, with a fluffy tail that's wagging excitedly. Alicia went through a phase in middle school where she learned every dog breed and their specific features, which means that of course, I did, too.

I bend to pat the dog, which is apparently all the invitation she needs to barrel me over. Calum makes no effort to save my life, so I have to detangle myself from the overly excited ball of fluff on my own.

"You don't," I say when I emerge, slightly breathless, "seem particularly excited to be here."

Calum eyes the dog suspiciously. "That's large."

"So are the ones inside. You sure you want to visit a place full of animals?"

"Yes," he says, and then, without further explanation, walks through the front door.

It's empty. Not of animals—there are rooms of cats to the right and reptiles to the left and Winnie the pig rests smack in the center—but we appear to be the only humans. When I've come on the weekends, it's been crowded with families and small children. But it's Wednesday.

Calum balks at Winnie, taking a quick step back and then several forward. "That pig," he says, "is wearing boots."

She is. A hat, too. And there's a blanket draped across her back. "Obviously," I say. "You've never seen a pig dressed for winter?"

"No," says Calum, "I have not." And then he does the strangest thing. He raises his phone and swipes open the camera.

I have never in my life seen my brother voluntarily take a picture. He is occasionally bullied into it by others, and he used to post promotional images for his web comic, but those were anonymous and for work. To understand how horrendous his social media presence is, all you need to know is he has only one personal account—Facebook—and his profile picture is his Knightley Corporations ID badge photo. But here he is now, snapping a portrait of Winnie the pig in her little black boots.

"It's for Benji," Calum says in response to whatever's on my face. "He enjoys it when I send photos of animals. Particularly when they're wearing clothes."

"This is . . . a normal occurrence?" An image of Calum stopping on his way to work to take a photo of a dog in a raincoat flashes through my head. I promptly dismiss it, because *what*?

"You're surprised I text my boyfriend on a regular basis?"

"Yes."

Calum rolls his eyes and turns his attention back to his screen. While he's busy apparently texting Benji about animals in hats, I pull out my own phone and connect to the Wi-Fi. In the time between talking with Dad in the workshop and heading out to Mr. Simmons's house with Calum, I messaged Eli again. I'd been thinking about Dad's question—*what are you trying to express with your art?*—and how I didn't have an answer, but how maybe Eli might. His photography makes you stand still and take notice. I thought he just had a good technical grasp of cameras, but maybe it's also that he has a clear vision of what he wants to say. So I texted him the question and then went off portrait hunting. My phone still has a UK SIM card, which means it doesn't work off Wi-Fi. But now that I've reconnected . . .

8:20 a.m.

(Eli): Is this about the thesis?

Okay, my fault. I should have elaborated. But I'm not really sure how to elaborate, because now that I think about it, asking what someone tries to express with their art is quite a vulnerable question, and is it too intimate of a thing to ask a friend? I don't want to overstep when I already did with the visa research. I mean, I think I overstepped? It was weird of me to look up ways for him to stay in the UK when he didn't ask me to. He seemed uncomfortable during that interaction, but he's also been texting me. Unprompted. Ever since I left for New York. I'm not sure what to make of all his initiated conversations, or how open we can be with each other, or where we stand in general. So instead of responding with something intense like *I don't know who I am as an artist, but your work seems very sure of itself and I'd like to know why?* I just write:

Me: Haha never mind!!

"Eli?" Calum's pocketed his phone and is looking at mine.

"*Excuse* me." I twist the screen away and out of his view.

"That was that boy's name. From the art class on your birthday. You said he was your friend."

"Congratulations, you've got a working memory." I shove my phone into my sweatpants pocket. "Why are we here, Calum? Looking at animals? How is this *remotely* related to the art exhibition?"

He frowns at me. "You're trying to change the subject."

"I'm not."

"Your face is red."

"It's *not.*"

He looks at Winnie the pig and then surveys the wall of reptiles over my shoulder. "Benji said you kissed someone."

I make a closed-mouthed sound that probably qualifies as a scream. Benji is not good at secrets. When I was twelve, he accidentally let slip that he and Calum were dating before Calum told me. Benji's also how I found out about Calum's anonymous web comic, and that there was some absurd point in time when my brother ran around London doing street art. To be fair, Benji didn't *realize* any of those things were secrets, and it's not like I asked him not to tell Calum about Eli. But . . . *urgh.* "Goodbye," I say.

Calum looks as displeased as I feel, but he mutters, "If you're dating someone—"

"We're not *dating.*"

"You kissed."

"That doesn't mean we're *dating.* Just because you fell into a fairytale love story when you were eighteen doesn't mean everyone does."

Calum shakes his head. "That is not—"

The rest of his sentence gets cut off by the front door slamming open. When I spin around, I see a woman on the threshold. She's somewhere in her fifties, with gray-blonde hair in a messy braid, leggings, and a large hoodie. Even if she weren't lugging a massive bag of animal food behind her, I've visited enough times to know she runs this place.

She stares at us in confusion. I'm about to apologize for barging in here without checking the opening hours when she lets go of her sack with a thump. "Calum *Clark*?"

My face snaps toward my brother's. Instead of going rigid with surprise, he halfway raises an arm in the form of a wave. "Ms. Rosen. Hello."

Calum knows this woman? Why does she know *him*? My eyes flit between them.

Ms. Rosen says, "I've seen your web comic, you know. The one with the giraffe? I came across it a few years ago, when you used it to shout out Glenna's Portraits. But I would have recognized your artistry regardless. You had such a distinct style, even as a freshman."

"You were a good teacher." Calum doesn't quite meet her eyes, but he keeps his chin high as her gaze travels over him. "I was hoping you might be able to give me advice on some paintings."

Teacher? I never saw Ms. Rosen inside the walls of Crescent Valley High, but Calum was a student a decade earlier than I was.

"There are several tasks I need to take care of before the farm opens at noon," Ms. Rosen says, "but I'm happy to chat as I work." She gestures at the bag behind her. "You're welcome to help with the feeding—I'd appreciate the extra hands. The cats would, too."

Calum narrows his eyes at the food. Considering his hesitation around animals—unless he's texting Benji pictures of them, apparently—I'm not sure if he'll agree to step into a room full of cats. But then he nods and helps Ms. Rosen lug the massive bag forward, and I don't even know who my brother *is* anymore.

Chapter Thirty-Three

We feed some cats. As Ms. Rosen shows us where to place the food and how much to scoop out, she tells us about herself. She's trying to pull Calum into small talk, and she's getting further with it than I anticipated. The gist of her narrative: Ms. Rosen used to teach art at Crescent Valley High, but seven years ago, she switched out students for animals. She loved her job, but the days started to blur, and she wanted a change.

"What did you end up doing for work?" she asks Calum.

He's careful around the cats, scooping food into the bowls and then backing away before they swarm. "Finance," he mutters after avoiding the tail of a particularly orange shorthair.

Ms. Rosen barks out a laugh. "Sorry," she says when he frowns. "A perfectly respectable career, but I wouldn't have pictured it for you. Why did you choose that path?"

Calum runs a hand through his hair. "It's practical."

Ms. Rosen nods. "Fair enough. Have you been living abroad? There's something in your voice, it sounds almost—"

"London. I've been there ten years."

"Quite the move. What brought you there?"

"University."

There's a pause—Ms. Rosen is doing the math, I think. Ten years ago, Calum was eighteen. But he left Crescent Valley two years before that. She opens her mouth—Calum tenses like he's anticipating her next question—

but she doesn't ask why he left. Instead, she says, "What brought you back?"

Calum turns away, nearly colliding with a cat. She's gray and chubby and watching him intently with bright yellow eyes. He raises a hand as if to pet her but ends up poking her softly on the forehead instead. She blinks at him, like *Didn't anyone teach you how to interact with me?* but then rubs her cheek against his wrist. "My family's art shop was broken into," he says finally.

"I read about that. A shame—your father does beautiful work. I commissioned from him a few years ago, and the portrait was well worth the four-month turnaround; he paints with such care. Have you been able to recover the losses?"

Calum's jaw clenches. "Ten portraits were destroyed. They were due to hang in a gallery in January. My family's been borrowing commissions from previous clients to submit to the exhibition as replacements, but I—would rather repaint the originals."

"*Calum—*" I start, but he ignores me, turning in Ms. Rosen's direction.

"You taught art," he says. "You've worked in a variety of mediums. I was wondering if you know a technique, or type of paint, that would allow me to complete ten portraits in a month and a half—"

"The originals can't be restored?"

Even though Ms. Rosen asked the question, Calum's eyes flit to me. "Restored?"

"Surely you've ripped a canvas while working?" she asks.

"I do not have much experience with canvas," Calum says, but I'm nodding. Mistakes happen. I've seen Dad patch a portrait with linen, and I've done it myself on occasion. But a tiny accidental rip is different from intentional gaping slashes. The same is true about the paint splatters. I've used a pallet knife to scrape up layers of color, but never to the degree that would be needed to revive the destroyed art in the shop.

"There's too much damage," I say. "We'd never be able to fix it all."

"Don't be afraid of battle scars," Ms. Rosen counters. "I told my students all the time: A misdrawn line or water spill might change the surface of your work, but it doesn't have to change the heart of it. If anything, mistakes add to your piece—new textures, unique imagery."

Calum looks over at me again. There's something very fragile in his expression. "Would it be possible?" he asks. "To patch them?"

I chew on my lip. It would be less of a workload than creating ten new paintings from scratch, but mending such battered canvases won't be an easy task. "I think you need to see for yourself. The damage, I mean. In order to make that decision."

The gray cat nudges Calum's arm. He pokes her head again. "Let's go, then," he says. "Let's see."

When we get back to Mom and Dad's, Calum doesn't head for the workshop. Instead, he beelines for the house.

"What are you doing?" I ask, running to keep up.

He doesn't answer, but his motive becomes clear soon enough. He bursts through the entryway and into the living room, stopping in front of Benji, who has graduated from repairing Grandma Glenna's pillow to sewing clothes for his shop. Benji's got his materials spread on the coffee table and is sitting on the ground beside it. On the wood floor next to him is a mug of tea. There's another one in Mom's hand—she's on the couch, and she and Benji appear to have been mid-conversation. Were they talking this whole time? We were gone for at least two hours.

"Can I borrow you?" Calum asks him.

"Always." Benji sets down a sheet of fabric and shakes out his hand. "Could use a break, anyway. Where are we going?"

Calum jerks his head toward the outdoors.

"Was everything all right with Mr. Simmons?" Mom asks. "Did you get the portrait?"

"Yes."

She waits for Calum to elaborate. He doesn't—he just takes Benji's hand and pulls him toward the front door. The second Benji's got on his coat, Calum steps into the snow. I'm not sure if I'm supposed to follow, but then Calum nods toward the workshop like *Hello?* so I step out after him.

"Right," says Benji as we trudge down the unplowed path to Glenna's. "If you brought me into the cold because you found who broke into your shop and we're to bury the body, I'll be disappointed. The ground is frozen, and digging requires arm strength. I have many strengths, but exercising regularly is not one of them."

Calum doesn't respond. He just takes Benji's hand again and pulls him along quicker. They're both much taller than me; I have to work to keep up.

"A surprise, then!" says Benji into the silence. "I like surprises. The suspense is building."

We reach the entrance to the workshop. Calum pauses. He looks at the door. Then he shoves it open.

It's warm inside. Bright. The damaged paintings are where I last saw them, overflowing at the waiting station. Calum drops to his knees beside them.

The portraits don't just have gashes and splatters of unwanted paint—some are also unfinished. Six are polished pieces beneath the destruction, but three have only the backgrounds painted, and one is all pencil.

Calum studies Mr. Simmons's anniversary portrait. Dad captured it in detail: the volatile expressions, the brightness of the classroom, the laughter in the eyes. It would have been lovely, but now there's a slash through the Crescent Valley High sign, paint in Robert's hair, and a jagged cut in Mr. Simmons's outstretched arm that flaps freely where it shouldn't. Calum touches the edge of the canvas and then draws his fingers back.

"Like I said." My voice is too loud. "They're bad."

Calum examines another portrait. It's the one I saw Dad working on in October with the black-and-white wedding dresses and intricate fantastical background. It was stunning, but now half of it is covered in bright yellow paint. "No," he says quietly. "They're not."

They *are* bad, though. You can patch over this level of destruction, but you can't ever fix it. "Do you know the slightest thing about painting restoration?" I ask.

Calum shakes his head. "But you do."

"Only enough to know they won't look how they were supposed to."

"New textures, unique imagery," he repeats from Ms. Rosen. "There's nothing wrong with that."

"They won't be pretty—"

"*They don't have to be.*" The intensity in his voice takes me aback. Calum grimaces and sits on his heels. He's not looking at me or Benji. He's not looking at the portraits. His gaze is on Glenna's itself—the wood walls, the old floors. "My art wasn't pretty, growing up. It wasn't polished like yours, like Dad's, like all the work in this shop. But it existed anyway, because I cared enough to make it." He swipes a hand at the canvases in front of him. "Mr. Simmons was right: A few gashes shouldn't determine whether or not they get to exist. I'd like to finish them. I'm going to finish them, whether or not you'll help. I'd—prefer it, though. If you'll help."

I sink down beside him. There's something about the intensity in Calum's expression that makes me want to hug him. I don't, because he's hardly ever okay with me grabbing him like that, and right now, he isn't asking me to. He is asking for something, though.

"I'll help you."

Chapter Thirty-Four

Calum, Benji, and I make a good portrait-mending team. First, we scrape off all the unwanted paint that was splashed over Dad's careful work. Next, I assign jobs. Benji has a steady hand. He's used to stitching intricate designs, so I give him the task of mending the canvases. After securing new linen to the backs to close up the rips, he uses glue and a very small brush to recreate the original texture of the material on the front. Calum has a good eye for color, so once Benji's work dries, my brother mixes the paint we need to layer overtop, and then I blend it carefully back into the portrait. The results are better than expected, considering we barely know what we're doing. But it takes two straight days to repair all the tears, and that doesn't include the time needed for the glue to properly set. Not to mention, there's also the large issue that several of the portraits were works in progress when they were vandalized. I could finish them nicely in a few weeks, but we don't have a few weeks. I go back to London in a few days.

Once Dad sees what we're doing, he offers to help. The whole reason Calum took this project on, though, was so our parents could reopen Glenna's, and soon Dad is busy with commissions of his own. Benji offers to take a stab at finishing the portraits; he often paints on the clothes for his shop, and to be honest, I think he'd have a better chance of recreating Dad's style than Calum does. But Calum waves him away, too—"I don't want to pull you from your work any more"—which means completing the figures and backgrounds falls to my brother.

He starts with the all-pencil piece because it's the only portrait that avoided unwanted splatters. As I doodle at the sketching station, I study him at the painting station. It's strange watching him work. The composition of the portrait doesn't look like Calum's art; it looks like Dad's. And yet something shifts as my brother applies himself to the canvas, because Dad is a careful painter and Calum is not. Calum's layers are darker and less intentional. His brushstrokes are not painstakingly uniform; they don't perfectly match the penciled outline beneath. I still see Dad in the concept and design, but the portrait feels different now. More complex.

"You were right. When you said I haven't been very fair to you." My voice is sudden and strange, disturbing air that has been still for hours. "You wouldn't have come back to Crescent Valley ten years ago, or five years ago, or three. You wouldn't have taken on these portraits. This whole week, you've surprised me, but . . . I shouldn't be surprised. I wouldn't have been surprised if I'd been looking at you properly back in London. I think the main reason I wasn't was because it would have meant admitting you're not stuck like you were when you lived here. And if I'd admitted that, it would have also meant admitting you've got everything I want."

That was way more than I planned to say. But once the cap came off, my words pulsed out like spilled paint, and now I'm left hoping it wasn't a mistake that I knocked over the bottle.

Calum sets his brush down. He turns to face me fully. It's been a while since he's looked at me like that—openly, without hesitation. The realization makes my stomach heavy, because he used to smile at me, and joke with me, and sit in easy silence with me, but for months he hasn't. I thought he was the obstacle in our communication; now it's clear that the obstacle was *me*. "What do I have that you want?" he asks.

I toss a hand at the portrait he's working on. "That looks like you, even though you're tracing over Dad's lines. You're sure enough as an artist not to lose yourself in his voice. If I tried to do the same, you wouldn't be able to tell if those were my brushstrokes or his. And—I don't know. Maybe that's fine. It's kind of like you said, right? When it comes to art, all that matters is if you care enough to make it. But—" I swallow. "I wish my work looked like me, you know? As much as yours looks like you."

Calum's brow furrows. "Your art is distinct."

I scoff, because that's either his poor attempt at a joke or his poor attempt at consoling me, but then he stands and steps farther into the workshop, leading me to the closed-off section that acts as Mom's office.

Aside from her computer, desk, and chairs, the space is crowded with shelves of old portraits that, for one reason or another, didn't make it home to their commissioners. I spot the one I did last year for Mrs. Thompson, who is generally an avid admirer of my paintings of her cats, but who thought, despite three revisions, that *Caramel Pudding's expression just still isn't right* and did not want to hang the piece with the rest of her collection. Once we reach a certain stage in the production of a product, we don't offer full refunds, but we do offer commissioners the option of donating the work to the Adopt a Portrait section of our website, where it can be purchased by someone else instead of being thrown out.

Calum surveys the top shelf and then starts pointing.

"You did that one," he says, gesturing at Caramel Pudding. He nods at a graduation portrait of a girl who was in my grade at school. "Dad did that one." He continues on, at least ten times more, assigning an artist to each work on the rack. He isn't slow about it; he never seems unsure. He gets every one correct.

At some point during this display, my mouth dropped open. I don't bother to close it, because the thing is, I know for a *fact* people can't distinguish my work from Dad's. *I* mistake my portraits for his on a daily basis, but Calum just identified our art too accurately for this to have been chance.

My brother isn't looking at me like he did something impossible. He's looking at my slack-jawed expression like I'm extremely dramatic. "Dad is a kind painter. When the lighting is harsh, he softens it. When someone is struggling to smile, he gives their expression more ease. It's subtle—I'm not sure he's aware that he does it."

"So . . ." It takes me a moment to process what Calum's implying. "You're saying I'm an *un*kind painter?"

"You're a more realistic painter," he rephrases. "You let the lighting be harsh. You don't care if it makes your subjects look dark or cold. That's how I can tell your work apart."

Well.

This is good, isn't it? It's groundbreaking, because all this time I thought my work wasn't distinct, and yet here Calum's saying it *was* distinct and I just couldn't see it. My problems are solved. Just like that. But if my art was distinct all along, I just put myself through a miserable few months for nothing. It was all for nothing, and it's my fault entirely, because instead of trying to push the familiar parts of me away, I could have been gathering them into my arms to show to people—to ask their opinions on what they saw.

Calum frowns at my face. "You were upset that your art wasn't distinct, and now you're upset that it is. It really is impossible to please you."

"I'm not *upset.*" I scowl up at the racks of portraits. They gaze neutrally back. "I'm just... frustrated. That I stopped working at Glenna's and went to school far away and took classes I don't like for literally no reason." There are also the descriptors he used: harsh, cold. I didn't realize my portraits looked that way. I never intended them to. "I'm annoyed that I dedicated my whole life to art when my work is... unkind."

I want sympathy. Words of affirmation. Calum doesn't give me either. He just sighs. "Do you regret moving to London? Do you regret discovering portrait painting is in fact what you would like to study?"

"Well, no—"

"Realism is less kind than fantasy, but that doesn't mean it is *un*kind, and it does not mean *you* are unkind." He gestures up at the shelves. "You are far too passionate about your subjects for your work to ever be mistaken as such."

"Wow," I say with as much sarcasm as I can manage, because it's either that or cry. "That's the nicest thing you've ever said to me."

"Surely not," Calum counters. "I mentioned your hair, that time, and how it looks so much better now that you've stopped dyeing random chunks of it—"

"Yes, thank you. It was lovely to hear my hair referred to as 'chunks.'"

"And I said you could come here with me. To Crescent Valley. Even though you were pissing me off—"

"Of course. Nice way to phrase that."

"And I was considerate with your birthday present—"

"The socks. Right. How thoughtful." I grin. "I missed you."

Calum exhales through his nose. "We've been together *all* day."

There's nothing funny about his statement. It's objective. It's true.

Still, I laugh.

Chapter Thirty-Five

On Sunday, I leave for London. Alone.

It's strange to be going back. It's strange that it's nice. I mainly chose to attend university in another country because I wanted to get away, but this week in Crescent Valley, I kept thinking of how it'd feel to return.

Just before I left for the airport, I got a series of texts from Eli containing all the photos of Benji he developed off the disposable camera. As I sit at the gate, waiting for the plane to arrive, I scroll through them. In the ones from my point of view, Benji's blurred in spontaneous laughter. In his, he's in full focus and staring straight into the camera lens, as though judging my lack of perception from behind it.

How embarrassing. I'm supposed to know Benji. That's the whole reason we landed on him as the final subject for our project.

8:34 a.m.

Me: I'm sorry!!!

Me: He looks like two different people!!

Me: I completely misjudged him!!!

Me: Maybe we still have time to find another subject???

Eli doesn't message back before I board the flight, which means I have seven wonderful hours to imagine every possible response I might walk off the plane to. At first, I assume he'll be angry. But it's not like I sabotaged the shoot on purpose. So I decide he'll more likely be disappointed that we failed yet again to capture a subject comprehensively. Except . . . the more I think about the contrasting imagery in the photos, the more I wonder if it has to be a bad thing that my perception of Benji was off. Dr. Lazar said people can't control how they are looked at. She asked, therefore, why it would matter how they are viewed. What if this opposing imagery is why?

Benji views himself as someone who is contemplative. He *is* contemplative—more than I realized—but that doesn't mean he's not also carefree. And my portraits and Dad's were indistinguishable to me, but they weren't indistinguishable to Calum. My brother saw something in my work that I couldn't. So maybe people are more than they can see on their own, and that's why there's value in analyzing the differences between a self-portrait and a portrait. Those differences are reminders that by stopping to consider other perspectives, we are able to get fuller pictures of ourselves.

I spend the rest of the flight trying to turn that jumble of thoughts into a succinct thesis. As soon as I land, I go to text everything to Eli, but before I can, my notifications come in. Not for messages. For calls.

He *called* me.

Eli's never done that before. Not to discuss meet-up logistics or complex essay edits. Not when his camera broke and he was standing alone in his room, holding its remains. The unfamiliarity of this development keeps me wide awake in the line through customs. I don't call him back in the airport, because it's chaotic and the signal is bad and I'm wrestling with my luggage. I don't call him on my way to the dorm, because I take the tube from

Heathrow and am not bold enough to disrupt the quiet of the other passengers. I don't call him after I've hoisted my bags up the front steps, because it's nearly ten p.m. on Sunday and, yes, Eli works erratic hours, but there's also a high chance he's in his room right now. It feels strange to press his number when I could just knock on his door.

So, I knock.

And then I immediately realize I should have dropped my stuff in my room first, because with my suitcase and my sweatpants and the wild bun coming loose from the top of my head, I must look like a movie character who just rushed off a plane to confess her feelings, and that is *not* the vibe I want to give off to someone who is my friend.

"You called?" I say when he opens the door. And then I blush, because who starts a conversation like that unless they are on the phone?!

Eli looks like he might have been asleep. He's barefoot, and his hair is a mess across his face, and he's in a T-shirt I know he'd never wear in public because instead of void black it's pastel green. His shoulders are hunched forward in a way that looks uncomfortable; I'm not sure why he's affected that posture until he pinches his shirt away from his chest.

"Sorry." I turn to go. "You called while I was on the plane, and I couldn't call you back until I was at the dorm, so I figured it made more sense to just see if you were here, but it's late, obviously, and I should have texted—"

Eli steps slightly aside. "You can come in."

"Oh! Well, okay."

His room is an organized mess. Printed PowerPoint slides litter the floor. Handwritten and typed notes layer his desk and chair in piles that look intentional. The pictures for our photography project are spread carefully under his bed.

"Finals," he explains.

"God. I haven't started mine. Except, you know. Photography. And ceramics. Does it count if I only started ceramics because the clay needs time to dry and I physically won't be able to finish my project if it doesn't?"

"We still have two weeks," he responds, which both answers my question and doesn't. He grabs the sweatshirt off the back of his desk chair and pulls it on before sitting down on his bed. I stand firmly between his notes on Sound Design and The Ethical Philosophies of Anonymous Sources. For a moment, there's nothing but lurching silence, until he says, "I didn't mean to freak you out with those phone calls."

"I wasn't *freaking out.* I was . . . lightly concerned."

"Fine," Eli amends. "You were lightly concerned, and you were texting in a lightly concerned way, so I called because I wanted you to know I thought it wasn't a bad thing the pictures of Benji came out so different from each other. It could actually be the point we were searching for in our project—arguably, people can learn more about themselves by considering the perspectives of others."

Seriously? I went through all those revelations on the plane just to have him beat me to the punch? "That's what *I* was going to say."

Eli's lips quirk up before he can settle them back into something more neutral. "You're angry we're on the same page?"

"I'm not *angry*—" Of course, it sounds angry when I say it like that. Eli isn't quite as successful at containing his smile this time.

"Maybe we should interview all our subjects," he says,

switching to a more productive train of conversation. "We can ask what they learned about themselves from comparing their two portraits. It would give us concrete evidence to pull from for the essay."

"I like that." It'll be more work during an already busy finals season, but it would add a lot to our project.

Eli looks like he's about to yawn. Or maybe I'm about to yawn. It's late, and even though a plane was responsible for launching me across the ocean, my body feels like it was the one doing the flying.

I turn to go—we can figure out the interview details tomorrow—but then I pause, because the whole time I was in New York, I couldn't stop thinking about our last in-person conversation. "I'm sorry, by the way. For last week. It was super weird I was researching your visa options to stay in the UK. You didn't ask me to do that. I overstepped."

Eli shakes his head. "No, it's fine. You just—surprised me. I'm used to having to research things like that by myself, so—I appreciated it, actually. I appreciated it a lot."

"What? Oh! Haha, no . . ."

Maybe this is how Eli felt that day I was crying outside Dr. Lazar's office. Not that he's *crying* now, but he's saying sincere things while looking at me shyly through his eyelashes, and I simply don't know what to do with that.

"Um!" I say, far too loudly, and flail my arms in the direction of the door. "Glad that's cleared up! So, I'll go now! Because it's late!" I fully leave the room before remembering that my backpack and suitcase are still propped against his desk, and have to do a horrific "Haha, forgot my bags!" while making a second exit.

Lovely.

Eli and I agree to split up the work of conducting the photography interviews. I set up a call with Calum for next week, while Eli plans to meet with Natalie. A few days after that, Eli and I will meet in person to interview each other. Since I already kind of questioned Benji about the differences between his portrait and mine, we decide to skip over his for the sake of time.

Now that photography's worked out, I can't afford to think about Eli anymore. If I don't get to work on the rest of my finals, I'll have nothing to show for this semester.

For ceramics, I have to craft a collection of four cohesive pieces and write a page detailing my creative process. I decided on mugs since I'm actually not terrible at constructing them. The good news: I shaped them all before leaving for New York. The bad news: I don't like my initial idea anymore. The plan had been to decorate each mug with a different type of flower—I took inspiration from these cute floral plates I found on Instagram—but although my sketches look pretty on paper, they don't feel like anything. There's no heart seeping out. So I spend another full day brainstorming, and in the end, I keep with the shrubbery, but add more intentionality into my work by having each mug represent a different place. I paint yellow gorse for Edinburgh. Crescent Valley is vibrant fall leaves. London is red brick and vines. The last mug I cover with a variety of orange flowers, because Alicia is a person who feels like a place. None of the mugs are perfect—they all have uneven edges, and my brushstrokes are messier than I'd like because I'm not used to painting on clay. But when I look at them, I remember home, and maybe that won't matter to anyone else, but it matters to me.

For abstract painting, I only need to create one piece,

but it requires a longer statement of purpose than ceramics. I struggle for two entire days to come up with a concept, because how do you create something that looks unintentional but does not feel unintentional? In the end, I play to my strengths. Instead of starting with an abstract design, I paint a portrait. A self-portrait. And then, while the canvas is still wet, I smudge it. I blur the colors together until the original image is incomprehensible under the new lines and curves. I title it: *Reset.*

So, that leaves metalworking. I started it last because I didn't want to think about it, but now it's Friday and it's due next Wednesday and I actually might come up empty-handed. After a full semester of lessons, I think I'm *worse* than when I started. Fear is a factor: The machines are loud and sharp, and I did not realize going into this course that there was a real risk of me losing a finger. Lack of interest is also an obstacle: Simply cutting out a circle requires enormous effort, and what am I supposed to do with a circle? I text Alicia a photo of one of my awful attempts and caption it *Blob Number 17.* She responds:

10:04 a.m.

Alicia Miller: BLOBS CAN BE ART

Alicia Miller: DON'T UNDERESTIMATE A GOOD BLOB

Alicia Miller: YOU GOT THIS

Except I really *don't* have it. After a morning of failures in the workshop, I give up and slump back to the dorm for lunch. It's been a week of me subsisting off handfuls of chips and old pizza and, on one questionable evening, an entire block of cheese, so I decide cooking something more nutritious might help out my brain. When I shove into the kitchen, though, I find Natalie already at the stove and Tessa at the table. They look as worn down as I feel: Natalie's pouring pasta into a pot but appears to have forgotten the water, while Tessa's laughing and saying, inexplicably, "But you didn't heat the sauce!"

Before I can intervene, the kitchen door swings open again. Henrold appears. My eyes bug because I literally haven't seen him since that first day on campus. He either never leaves his room, or we are on completely different class schedules, or he is a figment of my sleep-deprived imagination. He looks the same as I remember. He's even wearing the same outfit: brown trousers and a shirt made of suspiciously old-fashioned fabric. I don't *really* think he's a vampire, but I'm also exhausted and malfunctioning, and I don't *not* think he's a vampire.

Henrold takes one look at the three of us and backs slowly out of the room.

"Figures," says Natalie after the door shuts. "I think James is scared of me. Whenever he walks into the kitchen while I'm cooking, he backs away in the same manner."

I'm about to comment that if I only knew Natalie from that time I saw her melting Sour Patch Kids on the stove in the middle of the night, then I'd probably fear her, too. Instead, I choke on my spit. "Who is *James?*"

Natalie gestures at the still-swinging door. "Pet lizard? Lives one room over from you? Come on, love. It's December."

James? Henrold is . . . *James?*

I don't know what to say, so I don't say anything. I just laugh. I laugh until my eyes tear up, and then I keep laughing because Natalie and Tessa are looking at me like I've lost it. And maybe I *have* lost it, but I don't really mind losing it because now they have also lost it, and how nice, to be in London at art school in the middle of finals, shrieking with friends over nothing.

"There's—" I manage finally, and Natalie and Tessa wait with bated breath for me to finish my thought, because although it is noon and none of us have been drinking, it feels for some reason like we are all plastered at three in the morning, "There's no water. In your *pot.* But you just poured in the pasta." It's not funny, and yet it is extremely funny. It is the funniest thing I have ever witnessed, and I break down all over again. They break down, too.

In the end, I take a longer break than anticipated. Instead of waterless pasta, Natalie, Tessa, and I go out for lunch. Tessa suggests this place called My Old Dutch in Holborn, and it has *crepes.* I get a raspberry-and-lemon one and a hot chocolate with mint, and the three of us share french fries, and it's the best meal I've ever had.

"Did you finish ceramics?" I ask Tessa after reluctantly forcing my face away from my drink.

She shakes her head. "Figured it'd be the easiest to complete in a crunch—I'll knock it out this afternoon. You?"

"Yeah, but now I'm stuck on metalworking. I. Should've. Just. Taken. Figure. Drawing." I stab my fork into my crepe after each word.

"Next term," says Tessa, and I sigh. This semester was a learning experience. I don't *regret* branching out of my comfort zone: Like Calum said, it taught me the art I thought I'd hate is in fact art I hate, and that's not an unhelpful lesson to learn. But now that I've confirmed portraits are the medium for me, I want to study them properly. Next term, I'm taking figure drawing, oil painting, history of self-portraiture, and history of photography. Before you judge me for that last one, I'm *not* taking it on the off-chance Eli might also take it. I'm taking it because Dr. Lazar's teaching it, and—don't tell her, I'd never live it down—she makes some good points about art. I'm properly buzzing at the thought of next semester, but I can't get there before I'm finished here.

So, I finish. I chug my drink and get back to the studio and for the next five days, I metalwork the hell out of some circular bookends. They're terrible, and I'm not going to get a good grade on them, but hey. They're *made.*

On Wednesday night, a buzzing wakes me from the dark. I grab my phone with the intention of flinging it across the room and curling back under my blankets, but then I see the caller ID.

"Calum, it's the middle of the night," I hiss into the camera.

"It's eight p.m."

"In New York, maybe—"

"In London."

Oh. I glance at the time on my phone. "I was sleeping."

"And here I thought you were paddleboarding."

My eyebrows rise. "Was that a joke?"

He scowls. "*You* scheduled this call."

I did?

I *did.*

I sit up, grabbing my laptop from where it's resting at the foot of my bed. In the exhaustion of finals, I totally forget about tonight's photography interview. At least Eli and I created a Google Doc with questions in advance.

"When you were mending rips in the canvases, how did you blend the paint out overtop?" Calum asks while I pull up several tabs on my laptop. He tilts his phone, and my eyes burn with the sudden appearance of the afternoon sun out the windows of Glenna's workshop. I blink a few times to readjust my vision, and then I'm staring at a portrait.

At first, I don't recognize it. Then I realize it's the one he started while I was still in New York—the one Dad sketched but hadn't gotten to painting. It's a piece that suits Calum's skillsets. In the center are two women walking down a path, holding hands, a dog trailing behind them. But their backs are to the viewer and the focus is not on the figures—it's on the surrounding nature. Calum has painted trees in intricate shades of green and matched the warm brown tone of the dirt road to the golden highlights of the sun. His imagery isn't crisp like Dad's would have been. Everything's blurred and blended together, which makes the scene less realistic and more like a fairytale. He's pointing at an area toward the center of the painting—presumably where there's a rip—but I honestly can't see it. Maybe it's more obvious in person, or maybe he's been staring at the same few inches of canvas for so long that his brain is inventing flaws.

"It looks good, Calum." He looks good, too. I mean, he's too pale, and the circles under his eyes are as alarming as ever, but there's something less rigid about the sharp lines of his face, as though he's stopped clenching his jaw for the first time in a century. Fixing these paintings isn't a chore—it's something he wants to be doing. "You've missed this, haven't you? Art."

I don't expect him to respond, because it would mean admitting I'm right about something, but his eyes flick back to the portrait, and the look that passes over his face is answer enough.

"You could keep doing art. When you're back in London. I don't mean turning your whole life around to become a painter!" I add when he opens his mouth to cut me off. "But instead of data analyzing for a finance corporation, couldn't you do it for a gallery? Or a museum? An art shop? Or—right. Boundaries." I tap my mouth.

"I don't mind your suggestions," Calum says, which is so unexpected that I blink a few times to check if I actually woke up from my nap. "You can make suggestions," he reiterates, "so long as you're able to handle it when I decline them."

"*When* you decline them?"

"You cannot expect I will take all, or even most, of your ideas. While I find them amusing, they are generally unreasonable." He turns back to his painting as though he didn't just insult me. I'm about to switch course to the interview, but then he adds, "I am aware my job takes advantage of me. I don't plan to stay with the company forever, but it's stable. It offers high pay. It has granted me the ability to spend two months in New York. And while Benji's shop is very successful, he does not yet produce fast enough to make a consistent salary. I know he stresses over that, but with my job, there's really no need to worry. So, I will stay at Knightley for now, and we will be better off for it later."

That . . . actually makes a lot of sense. All these years, I thought Calum stayed in his job because he was scared of being unmoored. I do still think that's part of it—he could likely find a better company with similar pay if he put himself out there—but he's got concrete reasons for sticking with Knightley, and sticking with is different from being stuck.

"You wanted to interview me," Calum says after I let the silence drag out for a little too long.

"Yes!" It takes my brain a moment to switch gears. "Here, I'll text you the photos from the art pub." Once I send them, Calum sets down his brush to study them.

"How are they different?" I ask, and then position my fingers over my keyboard to type his response.

"I took one picture from my perspective. You took the other from yours."

"Right. Okay. And how are they the same?"

Calum hesitates. He runs a hand through his hair. "I don't know. They're not."

"There's no overlap?"

"I suppose I'm quite expressionless in your photo, as is the brick wall."

"Are you?" I pull up the images on my laptop. "You always look so relaxed when you paint. Look at your eyebrows. They're usually more tense."

Said eyebrows furrow slightly as Calum studies the photo again. "I suppose," he concedes, which *I* suppose is the closest I'm going to get to a "Wow, you're right!"

I glance at the last question on my laptop. Eli and I decided to keep our survey narrowed to only the information we knew could be incorporated into the essay. "What did you learn about yourself from looking at the differences between these portraits?"

"I . . ." Calum runs his hand through his hair again. He's hesitating, and I can't tell if it's because he's unsure of what he wants to say next or if it's because he's not. "On occasion—" he starts, and then stops, gesturing at his self-portrait. "I am told, sometimes—often—that I'm a bit like that brick wall. Maybe I took it to heart more than I realized, because I do feel relaxed when I paint. I didn't tell you that, but you were able to see it."

I scoff. "For the record, this is a great example of why my opinions are worth listening to. Obviously you are not a brick wall. You are far more transparent. Right now, for instance, you're thinking *Maisie is an incredible, groundbreaking artist, who is extremely knowledgeable and not even a little bit arrogant—*"

"Sure," says Calum. "Whatever makes you happy." But then he smiles, and maybe I'm not so far off, after all.

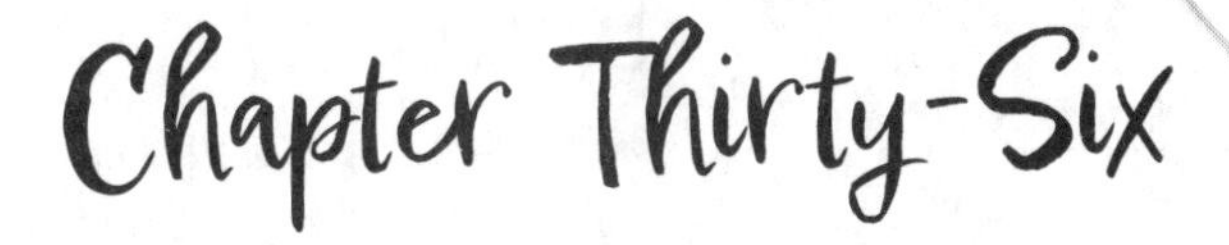

Chapter Thirty-Six

As finals come to a close, our campus lets out a collective breath. There's more laughter on the streets. People exist outside of the library. We have a full month break before the new semester begins, and it feels like the whole world is ahead of us.

Now that I've turned in my final for metalworking, I expect to feel some of the relaxed air that's whirling below my dorm. But I'm still heavy. Something is weighing me down, and after a bit of searching, I finally realize what.

Jasper the Camera.

Benji never got around to fiddling with the broken remains before we left for New York, and he and Calum won't be back in London until after the semester's over. For a moment, I convince myself I could just . . . forget about Jasper and hope Eli does, too. But I *can't* forget about Jasper when I know how much Eli loved him, and yet I *should* forget about Jasper, because *Hey! I spent many hours transforming your very important camera into something new that I hope can also be very important to you* doesn't sound like a casual friendship gift. It sounds like an I Still Quite Like You and I Am Coming On Too Strong gift. So I spend a day in awkward despair over that, until I remember what Calum said during our call: *"You can make suggestions, so long as you're able to handle it when I decline them."*

Eli might think me fiddling with his camera is me coming on too strong. He also might *not* think that. Either way, I'll only know if I ask.

2:32 p.m.

Me: Hi!!

Me: I've got some free time this week and know Benji didn't get around to looking at your camera before he went to New York

Me: I wouldn't mind working on it

Me: If you're okay with that!!

(Eli): Sure

For a moment, the clouds lift. Then they promptly fall back into my face, because I got the okay from Eli, but that doesn't mean I'll be able to *make* anything okay out of Jasper. Transforming a camera into something new is not exactly my area of artistic expertise. But over several days of pulling out my hair, I've created . . . something. Several things. And I could give the reinterpreted Jasper to Eli tonight when we meet up to interview each other for the photography project, but he might be horrified by the mangled remains of his most prized possession if I present it to him in this state…

I don't have much time to agonize over the decision. All too soon, it's evening and Eli is knocking on my door. The hood of his sweatshirt is pulled over his head, draping toward his eyes—as if he's cold, or like he came here with armor. His lips are chapped, and his skin is dry, and his hands are stuffed in his pockets. I'm looking too closely, but he's looking, too.

"Hi," he says.

"Hi."

He coughs. "Were the rest of your finals . . . fine?"

"My finals were fine."

"That's fine. I mean, that's good. That's good that they were fine." He nods, and I nod, and we're doing that awkward phone conversation minus the phone thing again.

"Can I . . . ?" He gestures into my room, and I realize I've been blocking his path forward.

"Yes!" I quickly step aside, and he moves to my desk chair, sitting on it backward like the last time he was in here, his arms resting across the top.

The last time he was in here, I could see through his T-shirt. Because he'd just showered. In my shower.

Super helpful, Maisie. Very productive train of thought.

I wrench open my laptop to our project questions. "How are your photos different?" I blurt, because maybe focusing on those pre-planned words will stop this unplanned spiral.

Eli pulls the pictures from a folder in his bag and holds them up—the one I took in his right hand, the one he took in his left. "Yours is candid," he says. "You didn't set up the shot. Mine is more intentional."

I write that down. "How are they the same?"

He hesitates. This is the harder question, we both noticed through conducting the interviews. Calum got caught up in finding an answer. Eli told me Natalie did, too, until coming to the conclusion that both her photo and mine had something bright in them.

"Your version of me is blurred," he says. "It's messy. But there's something urgent about that—like you really cared about capturing the image. I cared, too, in mine. That's why I was precise in how I lined up the shot."

Interesting. We had opposite approaches to our photos, but the intent behind them was the same. He's right—I did care. I wanted to take a good picture of him, and because of that, it turned out shaky, wild.

Last question. "What did you learn about yourself from looking at the differences between the portraits?"

Eli lays the photos on the desk, considering them from a new angle. "I like to take my time to conceptualize a scene, to figure out where I'm going," he says eventually. "I like the way my photos turn out when I do that, but your photo didn't do that, and I like it, too. So, maybe there's value in not always planning everything out."

After I type up his answer, I expect him to pull out the photos of me so we can begin my portion of the interview. But he continues gazing down at the desk, and then half turns in my direction. "I've done research. The last few weeks. On careers for people with photography degrees," he says abruptly. "There are more options than I realized—marketing, journalism, a variety of sciences. A variety of arts, of course. And then there's teaching." He shrugs in a way that looks like it's supposed to be casual, but there is too much tension in his shoulders. "I like teaching at the art pub. I think I'm . . . all right at it. And it's something I could do anywhere, in any country. So I started looking into what I'd need to do to get licensed. I also reached out to a few schools to see if I could assist or intern next semester . . . Anyway, it's nothing concrete, but it does feel like an actual direction. Instead of . . ." He flails a hand through the air. "So—I thought I should tell you. That."

I smile. It stretches my whole face. "Eli, you *are* a good teacher. That watercolor lesson you led was so impressive. It's not a medium you usually work in, but you obviously did your research. And you're calm. You explain things clearly. You got *Georgie and Ollie* to listen to you, which deserves some type of award."

His ears go pink. "Thanks," he mutters. "Anyway, your interview." He pulls out my photos and sets them on the desk beside his. "How are they different?"

I step next to him so I can observe them more carefully, and then hand over my laptop so he can take notes. "Mine's got you in it," I say, because that's the first thing I notice. "The other one's just me."

"How are they the same?"

In my case, this question is easy. I've known the answer since I first saw his portrait of me. "Even though I'm screaming and you're throwing paint at my face, I look... content," I say, "in both photos. Which is interesting, because I'm generally quite an anxious person, I think."

"You think?"

"Shut up."

He laughs. "What did you learn about yourself from looking at the differences between the portraits?"

That one's harder. Obviously, there are two people in my photo and one in his. Is there something to learn from that? Maybe, but it's also interesting how I shot myself in the dark, shrouded by blankets and a laptop and another person. It's almost like I was trying to minimize myself, but Eli shot me front and center, in direct sunlight, the brightness at my back almost causing me to glow.

"I'm . . . a lot," I say finally. "I know I can be a lot, sometimes. But your photo works *because* I'm a lot. If I wasn't lit as brightly, I wouldn't look as striking. So, it's not always a bad thing. Being a lot."

Eli's fingers pause on my keyboard. "Most people don't have the bandwidth to care about everything. It's cool that you do."

Yes, I am cool. That was a cool thing to say, and I am being cool about it. My brain definitely isn't short-circuiting, which is why I do the sudden normal thing of jabbing a finger toward him and saying, "Don't take this the wrong way, but I'm bad at metalworking."

Eli looks utterly perplexed, which—fair.

"Your camera," I clarify. "Jasper the Camera. The plan was to make earrings out of him, because—" I gesture at his piercings. "But I couldn't cut metal small enough, let alone fuse bits of camera to the pieces. So then I thought I'd try a necklace—I'm not sure how you feel about those, but you always wore Jasper like one, so it didn't seem too far out there . . . Anyway, I tried making a pendant out of the lens, but glass is fragile! It shatters easily! So, that didn't work out. But—and like I said, don't take this the wrong way!"

I lunge for my backpack and fiddle around inside until my fingers close around a small paper bag. I'd been debating throwing it out and trying something else—but although my next attempt could be better, it could easily be worse.

Eli shakes the contents of the bag into his palm. My cheeks heat even more, because they're rings. I made him rings. Circles, remember? After a semester of metalworking, the only skill I kind of mastered was concentric bands. I didn't know his size, so I made a bunch of different ones. Instead of stones in the middle, I fixed on the buttons from his camera. The results aren't pretty—I was going for durability—and they look very handmade. But I tried my best.

Eli stares at my creations without saying anything, so I blurt, "Not being weird, I just am a portrait," which is not at all what I meant to say, so I continue with, "I didn't do this because I like you," and somehow that is worse.

I cough. I stare very hard at Eli's shoes, trying to turn my rushing thoughts into proper words. "I just—those things you said. On Halloween. About how you left home and were having a crisis about it. I know how it feels. To lose pieces of your life. To re-find some pieces and realize they no longer fit together like they did before." My arms are tight across my ribs. "So, I didn't make those rings because I like you. I mean, I do. Like you. But it's fine if you don't still like me. My *point* is, this wasn't supposed to be some grand gesture. I just—didn't want you to have to throw away something that you weren't ready to lose."

At some point, Eli stopped looking at the rings. He started looking at me.

"I'm not usually that profound," I say inanely, because he's staring in a way that makes my insides feel seen, and I think insides should stay inside, actually, which—maybe that should be a topic for a new photography project, because it is, in hindsight, a terrible thing to be perceived—

"Would that be the title?" Eli asks. "*Insides Should Stay Inside?*"

Did I say that out *loud?*

"Stop *looking* at me," I beg, because I've lost total control of this conversation and am flailing toward the ceiling like a balloon without a string; because instead of a deadpan expression, Eli's eyes are bright and smiling; because when his lips grin down at me in that wide and free way, it makes me want to kiss him.

This time, he kisses me.

Epilogue

It's a Saturday in February and I'm minding my business when I get a series of texts:

6:58 p.m.

Calum Clark: Can you help
Calum Clark: Please
Calum Clark: The flat
Calum Clark: Now

That's not what you want to hear. I can only imagine Calum texting me for help if it's portrait related or he's on the precipice of dying, so my first thought is he somehow poisoned himself by attempting to make dinner and my second is he fell off a table trying to change a lightbulb.

Naturally, I rush to his flat. When I arrive, I don't find my brother lying passed out on the ground. I *do* find him sitting on the ground, staring helplessly about the living room, which appears to have been in a fight.

"What *happened*?" Books have been knocked off shelves. A large chunk from the plant in the corner of the room is under the coffee table. There are rips in one of the couch cushions that looks suspiciously like claw marks.

"I borrowed a cat."

I blink. I blink again. "You—*what?*"

"A cat," says Calum. "I tried to put her in a sweater, and—she did not like that. She did not like me. She ran under the couch. Now I can't find her."

"...Right."

I thought my brother had been doing better since

returning to London. The art exhibition was a success—the message behind the restored portraits was well received, and Glenna's has since been invited to contribute to several other galleries. Mom and Dad offered Calum a permanent job with the shop to coordinate with all the organizations. He turned it down, but he's been more inclined lately to pick up pencils to draw instead of to work. He's joined me twice this month at the art pub, and the other day, I saw him sketching something at his desk vaguely in the style of his web comic. But he *borrowed* a *cat*? And tried to *put it in a sweater*?

"Where—?" I start, then change my mind. "*Why?*"

"Benji likes animals in clothes."

"Sure," I say. "And again—*why?*"

Calum runs a hand through his hair. The back of it is scratched and bleeding. He doesn't appear to have noticed. "Rose isn't married."

"Calum, you could not be making less sense."

"Rose isn't married," he repeats, "so I wouldn't know, would I? How it looks to orchestrate a proposal."

"A proposal for what?" I ask, because my first thought is he's speaking in business terms, and my second thought is *Oh*.

Calum proposing was nowhere on my bingo card. I don't think it was on Benji's bingo card, but here we are. All things considered, a feral cat in a sweater is better than the *Shrek* disaster I walked in on in August. Probably.

"This." I wave a hand at the mauled couch and Calum's blood dripping into the carpet. "You're not supposed to do *this*."

Calum tosses something at me. I flinch, but then realize it's the tiny sweater. The neckline has been stretched. There's a tear in the hem.

"Would you try?" My brother jerks his chin at the knitted monstrosity. "If we can just get that on her—"

I throw the sweater back at him. "You *lost* the *cat.* How can I possibly do anything when you *lost* the *cat?*"

"We'll relocate her, obviously. And then—"

"Calum." I am two seconds from shaking him. "Let's regroup here. Let's fully think this through. Do you really want ten years of a relationship to culminate in an angry cat and blood all over the carpet? Does that sound ideal to you?"

He glances at his torn-up hand with vague annoyance, as though frustrated it had the audacity to start bleeding. "I believed," he says finally, "that I was doing something thoughtful."

"It is thoughtful," I say, because Calum went out of his way to find a cat and wrangle it home and procure a tiny sweater, and although this is a mess, it was not conceptualized without care. "Personally, I just—you know. Wouldn't want to be proposed to while a stray cat threatened to claw my eyes out. But maybe that's just me."

"It's not a stray," Calum says. "It's—"

He cuts off at the sound of footsteps on the stairs. More than one set.

"The cat," Calum hisses. "*Maisie—*"

The door swings open, revealing Benji and Rose, who appear to be in a heated debate over french fries. "Benjamin I-Forget-Your-Middle-Name Saito," Rose is saying. "You well know chips should be soft and thick—"

"*You're* soft and thick," Benji shoots back, "if you underestimate the little burnt ones at the bottom of the bag—" Two steps over the threshold, he pauses. His eyes flit from me and Calum on the ground to the chewed-up plant to the knocked-over books. "Hello," he says. "I appear to have missed something. Why are you bleeding?"

"We should get married."

Benji coughs, and then blinks, and then seems to malfunction internally. After a beat, he says again, albeit more faintly, "I appear to have missed something."

"You like animals in clothes," says Calum, "and there was an animal—a cat, I had a cat—but it's . . . I don't know where it's gone . . . Anyway, I didn't expect an audience, or to lose the cat. It's throwing me off—I'd like to try this again . . ."

Rose snorts and then claps a hand over her mouth. "Sorry!" she says when Calum frowns. "My dearest friends are getting engaged! The tears in my eyes are from heartful emotion. They are not from laughter. I would never laugh at such a vulnerable confession of love! How beautiful. How brilliant. Carry on."

Calum scowls. "Leave."

"I will not," she says. "I could never."

Calum focuses back on Benji. "This was a mistake. I'll be in Hyde Park, feeding myself to the swans. Good evening." He stands and makes for the door.

Benji grabs his arm. "There was a Shrek. A massive cardboard Shrek! That I built from scratch in August. And then there was a bear. A hypothetical bear, that I thought would make a scenic backdrop for an engagement." He takes Calum's hand. The bloody one. "The point being, misplaced cats are a step up from my efforts. The second point being, you need medical attention. The third point being, of course I'll marry you."

There's a sniffle off to the side. Rose covers her mouth again. "The tears in my eyes are from laughter," she says. "They are not from heartfelt emotion!"

"You are openly weeping," says Benji. And then he abruptly tilts his face away, which does nothing to hide the fact that he is also openly weeping.

Calum touches Benji's cheek and then his hair, and then they're both grinning, and somehow, despite the questionable start and trainwreck middle, it's the perfect conclusion. Rose is all but a puddle. I am more composed, if only because my family is ridiculous and I refuse to cry within a five-minute time span of anyone mentioning *Shrek*. For thirty seconds, this is a lovely moment. Benji laughs, and Calum smiles, and then they kiss, and then there's a noise. It sounds like chewing. I glance toward the plant.

"Bastard." Rose rounds on Calum. "When did you steal my cat?"

Acknowledgments

This is a weird book. Not because of the Shrek marriage proposal in the first chapter, but because I published a novel in 2021 about twelve-year-old Maisie, and then asked if I could write a new book where she's eighteen. That's not typically a thing that's done, because despite having the same main character, the stories have different audiences. They are classified under different age categories. They will be shelved in different sections of the bookstore!

Thank you to my editor, Meg Gaertner, for not only being into my experimental idea but for having such a clear vision for it. Remember when I submitted the first sixty pages and Maisie had no character arc?? Thank you for guiding her where she needed to go.

My agent, Eva Scalzo: Thank you for everything you do. I can't wait to work with you on more books!

To everyone at Flux who helped get this story into the world: Karli Hughes, Taylor Kohn, Sam Temple, and Rachel Vander Weit. I'm grateful for all your hard work! Thank you also to my copyeditor, Nevada Lewis, and my proofreader, Debbie Greenberg. Ana Bidault: I am obsessed with my book cover; you made it so beautiful. Pamela Nunez: The character art I commissioned from you kept me motivated as I drafted and edited this novel. I stared at it constantly while I worked. Dorian Weber: Thank you for your authenticity feedback on Eli's character!

My 2022–2023 Class IV students: You wanted to be in the acknowledgments of my next book, so here you go!

In all seriousness, I very much appreciated your excitement over *The Art of Running Away* and your entrepreneurial ideas for how I should market myself to become a famous author. (Maybe wait a few years to read this one, though—the characters are a lot older!)

Mom and Dad: Thank you for always telling your friends to buy my books even when I don't tell you what they're about. Mitchell: Your advice is invaluable. I genuinely wouldn't have finished this manuscript without our many impromptu, four-hour brainstorming sessions where you helped me solve my plot and character problems. And of course, the cats: Thank you for being cute and fluffy.

Finally, thank you to the cafés in Seoul and Suwon where I started drafting this book. After *The Art of Running Away,* I wasn't sure if I had what it took to finish another novel (I tried and failed for a few years!). But something clicked that summer in 2023, and I partially credit the English Breakfast lattes and 오미자차.

About the Author

Sabrina Kleckner is a teacher by day and an author by early morning and night. Her debut middle grade novel, *The Art of Running Away,* was a 2023 ALA Rainbow Booklist Selection; the 2022 Moonbeam Awards Bronze Medalist in Pre-Teen General Fiction; and a 2022 IPPY Award Silver Medalist in Juvenile Fiction. On her days off, she can be found traveling the world or gushing about her three cats to anyone who will listen.

Sabrina can be found online @sabkleckner and can be reached on her website: www.sabrinakleckner.com.

See how Maisie's journey began in . . .

2023 ALA Rainbow Book List Selection

2022 IPPY Awards Silver Medalist, Juvenile Fiction

2022 Moonbeam Awards Bronze Medalist (Pre-Teen Fiction – General)

2022 Best Indie Book Award Winner – LGBTQ Tween Fiction

Twelve-year-old Maisie is an artist. When she's in front of her sketchbook or apprenticing at Glenna's Portraits, the family-run art shop her grandmother started, the world makes sense. She doesn't think about Calum, her brother who mysteriously left home and cut ties with her family six years ago, or her parents' insistence that she "broaden her horizons" and try something new—something that isn't art.

But when Glenna's Portraits falls on hard times, Maisie's plan to take over the shop when she's older and become a lifelong artist starts to crumble. In desperation to make things right, Maisie runs away to London to reconnect with her adult brother, hoping he might be the key to saving the shop. But as Maisie learns about her family's past from Calum, she starts to rethink everything she's ever known. Maisie must decide not only if saving her family's art shop is worth it, but if she can forgive her parents for the mistakes they've made.